D0071630

Venusia

SEMIOTEXT(E) NATIVE AGENTS SERIES

Published by Semiotext(e)
501 Philosophy Hall, Columbia University, New York, NY 10027
2571 W. Fifth Street, Los Angeles, CA 90057
www.semiotexte.com

Cover Art by Marnie Weber
"The Owl's Evening" 1999
Collection FNAC (Fond National d'Art Contemporain, France)

Backcover Photo by Frances Scholz
Design by Hedi El Kholti

ISBN: 1-58435-026-1
Distributed by The MIT Press, Cambridge, Mass. and London, England
Printed in the United States of America

Venusia

a true story

Mark von Schlegell

for Frances

Prologue

Everything looked very much like it was supposed to look. A tectonic geology imperceptibly inhered. Its shifting mass traced a 35 kilometer/second ellipse around the middle-aged C class star. The planet spun slowly in retrograde, a quiet memorial to the cataclysmic collision that put it there. Off-world, its rotation would not be perceivable in the swirling of its perpetual clouds. Under them its oceans wrinkled like the lobes of an enormous brain.

At the meeting place of an ocean and a curling strand of mineral-rich soil, low fogs drifted against a ring of volcanoes.

Venusia's seven copper-bulbed towers crackled, igniting t-morning's blue-haired dawn. There followed a large hollow sound, a metallic exhalation. Along the apparently endless beach, the clouds slipped apart. Fresh light poured down through the new Hole onto the cracked rooftops and rubble-strewn alleys, as thick and as golden as syrup. The tall palms and trees, the flowering bushes and rising weeds, strained to soak up the hot glory.

A certain rhythmic movement flickered into mechanical life. Peculiar offices, businesses and culture-complexes opened windows and doors. Smoke could be seen rising from the stacks of the robot factories. Transportation systems ignited; irrigation lines sputtered and sprayed. Talking signs began to chatter quietly among themselves. From a window on Cherry Tree Lane, a dark-eyed woman gazed out on it all and saw only herself.

As usual, Dr. Yang had risen before dawn to organize her t-day. She had programmed her secretary's work, filed her research on new trends in neuroscopy. A Morituri-fluent neuroscopic councilor, Dr. Yang was like part of a robot factory herself: a mechanical thing kept in perfect working order. There were no wounds on the body of Dr. Sylvia Yang. Flowers managed her memory. Nano-technology, vitamins and entertainment maintained her health and relieved her depression and alienation as if she were no longer a living specific self. In the low gravity, there was little differentiating her from the holograms that performed on her patients' ever-present V-stages. She was less than a hologram. Her patients didn't need Sylvia Yang in particular. She was a general thing. She had no relationships, no friendships, no hobbies or dreams. Since attaining Q-level status, Dr. Yang couldn't even go out to Feed.

Every t-morning, bundles of flowers were delivered to high-ranking employees of the Crittendon regime for private consumption. The green packet was now waiting atop her deskmodule. At general Feed, out on the beaches, when the ordinary people clamored and hustled for their daily allotment, the flowers had about them an immediate, intense significance that transcended the general meaninglessness of life. But to have them like this, so easily, so without effort, was to be confronted with the blank absence the flowers replaced.

Sitting on the relax across from her deskmodule, there would soon be a patient. Green-skinned and twitching, he would be tapping dirty fingers on the relax-arm. Sexually aroused, focussed inward, this patient would likely make for an ugly spectacle. Still, Sylvia would lower the visor of her Morituri helmet and enter the fields of his n-scape. And there, in the smallest centers of his being, at the floating quanta of his remembering self, she would encounter a meaningless cloud of infinite combinations of a very finite set of possibilities. She would enter that cloud and by her perception fix it, as she had been trained to do.

She moved from the window. Before ponging Cindy instructions to send the first patient along, Sylvia glanced in such a manner at the flower-bundle on her desk as to cause the sentient plant on her window-side shelf to tremble. It wasn't just the shadow of the soon-to-come v-night casting its gloom. Beneath the conscious skein of her psyche, the plant detected in Sylvia Yang an immanent revolution.

For the first time in her life, Sylvia Yang did not partake. She dropped her privately-delivered flowers down the waste-tube.

For the plant, it was as if the future had claimed the little office in its death-nailed claw.

Like most Venusians, Sylvia Yang had heard the phrase "sentient plant." Yet, like most, she had never really considered that such a creature might be living in close intimacy with her. She certainly had no idea that the Crittendon regime had installed a sentient plant in every neuroscop's office in the colony. To Sylvia, the intermittently humming crystalline armature, and the tender plant it housed, was simply a curious adornment to her life, the gift from Station 5 that had accompanied her certification. Her attachment to it had gone unremarked upon. It was a living thing, worth her care and respect, less than a friend, more than a pet. She had never wondered what it might see through her if it could enter her mind.

In fact: the plant saw all. The wonderworld of the human senses. Sight: color, shape, volume, quality. Human time, so constant, miniature and all-consuming. The fluid solidity of apparent reality. The plant could even see and marvel at itself—its own tender, wrinkled leaves, arched branches and tensile roots, its own radial extension to the brilliant rays of glory to whose gaze all seeds are opened.

Despite its deployment by the Crittendon government, Dr. Yang's sentient plant had a will of its own. The plant had chosen her from the available opportunities. It had taken the plant a long time to find such a specimen as Dr. Sylvia Yang, neuroscop and Morituri-fluent. Living with her had increased its interest in the human species considerably. Her dedication to her duties was unimpeachable, her survival until now had been relatively assured.

She had promised to lead a long and stable life, cherishing the living things around her, imagining far and wide, never interfering with the larger decisions of the historical timelines.

But by dropping her packet of flowers into the waste-tube, breaking the precious routine, Sylvia Yang had just randomized both of their futures. It was like the first shot of a coming war. It caused the plant's gaze to range far and wide beyond the immediate scene. The other human perspectives coming seemed only further radicalized.

Meanwhile, the sun was going down.

1. DAY'S END, 101 V.E.

"Who controls the past, controls the future: who controls the present, controls the past."

— Party Slogan, Earth, AD 1984, C.E.

Chapter 1

Rogers Collectibles felt cut away from himself. But the part of him that was still here got him from the chamber to the den without falling back into the invitingly purring bed. It found the proper m-suit, an appropriate tie and prepared his anti-matter traveling pak. It took him from den to doorway and through doorway onto the very hot sand. It took him to where he didn't really want to go. It took him to Feed.

The rails had unloaded fat green blossoms into trenches cut fresh into the dunes. Rogers lit an LP, stood with the others lined up under the old morning sun. Already glutted, the children held hands in circles. Wild-eyed, they chanted their sound-churning songs.

> *Love, love, love. Love and flowers.*
> *Love, love, love. Love and flowers.*
> *The sun makes life, gives me power.*
> *Love. Love, love and flowers.*
> *Hands, hands, hands in flowers.*

A motion of a g-op's needle-rifle by the trucks initiated the crush. Pressed into the crowd, Rogers was forced towards the trenches. Adults were already falling in before him, scooping handfuls of the pale green petals into their faces. Elders and the weak ones scuttled at the edge on hands and knees, scrounging for discarded refuse.

He remembered suddenly that he hadn't intended to take flowers at all. A small businessman must retain his poise, no matter how topsy-turvy the times. Spitting out his LP, clutching his hat to his head, Rogers Collectibles tunneled down through the crowd.

Down into the unperceived, but already opening dimension, the place below where—when he found it—everything changed.

A pristine hallwayed interior, seemingly infinite, gave way to mysterious rooms and corridors. Porcelain walls gleamed in a soft, artificial light. Rogers walked quickly along one of the hallways. His limbs were stiff and wooden, as if he were a doll. He came to a halt at the corridor's dead end. There was no doorway, nowhere to go. He turned around.

Distant enough so that it seemed toy-like, a man-lizard peered at him through the telescopic sight of a long range needle-rifle. The green beam of its optical mechanism flashed as it stretched directly to the pupil of Rogers' left eye.

A gentle and erotic perfume, the distant scent of flowers, blew through the open air for some time before he realized he was off Venus Beach. Rogers swallowed, moved his limbs. He brushed the sand off his legs.

He hadn't taken flowers. He was still standing. Beside a concession stand, in fact. He tipped the vendor and made his way homeward to his ad-apt through the dissipating crowd.

By an older time, the Venusian colony was more than two centuries old. But on its own terms it was 201 days young. If Venusia were to set its calendar by the planet's slow rotation, a single Venusian day (a "v-day" the humans called it) would prove very long indeed, consisting of more than 243 Terran, 24-hour days. To counteract the unfortunate situation, the colony's robot factories manufactured Terran Standard Time by blowing a hole in the eternal cloudcover every twelve Terran hours. The regularity established an illusion very like time. Indeed, when the hot sun shone down through the Hole and flowers gleamed in the gold light, it was easy to believe a t-day was altogether different from the perpetual fog of Venusian evening. It wasn't, of course. Though it was a t-day morning right now, it was in fact very late in the v-day. But for a pregnant redness in the sun, one would never know a year-long night was coming.

Of the all the rituals with which Venusians marked their curious situation, none was more central to their culture than Feed. Like a castaway's calendar carved into a piece of driftwood, Feed was a communal marking away of days. Feed was what made the awkward time-scheme real. Feed organized the day. Feed spread out and into everything, and in the process did away with all other public rites.

When the sun wasn't shining, when the cold year's v-night had descended and time was all upside down, Feed was life itself. V-night's t-days were lit by a weak ionization of the local atmosphere, and at night the Hole to the stars opened up a huge and infinite darkness. One stayed indoors, except for Feed.

Take flowers, brother. Princeps Crittendon says we hang by the merest thread over savage gulfs of interplanetary death. Whatever can keep us here, living, breeding, marking our time, must be the end product of civilization. We must make Feed our religion, said the regime. We must dedicate ourselves to its observance. Nay though we walk in the valley of the shadow of death. Since Crittendon's industrialization of flower production and massed distribution, Feed had grown ugly and wild. Feed hung on to the sky with teeth.

It seemed to Rogers Collectibles that Feed hadn't always been so central to Venusian culture. In the first years, people had gotten by rather happily with a future to build; a grand, shared project. They seemed to have had many possible things to accomplish. He couldn't quite remember what. When the flowers had first appeared, he seemed to recall, they had not been made publicly available except on holidays: Princeps' birthday, Sunrise, Sunset, Founding Day.

Rogers had quit Feed three or four t-days ago. He wasn't sure how many. It was why he could remember all these things, why he could reflect at all. The new memories had the unfortunate effect of reminding him of how many other things he had forgotten. He expected that soon things would get easier. He hoped soon to remember everything.

There were only the side effects of quitting flowers to get beyond. The sleeplessness, the short-term memory blanks, the hallucinations. And the lizards.

The lizards were unfortunate.

Looking at his face in the mirror, Rogers saw that abstention seemed to have caused rapid aging. Longevity lines gripped his forehead down and around his increasingly prominent nose. At this rate, Martha would have a hard time recognizing him when she came back.

It hadn't cheered him, coming into the ad-apt, to glance over what was left of the inventory. Lamps, radios and oddities of every sort lay strewn about. There was no market for these things. The truth was that antiques, as a business, had little viability. Corporation Rogers Collectibles contained a single shareholder, himself. When he'd had to let Mandy go, his last working helper, Rogers had told her it was a temporary thing.

"No it's not," Mandy had said, chewing. "But I don't mind. I was wondering why we were working at all."

With a snap of her gum, she wandered out onto the beach. There was no farewell, no sorry it didn't work out. He'd expected at least to have maintained some social contact with Mandy. He'd enjoyed telling her things she didn't know, however disinterested she eventually became. But she'd disappeared, as if they'd never shared a moment together. He had never seen her again.

The future growth of CRC meant little to anyone in the general scheme of things. There were fewer and fewer clients and most of the old contacts no longer returned pongs. But Rogers was determined to keep the business alive. He had the feeling, for one thing, that Martha expected him to. It was his project and he happened to think it was a good idea. Just as there was still a past to be gleaned from evidence everywhere, there was still a future. Trends could suddenly turn. Things could change.

Rogers happened to have in his possession a key to a better future. A chance at enough K to bring in all that he'd lost and more.

When Martha came back, she just might find a comfortable home and a living partner. Rogers Collectibles intended to make good on these possibilities.

The key was an old blue, paperback book. There was even one old, rich and rather distasteful man to whom Rogers might well be able to sell it.

The population was only in the tens of thousands—and going down, it was said, every day. So you would have figured they'd have come across one another before. Yet in all his days in the business, Rogers had never met or even heard of Frank P. Hogart.

Yet long ago, he'd apparently found the old man's business card. He could no longer remember where or how. But he'd saved it, filed it away under *Collectors: Books*.

The card was actually printed; it had to be read to be understood.

> FRANK P. HOGART
> BOOKS RARE AND OUT OF PRINT
> BOUGHT AND SOLD
> 22A VENUSIA

Hogart was not listed, though a pong number was printed on the back of the card.

The old man had received Rogers' pong as if he didn't quite understand the technology. Not only was Frank P. Hogart a fool, but he was also impolite and nearly savage in manners.

"You disturb me for this? Melton's *Brane World* is hardly a rarity. Not only the most widely published book in Venusia—"

"Actually," Rogers objected. "That's Crittendon's *Reflections*. And this is a Terran copy of *Brane World*, Mr. Hogart. A 23rd century printing of the true story of Melton told in his own words, with a Preface by Ruby Greene."

The old man closed his eyes. He must have been very old, Rogers realized, to show so much age. "There's no such edition."

Rogers produced the book as if out from a hat. An object's sudden appearance often helped fix the collector's interest. "Look for yourself. This copy of *Brane World* has particular value, Mr. Hogart. The original Terran owners have penciled notes in on the first page."

"Eh?"

Rogers pointed to a handwritten phrase beneath the book's subtitle ("A Stay on the Paphos Loop"). He read it aloud. *"Is one 'grand lie.'*

"There's more," he said, shifting the book. "Beneath this someone else, a later owner, has written: *'But it's a good one.'*

"Yes, yes. Well I've never seen the edition before. You're claiming that this volume was printed on Terra?"

"New Caledonia, 2204, in fact. It's a first edition. Not the very first edition, but it's the first edition of a second printing. And the second printing is importantly different from the first.

"How so?"

"Because of Ruby Greene's preface."

At the name, the old man's eyes hardened, black and dry like seeds.

"I'll want to see this book for myself."

"I'm asking for 300 Klugers, Mr. Hogart."

"How soon can you bring it to me?"

Even with his lack of proficiency, Rogers had known right away what this book might mean to the right collector. People these days tended to forget the specifics of their history. But the name Ruby Greene sill carried weight. Girls were still named Ruby by the state, and important landmarks bore her name. In Rogers' own lifetime, Melton himself, Venusia's founder, had been more than famous. He had been like a god. Getting his start in the antique business, Rogers had first dealt in small likenesses of Melton and Morituri. But there was little interest in such things now. Crittendon's temp-procs forbade public ritual except on holidays and Melton had consequently fallen away. Reduced to abstraction, he'd been forgotten. Still, for someone who remembered, a Terran edition of Melton's first book would have a powerful resonance.

Since the day he'd picked *Brane World* up off a heap of a dead person's effects, Rogers himself had been possessed by a desire to read it. Which was why, in fact, he'd first forgotten to take the flowers. Struggling through the preface, he just hadn't bothered.

Young Peter Melton was poor and without connections. Melton was scientifically minded, dreaming of planets and interplanetary flight while other boys dreamed of girls and celebrity. He had signed up for the Merchant Marines because it was the only way for him to get into space. It was during the Fall of Nations, when the chaos in space matched earth's lethal brutality, that Melton's cruiser, *Barstow*, was docked on a Lunar orbit. As a non-military craft, the merchant cruiser found itself waiting for transport home that never arrived. When the United Collectives authorized its commander to raid the Danish Expansion's lunar domes, Melton and others rebelled.

This mutiny was led by scientist Ruby Greene, Melton's lover and superior officer. Ruby was both inspiration and mentor to the young officer. When she and the mutineers took command, they steered the damaged freighter towards Mars to join the libertarians. They never got there. The captain and the crew who had stayed loyal had managed to damage the ship's long-rage engines. *Barstow* made an emergency landing on the asteroid Paphos, then passing near Luna. Ruby decided to set up temporary shelter on its surface, and she set about organizing necessary repairs.

Melton loved to spacewalk. He'd even made a temporary lab on the surface of the asteroid. One day when he was there alone, the ship lifted off without him. There was no answer on the radio bands they had decided upon in case of emergency. No explantation whatsoever. He was simply abandoned.

Peter Melton found himself castaway on the surface of the rapidly traveling, inter-system asteroid. He determined to survive. On the rock, with the materials pre-selected by himself and Greene for just such an emergency, he managed to erect "Tee-Pee", the legendary life-support shelter and rudimentary greenhouse. He kept a log of his days, if only to keep a semblance of sanity, and broadcast his experiences on Ruby Greene's private bands. Most of the time he speculated on what had happened on board the *Barstow*. The inconclusiveness of Ruby's abandonment drove him mad. As his messages back were met only with silence, and the asteroid took him farther and farther from Earth, he began to believe she had left him there purposefully.

Sixteen terran-years later, when he was received by a collective refugee ship on a return pass from Venus, Melton had forgotten how to speak.

Earth healed him. He brought himself back to human language, he said, by writing *Brane World*.

The book made him briefly famous and quite fabulously rich. Its early chapters, describing the corruption of the UC Navies, and contextualizing Terran politics from a spacer's perspective, caused a sensation. Spacers then were in vogue. Movies were made; interviews held. Strangers approached him with paranormal plans and ready funds.

"Gravity," the book's first lines read, "is the weakest of the known forces. But it is also the strangest." The book contained rudiments of an astrophysical revolution. Much skepticism was put forth by the scientific community in denial of Melton's astronomical claims. Latter portions of the text were described as the ravings of a man who'd flown solitary too fast, too long and too far.

Engulfed in rapidly degrading global eco-politics, faced with the total and complete moral failure of science, people couldn't muster the imagination necessary to believe in inter-dimensional travelers, atmospheric oddities, or talking plants. And because *Brane World* challenged one of astronomy's most sacred totems—the uninhabitability of Venus, second planet from the Sun—Melton was held, for a time, up to ridicule.

Then he was mostly forgotten.

But certain of his observations chimed with possibilities that Hugo Morituri, the celebrated "super-mind of nano-engineering," was brooding upon in the South Seas. At Morituri's invitation, Peter Melton came to Tahiti. They embarked on a year-long study of all known data concerning Venus. At year's end, the scientist was convinced. The Melton & Morituri Corporation, M&M, was forged for the purpose of settling that planet. Venusia was born.

From their South Pacific base, the Founders began preparations for emigration, gathering preselected followers from the dispossessed of all the System.

According to the Preface, Ruby Greene surfaced in Canada around the same time Melton first returned to Earth. The controversy concerning the first edition caught her attention and she wrote the preface as soon as she read it. This edition of *Brane World* was privately printed by a Revolutionary Communard in Canada after the Fall. The so-called ORD, the "Order of Dawn" published an expanded edition with Ruby's corroborating preface, one year after the first ships set out in 2204.

It was Ruby Greene's presence in the text that made the edition particularly valuable. Ruby had slipped out of history when the *Barstow* had first left Paphos. There was no mention of what had become of her in any records Rogers could find.

The old man snorted. "You're not even human. You're a fucking flower. You know nothing of history."

"I'm learning to read. I've read the Preface myself. There are number of antique V's and sound recordings I've come across relating the legend of Melton, the Founder. They helped me along, of course. I've picked up enough scraps of information here and there that I can safely say I know as much as anyone of my generation about these matters."

"Hogwash," growled Hogart. "You've convinced me your "first second edition" is a damned fake. Ruby died. She died in space, on the *Barstow*. Do you hear me?"

"I hear you quite well. But you're wrong. Ruby Greene didn't die. The officers the mutineers had captured persuaded the guards to set them free while Melton was off-ship. Ruby and her crew were jumped, imprisoned and taken to a Lunar prison. It was there she claimed to have received radio signals from Melton on the wavelength pre-selected in their original plans. She was unable, of course, to respond."

The old man's eyes closed amid a cluster of the softest, wrinkled skin.

Rogers continued. "He sent out radio letters to her on their old channel, you see. Every day, like a diary. Ruby Greene had taught him everything he'd known of science, of life and more. He was young and clearly in love with her. Even though he believed her dead, he spoke to her. Sent her messages, accusations, descriptions of what he perceived. The thing was, she received them all. And, unless he saw this edition, and it's doubtful he did, he never knew."

Hogart leaned back away from the Iye. His image was somewhat distorted.

"Do you understand what you're saying?"

Rogers noted a tall, twin-pointed cap fixed tight on the old man's head. It was as if he had horns.

"I believe I do," Rogers said.

"I need to see the book, to prove with my own eyes you're lying. Block 22a 11PAM your time tomorrow."

Chapter 2

What was the time? Nothing was working like it used to, not even his watch, which seemed to be suffering some sort of generalization corruption. Outside the kitchen window, the big sun had already eaten up half of the morning's Hole. Along the beach, the throngs were still dispersing. Day's End flowers were the finest of year. For a moment it was as if a part of Rogers Collectibles, an alien, animal part, was still there. Twisting up amidst the soft, green petals and their bitter flesh. Rolling in the muddy trenches.

Rogers braced himself for a sudden descent into another world. His body turning wooden, doll-like. Lizards pursuing him down ambiguous hallways—the dreams of the flower addict. The terrifying sense that he wasn't real. Just thinking about it caused Rogers to sweat.

But it didn't come.

He lit and LP and tapped his watch once again for the time. The watch mistook his intention and switched on the stage. A Johnny Ho segment came noisily alive on dencenter V. Johnny Ho leaping, Johnny Ho soaring, Johnny Ho running faster than the eye could see. It was bizarre the things the freak could do and, apparently, entirely true.

Everything on V—with its holographic solidity—was true, truer than Roger's own fantasy of a daily life. What were his useless collections worth when a man could run faster than the Iye could see? People like Rogers, the little people, were machines, receivers of holographic immediacy. Freedom didn't apply. As Johnny Ho hung for the moment aloft, arms outstretched, launching a dizzying cliff-side leap—Rogers told his watch off. But it didn't respond.

The multitudes boomed out as one: "Ho! Johnny Ho!" and the bird-like man fell through the air.

VMC "Leave-It-To" Larry Held narrated, with familiar droning irony. "Look at that, hoppies," he whispered. "He thinks he can fly. Look in wonder, my hoppies."

Rogers walked into the den and thought off the V manually.

"Watch. Time?"

"Late morning, sir."

"What time in the morning?"

"10:30, sir."

"Exactly?"

"10:36, sir."

"I take it that it's 10:37, then. Which, for your information, is near 11. Quite near, in fact. As I told you yesterday, I have a meeting at 11 and I should already have been on the way there."

In the temporary office he'd constructed out of what would someday be Martha's studio, Rogers located his indivsafe and breathed on its grid. After an annoying second's pause, the little door slid quietly open.

It was still there.

Rogers held the blue, paperbacked *Brane World* to his nose. He inhaled the faint pungency of its living molds. He checked to see if the two hand-written notes were still there, particularly the second one. The "but it's a good one." It seemed like someone very wise had written that, someone who understood more than he did about what a book could be. Someone he'd like to have known. He buzzed the soft pages with his thumb, watching a three-dimensional blur rise up from the passing words.

He shook his head of the rising dizziness. It wouldn't do to experience a lizard hallucination now. It wouldn't do at all. His entire future was at stake.

Rogers fixed the book in his anti-matter pak, and hurried to the harness. There was little time to make himself presentable.

"How about a shave?"

"How about 900 Klugers?"

"Eh?" It was an old mirror, and easily confused. Indeed, the situation was difficult to comprehend, even for Rogers himself. The point of a needle had been inserted into the pupil of his left eye. The needle was cold, and apparently sucking something from his eye into a shoulder-device worn by a human-sized lizard.

"Ah," said the lizard. "Id's awaeg."

Rogers, outraged, pulled his head away.

Surprised, the lizard also leaned backwards. The needle slid out of Rogers' eye with a slick, fatty snap. Aware that a hand somewhere in the future was gently slapping his face, Rogers Collectibles (who was committed to keeping composure at all times) tried to keep focus on the enormous, slithering thing. He failed.

The slapping hand seemed to be attached to the thin arm of a beautiful girl. Suddenly nauseous, Rogers Collectibles swallowed hard against the instant transition to a state of high speed. Acceleration weighed heavy, and everything swirled in a dizzy, merry-go-round melt. He found himself hooked into a railbus, arcing up and along an arch from the city below.

Rogers focussed. The girl's eyes reflecting his own, her confrontational gaze and crackpot frown, helped him fix his position.

"Welcome back to reality," she smiled. "Are you all right?"

"We're on a railbus."

"Of course we're in a railbus." She swung in beside him. The warmth of her body touching his shoulders, the gentle scent mixed up in her hair, brought on a sudden, bewildering sensation.

She was looking at him. "What are you wearing on your head?"

"It's a hat."

"You should try to attract less attention," the girl said. "You were talking in your sleep. They're apt to re-educate you for something like that."

"What was I saying?"

"Something about a shave. It looks like you never got one by the way."

"How far have we come?"

"You've already made a full circuit, we're looping back. I'm getting off at Castlestop. What about you?"

Through the port-hole nearest his head, over the railside shops and artstalls of inland Venusia, the Castle seemed distant and small, a scale model of itself under an artificial sky.

"Do you live in the Castle?"

"No," she smiled. "Nearby. But someday I will." And then, whispering close to his ear. "Did you miss morning Feed?"

Rogers didn't answer.

"You're an addict, aren't you? You're a desister. But you're not so far gone yet. How many days has it been?"

"Listen, thanks for the interest. But you don't know what you're talking about."

"You don't understand," she said. "I'm a journalist. My name's Martha."

Rogers Collectibles tapped his wrist. "Time?"

"Late t-morning, sir."

He remained composed. They were in fact on the railbus, swinging out in a long arc over the city. His hallucination had occasioned a short-term memory loss. The young woman remained close to him, as she had been, as she should be. Rogers felt very peculiar. She grew as you knew her, he sensed. After the first shock, her thinness filled out. It was like the person you thought you first saw; that bony young creature was already a ghost.

"My name is Martha Dobbs," she was saying. " You may have seen me on Larry Held's "Windows on the Weird." I roam around and catch interesting people on live-broadcast reality V. I have a flying Iye. It's always ready to go."

She was observing him. Too closely, in fact.

"That's a funny old watch," she said. But when Rogers glanced back at her, he saw that things were already changing.

He was falling to pieces. The memory of her face fragmented into a thousand identical images of itself, all large-eyed and young, spinning mechanically around till they inhered, slowly, into an uncertain wash. Flickering down then and fusing, finally, into the head of a single, q-suited lizard.

Rogers felt stiff and unreal. A desperation took hold of him. He reached out to touch the arms of his chair. What was this world? Why wouldn't it leave him alone?

By its look and feel, the wooden desk at which the lizard sat was a priceless Terran original. The worn ruddy red of its top shone with the wisdom of age. The object's great mass had a gravity to it. Rogers preferred looking at it than at the lizard. But the forked tongue slithering lightly along the feathered jaw was hard not to see.

"You'll plobably thinging you'll belly obzervand," the lizard said. "You bill dot bebember though. You debber do."

He would remember the lizard, he knew. But he imagined all this had something to do with not taking the flowers, so he said nothing.

"And whad is this?"

The light from the porcelain hallways shone through a half-opaque window in the old wooden door to the left, enough to illuminate the head of the lizard inquisitor. Other than that, the room was dark. Rogers Collectibles lit an LP. He had the feeling that there were more creatures lurking, watching from the shadows.

The Lizard leaned back. Its old chair creaking with age, the thing fixed him in its ambiguous, fish-eyed gaze. It held a blue-jacketed book in one claw.

Rogers had to speak. "That book belongs to me," he said. "You can't take it."

Chapter 3

Rogers Collectibles was an unremarkable patient. Among the scores of neurotics examined by Sylvia Yang were citizens who showed a proclivity towards economic dissolution. Rogers was one of those who seemed to pursue failure with intent. He had come to her a handful of times over the last three years, a quiet eccentric who had reluctantly submitted to several scans. The scans had shown a neurotic interest in the affairs of his antique dealership, one that could grow into possible psychosis, she'd seen. Especially considering the accidental effects of a career involved in handling objects of the past. But Rogers did seem to have a genuine regard for the junk he peddled. If a patient had something to live for, however delusional, Sylvia would rather not interfere. With Rogers, she'd never pursued treatment.

In session Rogers had spoken repeatedly of a "Martha." The doctor had assumed the "Martha" was a standard object of ficto-transference in the ordinary circuitry directing Venusian trauma away from consciousness. Most citizens had erected missing loved-ones in their psyches. For the Venusian-born, like Rogers Collectibles, such delusions were often necessary for survival. Without family and certain origin, one had to generate actual false memories to maintain a functioning psyche. Sylvia herself felt a great absence in her life, but her work with other minds demanded she allow her own a wide and abstract presence, empty of fantasy.

So when a Citizen Martha Dobbs ponged from the rail-station (Rogers' watch had given out the name of his neuroscop) and informed her that Rogers had collapsed into a state of catatonic consciousness, Sylvia reviewed the facts of his case with interest.

The girl "Martha" must have been real after all. Rogers Collectibles must have managed an actual relationship.

When the two of them arrived at Cherry Tree Lane, Dr. Yang ushered Martha Dobbs into the office, leaving Cindy to revive the zombie-like Rogers in the lab. Sylvia was taken aback by the young woman's glamor, her large mascara-lined eyes and the length of her limbs.

"I must tell you that I'm surprised," Sylvia said. "Rogers Collectibles always talks about you. He insists that you'll be coming, expecting a happy home ready and waiting. But I never pictured you as a real, breathing woman. But you are. And so beautiful."

"Please, thank you. But it looks like he's not very sure of much that's going on."

"Maybe the strain of supporting an imaginary, fetishized version of "Martha" when you are actually so very real has caused him to relinquish mental control of received reality. It's possible. He could be seeing all sorts of things."

"Listen," Martha Dobbs cut in. "I'm a reality-V journalist," She took a relax, crossing her long legs. "And as to me and him, there's been some mistake. The Martha thing is a coincidence."

A mistake? Had her decision not to take her morning flowers already bred such chaos? Sylvia frowned as Cindy led Rogers Collectibles, somewhat rumpled and the worse for wear, into the office.

Rogers, having just understood that he was not in a lizard inquisitor's cell, but in his neuroscop's office, opened his mouth to object.

But he was held by the sight of Dr. Yang's grey-tinged black hair tumbling out from her Morituri helmet. Her eyes surprised him with their dark intelligence. He decided it would be better to volunteer no disorderly behavior. Things were bad enough already.

In a relax by the window, the blonde girl from the railbus was looking up at him from her pretty, pointed face.

Rogers couldn't help himself. He turned to the Doctor. "Could you please return my pak? There's an important engagement—"

"Mr. Rogers," said Dr. Yang. "Be calm. Please sit down. Your belongings are on the table."

"I am calm. Quite calm."

Reluctantly, Rogers took the proffered relax directly across the doctor's deskmodule. He put his hat on his head, fastened his watch. Took up his pak.

"Is that hat one of your antiques?" asked the doctor.

"Yes."

"I see. How are you feeling?"

"Very well, thank you."

"Do you know why you're here?"

"I suppose I passed out on the railbus. I didn't sleep much last night." He looked at Martha Dobbs. "What has she told you?"

"Nothing," said the neuroscop. "She hasn't told me a thing."

Rogers wondered. "I only met her on the bus to-t-day. If it is still today. And I really—"

"It is," his watch said. "12:45PAM."

His heart sank. "Wonderful," he muttered. "I've managed to miss my appointment with Frank P. Hogart. The most important deal of my career."

But had he missed the appointment? Gripped by a sinking certainty, ignoring the women, Rogers opened his pak and materialized its contents. The book was not there.

"Please," he said. "Prescribe me some medication. I'll be sure to take it when it comes. I'm very sorry to have bothered you both." He stood up and took off his hat. "I'll be leaving."

The two women were staring at him.

"What is it?"

"I'm afraid we have to talk, Mr. Rogers. It's a formality, but the only other option is to recommended re-education."

Rogers sat back down.

Outside the office window, the sun was swelling. Red light bathed the cells of the windowside plant in glory. Resplendent with energy, the plant turned on its pump to circulate water throughout its crystalline armature.

Doctor Yang lowered her visor. The helmet's twin pincers locked at a point directly in front of Rogers' forehead. He imagined the head of a giant white insect gazing across at him.

Maybe he did need help, after all. Maybe there was something she could do. "Time is changing," he wearily explained. "Or my memory of time. I will be somewhere, and then suddenly somewhere else. I feel unreal, sometimes, like a doll. I have black-outs. Blocks of life seem to disappear. It's like I've just stepped into another time and space, but I haven't gotten there from the usual way. From A to B I mean. Not even to C. Sometimes I'm not sure of when which things are occurring and in what order they do. For instance I came to on a railbus today, but I have no memory of boarding it. The last thing I knew I was shaving. And now I'm in your office and I don't know how I got here. At some point did I get to my client and give him my book? I don't think so, though the book is evidently gone. I can assure you, meanwhile, I'm quite stable, mentally speaking. You can see I remain composed. I know who I am, what I need to be doing. I know, for instance, that I've never met this person before today. This Martha Dobbs." He turned to her. "I know that. You are not my Martha."

But as Rogers turned to look at Martha Dobbs, he was disturbed to see something familiar in the smiling way she returned his gaze.

"What does your Martha look like?"

Though Rogers easily grasped a non-pictorial essence in his memory that was, simply, Martha, no beloved image came to him. There was warmth, even a kind of soft smell he remembered. An appreciation of fine things, surely. Very personal things. But nothing more specific. Nothing at all.

"Think of Martha. Right now."

Rogers concentrated on how the very word Martha caused his heart to change its rhythm, his body to feel the tingling happiness of home. But his mind, as if intent on driving him crazy, conjured up the image of the girl from the bus and not Martha at all.

Suddenly enraged, Rogers smacked himself on the head.

"Calm down, Citizen Collectibles. She is a Martha," said the ruby lips of Dr. Yang, visible from below her helmet's creamy visor. "She showed me her tag. Martha Dobbs, Journalist."

"Surely you can see with your helmet that the name Dobbs means nothing to me. My Martha is older than this girl."

"I'm an adult," said Martha Dobbs, with a curious smile. "Older than you all seem to think."

"It is true that you have no memory of the name Dobbs before today," the doctor admitted. "Perhaps you prefer to call her Martha Collectibles—"

Martha Dobbs giggled.

Again Rogers lost composure. "And do you see giant lizards there, Dr. Yang?" he shouted. "In porcelain hallways and dark offices? Running around in my head? With little feathers, tongues flickering down along their jaws—"

He stopped speaking, terribly embarrassed by the outburst. The pincers atop the doctor's helmet curled to meet one another at the tips. Rogers could almost physically feel their interference in his neuroscape.

Lizards. It had been a long time since she'd heard of them.

TEMP-PROC 112A: IN CASE WHEREIN SUBJECT REPORTS INTERACTION WITH LIZARDS, AGENT IS REQUIRED TO INITIATE IMMEDIATE RESET OF SUBJECT'S MENTAL PATTERNS BY WAY OF MORITURI APPARATUS.

Orders couldn't be clearer, but Sylvia held back. She lifted the visor without blotting Rogers' mind.

"There are no lizards in your memory," she said calmly.

"How could I refer to them if they weren't there?"

"There are no lizards in Venusia. But we have the word "lizard" in our language, thus the idea exists in all of our minds. You imagined them. And memories of imagined images are not true memories."

"I didn't imagine them. I saw them. I assure you. I spoke to one this morning. Your console should be able to tell you that I'm not lying when I say I have seen lizards. Large talking lizard-men, in fact. I was speaking to one of them when this Martha brought me here."

Sylvia was surprised to see that the journalist had unpacked a flying Iye and set it hovering above her head. The little silver ball was turning, tracing the entire office in 3-D.

"Well how about that, hoppies?" Martha Dobbs was saying, in a new, artificial voice. "Large talking lizards, he says. Welcome to the office of Dr. Sylvia Yang, certified neuroscop and Morituri Fluent—"

"Excuse me, Citizen Dobbs," Sylvia interrupted. She took off her helmet and looked into the Iye, shaking her luxuriant hair.

"*Shhh…*' The machine whispered. "*Go on as if Iye wasn't here.*"

Sylvia didn't like it, but the Iye's anonymous power had sent a thrill tingling through her face, all along her skin; down, even, around her legs. She shifted uncomfortably in her chair.

"Hey, turn that thing off," Rogers said. "This is private."

"Be assured that Citizen Dobbs will honor this office's confidentiality, Mr. R. It is right that this interview be recorded, because there are many others out there who may benefit by hearing what I have to say. Look at yourself, sir. You're a shambles—mentally, physically and spiritually."

This outraged him, she saw. But she went on, finding her voice. "Though you've not seen fit to tell me honestly, you have no memory of taking flowers in the last four t-days. Extensive abstinence from Feed is expressly illegal by perm-proc. Mr. R., you're still in control of yourself. You've done nothing yet to hurt yourself or others. But you're experiencing psychotic breakdowns. I must insist that you go to the next Feed. If you don't, re-education will be a necessity. For now, we'll give you a temporary re-set."

He stiffened.

"Citizen R., the flowers, though not narcotic themselves, perform for us many of the services of narcotics. They relieve us. They allow a sensory constant in our anomalous lives around which we can begin to organize our emotions in time. Without the flowers, we simply fly to pieces. The flowers link us to one another in shared experience, they weave a shared community. When that constant is removed from your individual life, Mr. R., when you see fit to stop taking flowers with the rest of us, the world we share will necessarily collapse around you."

"Very good," said the patient. "Point taken. I'll feed this evening. Now if we're finished here I'll be on my way."

"That's it," Martha Dobbs whispered. She rose happily from the relax by the window—the Iye turning to catch her. "Thank you both so very very much."

Sylvia bit her lip. Was she such a capable hypocrite?

For the plant, it was beautiful loving Sylvia Yang in the present, without worrying about the shape of the future. Yet the inflation of beauty exponentially increased life's fragility. Sylvia was beginning to observe and remember, to trace causal relations in her mind that were no longer directly perceivable. Her future (and the plant's own) seemed to be governed by the new perceptions of these others, the antique dealer and the reporter. Now, for instance, Martha Dobbs' flying Iye had not only recorded the scene but was already spreading it on live feed over all Venusia.

The sentient plant trembled as it traced the broadcast waves undulating irretrievably out into the frozen volume of space, thereby solidifying their fact as receivable history.

The plant disliked thinking about human destiny. Destiny, as a concept, contradicted its own immediate experience of time. Living within an infinity of interlocking parallel universes, the plant could grow equally in them all. The human stream moved too quickly, changed too fast between, to impose a single idea of growth upon the possibilities.

The plant was particularly distressed to see the broadcast had already reached places m-op Niftus Norrington was traveling. This Norrington was precisely the sort of human the plant wanted nothing to do with. There, in his dreams, beneath the shadow of a three-headed spear with a prong shaped like a tongue, the angry little man had finally managed to grow taller than the monsters attacking him. And Martha Dobbs' broadcast, live fed across the colony, had awoken him to a world in which he didn't so easily belong.

Chapter 4

A pea-green office. A reality V. A gorgeous neuroscop. An unshaven screwball sitting up straight in a relax as a journalist repeated, "large, talking lizards." A flying V projecting the little scene over the bed, staging its fact, drawing him back to the waking world.

M-op Niftus Norrington wished Melody hadn't thought-switched on the V, but she'd done it before he'd opened his eyes. Now, of course, he'd opened them. Now it was too late. When he made the monthly scan, the g-ops would see what he'd heard and perceived—the ridiculous scene burned into his brain like a brand.

"I see lizards, Doc, lot's of 'em."

TEMP-PROC 112A: IN CASE WHEREIN AGENT LEARNS OF SUBJECT REPORTING INTERACTION WITH LIZARDS, AGENT IS REQUIRED TO INITIATE IMMEDIATE RESET OF SUBJECT'S MENTAL PATTERNS BY WAY OF MORITORI APPARATUS.

Niftus Norrington was less than a meter tall. Niftus Norrington was a dwarf. But he was also an m-op. M-ops entered society as a citizens. They were intended to pass through questionable crowds and collect information to be gleaned at monthlies, when the g-ops scanned their brains. Usually, he was directed to a particular location, or individual. It didn't happen so often anymore.

But a lizard outbreak was a true rarity. An m-op, when he heard anyone mention seeing lizards, anywhere, ever, it was his duty to locate and blot that person's mind. The harder he searched for the subject the better, from Station 5's point of view. They'd want to see everything the lizard man might have touched. However attractive she might be, this neuroscop was the typical Venusian professional. She didn't know about the lizards. She said she'd give the patient a temporary reset, not a full-on re-education blot. Dirty work was for dirty people to do.

The thought of the Doctor's pretensions outraged him. Norrington muted the V and pushed Melody's huge legs off of his torso.

She whined, "It's second Feed already?"

"Shut up," he said. "You're sleeping."

Melody, the way he looked at it, was less useful than an animated doll. But she had some interesting possessions, chief among which was her holo-mirror. Nifty had dislodged it from her harness-chamber and set it up in her den, so he could see himself properly—in full. Standing before his manifested self made him strong; his self became stronger by facing him, as if it projected itself though the apparatus from another universe, equally real. Nifty and his holo-self took strength from one another.

Their hair was braided into long spoles, exposing broad, ponderous brows. Their hard chest muscles gave way to rippling abs and mountainous biceps straining. Together, they shared the rick of a full-sized man.

Nifty slipped on a natty n-robe and stepped into his familiar sandals. He was ready, at last, for the helmet.

Very slowly, he turned and looked around Melody's ratty little ad-apt. He opened the closet. There, on the top-most shelf, the blank, dark face of the Morituri helmet looked down as if it knew he could never reach it.

He clenched his fists. "Melody?"

She'd put it up there as joke, but she wasn't laughing when he yanked her out of bed. When she stretched to reach the helmet on tip-toe, her pock-marked bottom was full in his face.

"You're so rude," she said.

Nifty dropped to all fours behind her. Grasping the helmet, she came down on her heels, leaning, ever so slightly, backwards. She toppled easily over his body. When her head hit the carp with a dull thud, he chased the helmet rolling across the floor.

And now she sat up all teary. Warming up for a good screaming, he saw. A good let-the-little-freak-have-it fit. "Asshole! Midget!"

Nifty didn't let it get to him. He felt better already. He fixed the code-Q Morituri tight on his head and lowered visor.

"Helmet," he said.

"Sir."

"There's an investigation to attend to."

"So it seems, Sir. If one might point out, however, that we've missed First Feed again, Sir."

"There's still time for Second Feed, isn't there?"

"Yes, Sir."

Nifty detected a pregnant tone of condescension in the "yes", but he let it go. A code Q Morituri helmet was a classy piece of machinery. It inspired patience.

Tech-code Q superceded order P and below. Those without Q were unaware of Q's existence. The gangly-limbed squares who brushed past him on the beach, even those wearing helmets, had no idea what this "little fellow" could know about them if he chose.

Mostly, he didn't choose. Niftus Norrington rarely scanned unless he had to. What might have been amusing in the singular soon proved monotonous in the general. Limited to labels like "midget" or "shrimp" upon meeting someone slightly vertically challenged, Nifty's contemporaries spent most of their energy convincing themselves of their own "normalcy." They were pro-grammed into frightening symmetry. The more Nifty saw of these people, the more he believed they altogether made up one, single, gigantic, stupid animal—too big and listless to be even self-aware.

Before he'd been awarded order Q, of course, Nifty would have given an inch to get inside a woman's head, to be able to control the mind of a woman. He had a thing about women. But that was before he knew what a neuroscape was. Navigation of the female 'scape demanded such attention to detail, such careful movement that before you knew it, it was manipulating you. In the mysterious nimbus of autonomous thought-points, you had no idea which modality to access for sexual fantasy. Even assuming you found something like it, you'd find yourself in no time lost among pointed demonologies about pointless events that had nothing to do with sex at all.

The Morituri interpreted mind-waves pictorially. Because it transmitted them via the cortex, it had the potential to work like an interactive V. The helmet could add the immersion of actual mass and volume to the observing gaze. Wearing the helmet was the purest extension of a certain kind of desire that remained unfulfilled. You couldn't stay with it. After a wide open moment of promise on first penetration, the vista gave way to something as flat as a map. Bodies in motion turned into traces of line and snippets of sound. These, of course, were more easily managed.

In this environment, Nifty could navigate the infinite maps. By fixing one memory, he could infer and draw out other memories that were out there. Paths opened up, often providing their own locomotion. He could move instantly, beyond space and time, guided by pure intuition and the limits of his own imagination. He could find a single phone-number from the past in less than a t-second and never remember how he'd done it.

Of course if things got too tight, there was always the blot. Sometimes regulations required it. This was an electromagnetic burning out from inside; a quantum escape from n-scape reality. Since the neuroscape was simply a cloud of possibility supporting consciousness, consciousness couldn't know what had occurred when it was momentarily swallowed. From the ineffable blankness of weird possibility, you emerged baptized and clean, landed on the shores of your most probable existence. Only after several hours (whole t-days for some) did your specific life reassemble around you. Flowers helped a great deal. You gathered yourself back feeding.

Niftus Norrington had worked very hard in the lower eche-
lons of security to raise himself to order Q m-op status. He'd
done the dirtiest work there was. Hauled corpses, cleaned trenches, fertilized. When he was finally promoted to m-op, Nifty's size
had been an asset. Because a dwarf wasn't a real man, he could be
trusted with order Q knowledge of the human mind. A dwarf was
easy to control.

Nifty's order-Q helmet did gave a lift to his walk. It was like
wearing an invisible platform shoe. It wasn't necessarily a healthy
thing to base your life upon, maybe, but this helmet was all he had
on the world. It was his private piece of the Morituri Revolution
and he intended to keep it and use it everyday, even if it meant
scrounging around the colony in search of an anonymous lizard-
scoping psychotic. Because if he didn't find Citizen R. and wipe his
mind, they'd take it away from him.

At Feed, the helmet awarded valuable anonymity in the trenches. Face concealed by the visor, spoles tied up and bound, a
helmeted Niftus Norrington could pass for a child and make his
way to the front and feed early. Kids were easy to throw around and
when grown-ups got in the way he could slip easily around them.
He could get the freshest first flowers.

Close in the sticky fray, his visor up, chewing thick-pressed
bunches of petal meat under half-raised visor, no one ever noticed
the "child's" thick hands and rough strength, nor the vast amount of
flowers he consumed. Niftus Norrington could consume more of the
thick green petals than a man twice his size. He was a master feeder.

"Address on Dr. Ying," he was saying, still a little disoriented
by flowers. "Dr. Something Ying."

"Anti-ager, Sir?" the helmet inquired.

"Neuroscop. I don't remember her first name. It's a woman,
Ying—"

"Yang. Dr. Sylvia Yang, Sir, neuroscopic councillor, Morturi
fluent."

"Fluent did you say? I doubt it."

"It is a questionable designation, Sir."

The memory of the doctor's office on V came to him, with all its professional superiority. Apparently they had dyed Johanna Zeep's hair with tinges of grey and implanted the star into the neuroscop's role. Nifty had no problem with Johanna Zeep, no problem at all. But he doubted the real Dr. Yang would turn out quite so leshy.

"Address?"

"Block 13b, Sir. Cherry Tree Lane."

"Make an appointment. We're going now."

The helmet over-rode his lift-visor command.

"Sir," it said. "Required communication 28."

"Shut down."

The helmet continued. "Dr. Yang enjoys the use of order-Q technology. Not permitted to scan or in any way inform her of the nature of investigation. Nor should she be allowed to scan you, Sir. The dangers of neuro-feedback outweigh—"

Nifty removed the helmet from his head manually. It wasn't the machine's fault it had been programmed this way. So he wouldn't use the helmet when he interviewed the doctor. He wasn't worried.

Under the shade of an avocado tree, Nifty bought a fruit ice from a vendor and requested a large bag. He covered the helmet with the bag so that it looked like he'd simply purchased a coconut. He ate the ice, thinking of how easy it would be to trick the doctor into telling him where to find this Citizen R. who saw lizards. He'd mind-blot the lizard-man good and quick. With any luck, he'd be done by evening.

"Are you angry? Say something."

Rogers Collectibles could already smell Ishtar Ocean. The odor was sulfurous and nasty, it cast its ancient ugliness over everything. He walked with Martha Dobbs down a shaded lane, taking refuge from the hot sun. She hadn't packed up her flying Iye and it was following them on radio tether like a pet.

The girl reporter was in high spirits. "Thank you, so much," she said. "I'm so glad I got in there. Larry ran it live."

She gripped his arm and turned to him, her fingers digging into his flesh. "You were great."

"Forgive me if I can't match your enthusiasm," said Rogers, pulling away. "Do you realize how this looks for my business? I admitted losing an object, admitted hallucinations, abstinence, missing an appointment. Who do you expect to work with me after that? I don't believe I gave you the authority to broadcast—"

"Oh don't be so paranoid. People want to see things as they really are. You were so honest in there; it was remarkable, funny. What's wrong with that? Your hat is hilarious. You're going to keep looking for your book, aren't you? Maybe someone saw the broadcast and will return it to you. Maybe someone wants to buy a watch or a hat like yours."

They stopped walking and she stood there before him, blinking her thick blue eyes. She really seemed to believe what she was saying.

"I suppose it's possible," Rogers admitted. "But they won't know how to reach me because of the Doctor's anonymity policy."

"I like you," she said. "I want to film more of your life."

"Is the Iye feeding this?"

"No."

"Good. Listen. I just want to make sure. I have no reason to believe I really understand anything these days. You're not my... you're not .... You see, there is a Martha in my life—"

"I've never seen you before, if that's what you want to know," Martha Dobbs said. "I'm not your Martha. At least I think I'm not."

"What do you mean, you think you're not?"

"Who knows what memories are real, these days? When I saw you on the bus, your mouth hanging open, talking to yourself. It was the strangest thing. It was like...."

"It was like what?"

"I don't know. Déjà vu."

Rogers felt himself reddening. "You don't know. Jorx Crittendon, how could you not know? I know you're not my Martha. My Martha wouldn't...." He held himself from finishing, out of politeness.

But her face flushed in anger. "Maybe it's time you got over it."

"Got over what?"

"This Martha thing," said Martha Dobbs. "Maybe that's what's giving you Lizards. Maybe you should find a new Martha."

He'd touched her pride. It was charming to see the flash in her large eyes.

"Are you engaged this evening," he asked. "For dinner?"

Chapter 5

"In cases wherein patients refer in any way to meetings with lizards, dragons, snakes or reptiles, by any degree of reference, I swear that I will immediately report said reference to Station 5, confidentiality—"

Sylvia switched off the tin-voiced deskmodule.

Confidentiality disregarded. She knew the code with respect to Lizard outbreak but presumed Rogers Collectibles would be blotted without her having to do anything. Now that it had been broadcast it wasn't her responsibility alone. She disliked blotting, she disliked m-ops and g-ops both, and she admired Rogers and his reporter friend. She wouldn't be a part of it.

The paranoid suspects that events outside himself are organized according to his needs and fears. A psychotic knows it. Sylvia had the feeling that Rogers and Martha Dobbs were connected to her in some secret way, as if they shared something criminal and strange between them. She'd only missed one Feed. Had her neuroses already begun to encroach on the real? Doubtful. A psychotic doesn't consider the fact that she might be psychotic.

Cindy was ponging, but Sylvia's thoughts focussed inwards. She had no interest in patients.

Perhaps she was psychotic. Had the little disruption—her not taking flowers—now triggered an avalanche of improbability on her ordinary life? Already she was cheating on her professional vows to the Evening Star. She'd lectured the colony at large on the evils of abstention, yet she herself had abstained. She'd not blotted Rogers, nor reported him to Station 5. And she was already itching to go farther, to cross more boundaries.

Second Feed was most likely beginning now. Her bundle had been meant to last all day, but it was gone and she knew what she had to do.

Sylvia let herself out the back door to her office. Without entering her ad-apt across the way, she passed quickly along Cherry Tree Lane, only turning beachward on 13th Street.

The inner-city streets were nearly empty. She might well be noticed and rounded up by the authorities. Wrapped in a warm d-cloak and veiled from the sun by a flower-print halox, she hoped it would appear that she was a harmless late-sleeper hurrying beachward for dregs. Nevertheless, any standing g-op could scan her and detect her a-social intuitions. Though she really was hurrying towards Feed, had done nothing extraordinarily illegal, Sylvia felt a paranoid chill color all the observed.

Always within one's peripheral vision, armed government-operators simply let it be known they were near. Sprinkled here and there, helmeted, weapons slung lazily over their shoulders, they darkened the city's general peace like individual droplets of death. It proved remarkably easy to control a people who, so long as they took flowers regularly, had the easy ability to live close enough to forever.

Already, not feeding had affected Sylvia's perceptions. Ordinary things were dropping away. She slowed in an overgrown public garden, whose trees stood taller now than the Castle itself, and stopped to observe a commotion she would not have noticed under normal circumstances. A gang of adolescents had circled around an addict, who'd made herself a shelter behind some benches. She was an old woman, a witch most likely. Her white hair was matted with mud and her filthy brown robe was soiled and torn. Aroused to a state of unstoppable sadism, the youths had thrown her down in the dirt. They were kicking her. One yanked up her robe to expose her thighs. The woman began to laugh hysterically though the situation wasn't funny at all.

Sylvia followed the witch's wild eyes towards a very odd sight. Up in the air, framed by the park's great rectangle of trees, there was a blurry cloud, the optical effect of a great and concentrated heat. From out of it a house-like cube of steely glass bricks came into focus, completely aloft. The tawny cube had more gravity than a holo-v projection, but was apparently not ordinarily visible. As she looked she saw it wasn't quite a cube, but something mathematically absurd—an object that folded around its own X-axis. It made her feel sick to look at it, and she turned her head down.

She found herself standing somewhere far away. A wide grassland, rich and mud-soaked, stretched around her.

In the distance, a creature—a man-like lizard—was approaching rapidly.

A voice rang out, high-pitched and close:

"Dr. Yang?"

Breast cheerily exposed, cheeks warm with Feed, it was Cindy, returning from the beach.

"Is everything O.K.?"

"I was just admiring the view," Sylvia said.

Having no reason to doubt her employer, Cindy turned to take in the view. The scene had reverted to a more probable present. The structure in the air was gone. In the park, two g-ops had arrived to disperse the commotion. They'd hog-tied the old woman, and, to the delirious jeers of the boys, they now poked their needle-rifles into the back of her neck. At the sound of their rifles, the loud hiss, the woman's head kicked and split open. Her brains spilt out on the grass.

"What leshy palms," Cindy said admiringly. "I love these afternoon days."

"Yes," Sylvia answered. "It's a fine day."

"Should we be getting back to the office?"

"We should."

When Sylvia eventually returned to the office, she had no idea of the commotion she'd aroused in the sentient plant on her windowside shelf. The plant disliked dilemmas intensely. Yet it found itself caught between two possible actions. Neither promised much certainty for its continued growth. The plant understood that Sylvia Yang's departure into the n-scape (it had followed her as she walked) had been triggered by not taking flowers. Her growing ability to remember hallucinations, maddeningly, had made it harder for the plant to inhabit her present mind. Already it detected memory-traces blocked from its gaze. Vines were knotting together; streams were cascading against streams, interfering with most-probable particle distributions.

Human time was so disturbingly minute. One could only reflect on the specimen's actions after they occurred. Two missed feeds meant that Sylvia Yang had broken the law. By PERM-PROC, the plant was required to report her abstention to Station 5. It would also be expected to blot her memory to the point where she didn't remember not feeding. Should it be found to have defaulted on these responsibilities, the plant might well not be allowed to live through the coming v-night. It would certainly be forbidden reproductive rights—a fate far worse than death.

Yet should the plant report her, the incident would result in Sylvia's re-education. She would lose her job, her function. The plant would lose its happiest garden. Yet honestly perceived, the dilemma was not insurmountable.

Immersion was the answer. If it was willing to cut off all intervegetative communication, a sentient plant could enter the nearest consciousness stream in full and would not be required to report until it was pulled out. It would mean descending into where the relative solidity of quantum probability management could be pulled by any interlocking point-of-view into the chaos of relativity between streaming minds. The plant could only, while immersed, communicate among the minds through which it reached.

Technically fraught with ambiguity, legally, immersion was clear as day. But it was a radical step. If the Senate approved, the plant would be unable to disengage from human spacetime until the Senate pulled it out.

The plant doubted that the senate would disapprove. Already, many factions were protesting various offenses of the Crittendon regime against the Plant-Human Fair Labor Agreement subscribed to since the colony's founding. Since the ultra-conservative new plants had sacrificed their so-called principles by allowing Crittendon's industrialization of flowers, the Senate had approved the majority of sentient immersion petitions, in order to monitor the increasing relation of human and vegetative biologies beyond the ordinary bounds of Oan law.

Still, the plant had no connections within the senate and if the Crittendon regime discovered its failure to report the doctor, even during immersion, it could be legally eradicated—and the privelege of its entire species jeopardized.

But the plant had already resolved to immerse. It would have to do its best to preserve its life with the exertion of its own individual will. Sending off its last signals, bidding farewell to the interlinked vegetal field, the plant asked its constituent parts to generate energy enough to launch full immersion into Oa's human dimension.

Unfortunately, the nearest human, the patient already waiting for the doctor's return, was the most potentially lethal specimen the plant had yet encountered.

Niftus Norrington had instructed the helmet to schedule the appointment as soon as possible. The helmet he trusted, but the possible lagged. Nifty let himself into the office on Cherry Tree Lane a half an hour early. The secretary's deskmodule told him to take a relax.

Nifty disliked waiting intensely. The forced optimism of places built for waiting immediately depressed him. Warm red relaxes, easy chairs and paddle-socks filled the piss green room. The carp was organic and too warm. Ugly indoor plants drooped dryly in the corners. He sighed.

At work now and obliged to keep the material peace, Niftus had to be a good little citizen. He fell into a relax and took up a copy of *STAR!* megazine.

How delightful. The cover showed him with his arm around Johanna Zeep, the famous V star. He was taller than her by half a meter. Page six showed him giving it to Johanna from behind.

The headlines chirped:

"NIFTUS IS NUTTS!"

"NOBODY NASTIER THAN NIFTUS!"

"NIFTUS OR NOTHING!"

"NIFTY NETS NINE NUBIAN NUNS!"

Niftus Norrington was quite a guy.

"May I help you?"

Dropping the megazine to cover the bagged helmet on his lap, Nifty looked up to find a woman standing before him. The sight surprised him and took him momentarily out of himself. Her face was clear and strong, with green and shining eyes. He had seen her on V, he now realized. It was really the doctor they'd showed. But she wasn't like Johanna Zeep at all. Johanna was fairer, slighter, a lot less woman. This neuroscop had her own kind of beauty.

He noted the grey streak in the doctor's long swept-back hair, her confrontational gaze, her remarkably shapely breasts. She looked down on him curiously, without judgement.

"Have you an appointment?"

Nifty put out his LP. He stood up. He was about half as tall as she was.

"Yeah," he said. "2:30."

"My secretary's freshening up. Please follow me."

She turned, monochromatic D-robe wrapped tight around the hips. The sight had him sinking toward just the sort of neuroscopic interlude he'd rather avoid. He followed her without looking.

Nifty hadn't been to a shrink since the visit required one month after his promotion. Since then, he had resolutely avoided counseling. He was damaged goods and he knew it. Do you resent tall people? Do you feel all alone in the world? Of course. What was the point of talking it out?

But Neuroscops located your weakness and exploited it. They drew out that part of you naturally inclined to believe it was possible for you to have a single friend in the universe.

The doctor had crossed to her deskmodule and was already readying her Morituri apparatus for scan. Her hair hung long down her back, just touching her perfect ass.

Control yourself, Norrington. Don't get distracted

Nifty sat warily down in the already warming sucker's seat, resolving to get immediately to the whereabouts of Citizen R. But with his legs dangling over the carp and his helmet wrapped up like a coconut on his lap, he felt ridiculous.

Dr. Yang's helmet was standard issue white, imbued with the tiny logo of a blue eye inside a blue triangle. She took it in her hands.

"Actually," he said. "How about not scanning me this first session? I'd just like to talk."

She raised her eyebrows, surprised. "It's standard procedure, I assure you. I won't know anything about your case without a scan. Your name and occupation, for instance. Your background."

"That's OK. I understand that."

"I assure you everything learned through the helmet remains strictly confidential. It's expressly illegal under perm-proc for a neuroscop to remember what was read without wearing the helmet again."

Nifty lowered his voice, leaned forward.

"Doc, I'll be straight with you. Those helmet things don't pick up certain memories I've had. The ones that really bother me."

She sighed. She was tired, evidently, he could see it round her eyes. This was one more annoyance in her long and interminable day. She looked away.

He went on. "I see lizards, Doc. Lizards."

She looked back at him in a way he couldn't read—her dark eyes widening, drawing him inward.

"You're lying," she said.

"Look," Nifty said, reddening. "I'll be honest. Why I'm here is I saw you on Leave-It-to-Larry's "Windows on the Weird" and I saw that guy on the couch. I forgot his name. What was it?"

She didn't answer.

Those green eyes: it was like she was scanning him without a damn helmet. Nifty attempted to look pained. Acting wasn't hard. Hard was tossing full-grown human bodies into a volcano. In his youth, he'd worked in entertainment. Nifty could act with the best of them. Why couldn't she believe him?

"You see I also have these dreams of lizards. Hundreds of them running around in pits, fornicating. Like this." He wriggled his fingers in illustration.

The doctor shook her head. "I will never tell you my patient's name, Mr. whomever you are. As a professional neuroscop—"

"Damn, Doc, look at me. I'm so small. I'm lonely. I could use a friend."

"What exactly else do you want from me, Mr.—?"

"Norrington. Niftus Norrington. I see lizards."

A very slight smile had curled her lips. Could she could see right through him?

As if on cue, Norrington turned to the window. In the gentle breeze, the cherry tree leaves outside all seemed to be nodding in towards the window. There on the sill, he saw the sentient plant basking in an orb of sunlit crystal, its strange leaves vibrating quietly.

"—*Greetings*," it said, in his mind.

Niftus Norrington despised sentient plants. When he found them interfering in his thoughts, he was usually possessed by an unstoppable urge to tear the nearest vegetation from its Venus and eat it raw, sentient or not.

He whispered. "I should—"

"*Shhh,*" his mind said. "*—The doctor doesn't know—I'm here.*"

"What do you do for a living, Mr. Norrington? Are you employed?"

He turned back to her.

"*—She likes—you,*" the plant articulated.

"I'm entirely a free agent," he said. "A beacher."

"You've never really seen lizards, have you?"

"*Want name of man—who said—Lizards?*"

Yes. Tell me now or I'll break you.

"Mr Norrington?"

Nifty wiped sweat off of his brow, mustering patience. "Trust me," he said. "You have no idea how significant it is that I'm here at all. I happen to hate neuroscops. I happen to think people like you just keep people like me in line. Just so you can get your private flowers and kredit and watch your V's without any danger to your own precious hide. My name's Niftus Norrington, Dr. Yang. They call me Nifty. I'm a little man. I'm not rich. But I assure you, I'm not a problem to be trifled with. I'm losing control. I could threaten communal security. Look at me, I'm under no illusions as to the chances I've got at a normal life. And now I'm seeing lizards. Doc, why would I lie? Have you ever seen a lizard? Have you ever seen its black and glittering eye, its forked tongue slathering up its long, feathery jaw? Have you ever seen its razor-lazer—"

He held up. The vision was too clear. It was like he had actually just seen a lizard.

"*We make—a deal.*"

Nifty went on. He had little interest in making deals with chloryfil. "Doc, if you haven't seen a lizard, you don't know how important it would be to meet someone else who did—"

"But Niftus," she said quietly. "I have seen lizards."

What the hell was this? Did she realize what she was saying? Did he have to blot her now too?

"*—You blot—her. I blot—you.*"

Cold sweat trickling down his neck, Nifty tried again to reason. "Another male, a possible—"

"Perhaps we should get to the real business you came in here to discuss, Niftus."

He closed his eyes. How typical.

"Your size."

So presumptuous. So very presumptuous.

Nifty sighed. He shifted uncomfortably in the relax. The Doctor was looking deeply into his eyes.

He turned his mind to the plant, but spoke aloud.

"OK. What do I have to do?"

"—*Tell her. She's beautiful. Tell her—she reminds you. Of the V-star Johanna Zeep.*"

"Tell me the truth."

Chapter 6

When Rogers Collectibles arrived home he found a g-op leaning in the center of his den, puffing a lungprotector. The g-op's body was a holo-projection, but no less shocking for it. The rising smoke around the green-faced man was delineated by the broadcast so that he appeared to be inside a kind of swirling egg. Morituri technology had a way of being more real than the people it served.

The g-op rose, clearly annoyed. "Rogers of Rogers Collectibles?"

It was not a time to make trouble. Rogers removed hat. "Yes, that's me."

"Are you the owner of a copy of a book by the name of—"

The g-op paused, and a clearly electronic voice articulated: "*Brane World.*"

"Yes I am," answered Rogers truthfully. "But I've lost it."

"You've lost it?"

"That's what I said."

"Did you register the book at the time of your acquiring it?"

"I forgot," Rogers said.

"You forgot."

Entirely true. The g-op's console winked green.

"I'm sorry," Rogers said, emboldened. "But is the failure to log an acquisition statement an offence warranting this intrusion?"

"The law, idiot, is not for you to dictate. If this book turns up, you foarking bring it directly down to Station 5 before any transactions occur as to its future ownership. Do you understand?"

"I understand."

"Don't think you have any rights in this matter."

Rogers nodded.

"You're running on borrowed time, Rogers. I wish I could blot you, I really do. I know what you are. You're a dirty addict and you see lizards. But I can't. When you find this book, bring it in."

Before flickering out, the g-op stamped his LP into the holo-floor as if it was Rogers' own carp.

He called his bank and checked his Kredit. There was no record of a recent transaction. Perhaps not taking flowers was a bad idea. Rogers had lost *Brane World*. He'd missed meeting Hogart, thereby in all likelihood losing a promising new client. If he'd gained on memory it was only to enjoy a new understanding of what he'd forgotten. Now the g-ops were presumably watching his every move. He'd lost his invisibility, his freedom to come and go as he pleased. They could continue harassing him forever.

But a small businessman couldn't simply jump ship. Even if the ship was going down, it was the captain's responsibility to take it down to its final orbit. Rogers had to find out what happened to the book. It did exist, after all; he'd held it in his own hands. It could be recovered, then be registered. It was still entirely possible that he would make the sale.

Rogers lit an LP. Find the book. Maybe in one of his delirious episodes, he had misplaced it in the ad-apt before setting out in the morning. He turned the place upside down. To no avail.

Intuition told him the book was lost in the outside world. Perhaps Frank P. Hogart of block 22a already had *Brane World* in his possession, somehow. Maybe they'd met, and the old buzzard had tricked him, snatched the book and blotted his memory.

He ponged Hogart. The old man, of course, didn't answer.

He lit another LP. There was still Martha Dobbs. Though the thought of any Martha caused confusing physiological shifts in his body, this one did seem to offer a way forward. He'd made a date with her for the evening. Perhaps it wouldn't be such a bad idea to encourage her to broadcast his search for the book.

The more he considered, the more it made sense. Such exposure could extend his inquiry into ten thousand ad-apts, beachside shanties and dens. It could reveal Hogart, if a suit was necessary, as a shady operator. Plus, the g-op's would get the message that he was doing his best to locate the thing. Maybe "Windows on the Weird" could help give collecting some respectability. Trends change, after all. Who knew? Martha Dobbs and her quick big eyes, her long legs, could certainly help set styles.

But what was it about Martha Dobbs that threatened his private day-to-day existence? Why was he already frightened of becoming more deeply involved with her? There was something about her, something between them, in fact, that touched his heart with fear.

Rogers grinded out his LP butt, and shook his head of the feeling.

G-d knew it had been some time since he'd been close to a woman. Walking with her in the dappled shade of the flowering trees, his hand brushing against hers, he'd felt the breath of something private and secret between them. Something old and familiar.

If you sliced Venusia a certain way, it would look like a labyrinth. Every person at every time occupied a point along a complicated series of hallways, avenues, stairs, elevators and doors. Together these points, these persons, passed through the maze in time, tracing out Venusia as it had been provided. Now, for instance, Rogers was in his ad-apt thinking about Martha Dobbs. Where was she? Most likely far away, engaged with a project that had nothing to do with him.

But still he believed that they occupied a closer relation than this view suggested. He could smell her near him, still feel, in his own hollowness, the closeness of her spirit inside his chest. Venusia wasn't a labyrinth at all—the thing that you were looking for was inside of where you began.

Because if you took the maze and then lifted it up, folded it on a vertical axis, it would no longer be like a maze. The architecture was simply a blind slice—a hologram prison with no real walls. From the new point of view, the lifted, folded maze, he and Martha Dobbs could actually be occupying the same point—already tangled up in time.

Strange thought. It was as if he'd suddenly glimpsed down on himself—and saw this glance as a part of something else—something larger and looming. As if he were not a part of himself at all.

Rogers Collectibles shook his head and stabbed an LP into a brimming tray. He resolved to make it through the afternoon without further hallucination. There was one sure way to keep himself sane. He took out the copybook with which he was teaching himself reading and writing and set up to work at the makeshift desk in what had been Martha's room.

The print copy of Crittendon's *Reflections* had the pre-transition M+M stamp on its first page. It was an object of value in its own right and it gave Rogers pleasure to open it on the table. Though he disliked the Princeps and much of what he stood for, he admired the man's early writings. Rogers wrote out the following passage from where he'd left off, still at the beginning of the first chapter:

> *There is no "mankind." In the new peril the very word mankind has changed. There is only the everydayness of the present. There is no past, because the past has wiped itself away. We divide the names of things from the things that exist to allow those things their freedom to change. Primitive literacy is redundant. Mere words are expelled. We inaugurate a world of pure presence. The mind that intrudes itself between ourselves and those memories too terrible to know must keep us moving beyond the grasp of their claw. To control the flow, it will be necessary that political order be imposed always temporarily. The state shall enjoy direct, creative access to the real....*

Rogers couldn't quite understand the sense of Jorx Crittendon's long-forgotten words. But as he copied them out onto a yellowed copy-book, his hand throbbing and twisted, he felt like a practitioner of the most arcane of arts.

It passed the time, certainly, and kept the lizards away, trailing out long-silent thoughts from the tip an antique miracle-pen. Just when he'd let go of his worries (the past and the future), just when he'd forgotten everything, that Rogers Collectibles received a return-recorded pong from Frank P. Hogart, bookseller.

It looked as if not a minute had passed since the old eccentric's last communication. He wore the same soiled robes. The same, two-coned hat sloped over his brow (though transmission cut if off half-way). He was a big man, and, although bent, he looked a hell of a lot larger den-center than on watch-pong. He was remarkably pink-skinned, and Rogers, who was a light green, reflected that if Hogart was rich enough to afford pigmentation, he could certainly come up with the necessary Klugers. There was no reason for him to steal a book.

"Rogers," growled the hologram. "I want to see this book. T-Tomorrow; 11 A.M. your time."

Odd that he didn't mention the missed appointment.

The image of Rogers grew distant. On Cherry Tree Lane, still entwined with the short, compact body of Niftus Norringtion, Sylvia Yang's mind was turned inward. It was almost impossible for the plant to form a distinct image of her thoughts. Niftus was perfectly proportioned, masculine, even handsome. His eyes had a spark of wild life. But it was as if he came from another, smaller dimension. He was like a cartoon. Yet, oddly enough, somehow more perfectly real than she was. Inexplicably, in his presence, Sylvia felt it was she herself, somehow, who was the freak. His comments on her profession had affected her deeply, so in tune were they with her own opinions. Most of all, in his unguarded manner, the defiant returning of her gaze, Niftus Norrington had brought her an awareness of her body and its relation to herself that was entirely unfamiliar. It was taxing for the sentient plant to understand what was happening to her. Its constituents were registering thousands of individual complaints. The plant wondered how it could withstand the future. Already, it had jumped between so many entangled streams that it could barely recognize its position.

It had sought to bring Doctor Yang and m-op Niftus Norrington into close emotional contact in order to gain her a champion and deflect the m-op's attention from the legal fragility of her position. Certainly the Doctor herself, after her unusual t-day, was powerfully affected by the little man's algorithmic efflux. But the m-op, if anything, proved more lethal than ever—more self-contained and radically opposed to the plant's interference. Realizing suddenly that its armature was damaged and its way to the sun was newly blocked, the plant saw in Sylvia that, after their lovemaking, the little man had already tried to kill it.

Later, Sylvia found herself remembering the little man's black-green eyes, the rich spoles of braided hair that curled off his forehead and down onto his shoulders, the angry strength of his strong, small arms. It made her feel stiff and doll-like. The way she'd felt near that park, when just for a moment she'd been standing in a wide and grassy field.

Had she really gotten down to her hands and knees like that? Given herself so entirely to his thrusts? Where was she heading with such abandonment? What wild place was calling? Her heart was pounding.

She collected the disks and objects that lovemaking had knocked from her deskmodule. Before leaving, Niftus had lashed out at her favorite windowside plant and knocked it to the floor. She lifted the poor thing up and put it back in the sun. She hoped its crystal armature was not damaged.

The plant had come with the office. She paid little attention to it, though it made her happy knowing it was there, living. Like a quiet friend and comrade. She disliked looking at the plant too closely. Roots exposed, spread out against the crystal, curling sensuously around the little clay balls of its interior, there seemed nothing hidden about the straining thing. The pale roots and leaves were virtually indistinguishable, radiating out from its thin, tensile center like twitching nerves. To see it fallen, a good deal of its water spilled out onto the carp, was to see the danger Nifty Norrington might pose to her own existence.

> Petals past flowers, flowers past petals
> Each of a kind, all intertwined
> Petals past flowers, flowers past petals
> One of a kind, all intertwined....

Singing sweetly (the plant vibrating in sudden, painful delight, tasting its budding tiny deaths as pure extension...), Sylvia refilled its water and wondered again at what was happening inside of her.

She brushed her robe over her hips, felt Nifty's wetness still upon her thighs. He had left her on the floor like a used thing. It excited her. Remembering, she felt herself breathe, smolder with a new power. This person, this sexualized creature she'd become—it had little regard for any law but its own. Had she really told him the name he'd wanted, Rogers Collectibles?

How easily one midjudges the height-impaired. Standing above her, Niftus Norrington had belted his robe back on and laughed quietly at her humiliation. He wouldn't report her himself, he said. He wasn't like that. But come monthly scan they'd find her out.

"I'm an m-op," he said. "You should never have told me his name."

The full horror of her position now came upon her. And a shame, the terrible shame of knowing she wanted more. Sylvia covered her face with her hands. To know that it would all be on view—that she had already crossed such lines. It changed her, opened up the crack the lack of flowers had forced in her mind.

She was standing in a dark and dirty room, with soft lamps lit all around. Their flames cast weird, fluid shadows on the walls. It was somewhere very far away. Heavy smells came down on her like things. Her hand was holding a small weighted object, compact and triggered. A weapon. Outside, the sounds of gunfire.

Her lips moved mechanically.

"Sylvia," they said.

A new self, a kind of wind blowing through her chest, extending through her architecture.

The Green Man across from her smiled. She wouldn't be able to kill him though she wanted to. There were things growing into and out from his mouth and eyes, from his ears. Things grotesque, squatting, hungry and absurd. They gathered in a circle around her, whispering.

Sylvia's hand had caught into a claw. Her fingers burning, pulled her back to her office, to her anchored deskmodule.

"Dr. Yang?"

Sylvia didn't look up at Cindy.

She had scratched four letters with her nails into the dark surface of her desktop. Her nails were sticky with blood. She couldn't read or write, but she recognized the awkward shapes of the letters they'd carved.

A, E.

Was she a puppet on a string? "Ae," her lips whispered. "*Ae.*"

Chapter 7

No flowers and fade; she missed Evening Feed. The Green Man, a boy reading…. Perhaps it was Rogers Collectibles' strange ad-apt, his old-fashioned bed, but Martha Dobbs' dreams had rarely been so vivid. They were like memories come alive. In one dream, she'd pictured herself at the foot of a funeral pyre, hands over her eyes, receiving its hot warmth on her face. Her parents thrown onto the fire? She didn't remember her parents. She'd never lived with them. In another dream, there'd been a wild-eyed young woman, called Ae standing in the center of a circle of light.

Why was she seeing such things?

Martha Dobbs lay awake. It was late now, and quiet. At dinner, she'd talked with Rogers Collectibles about her Aunt Lila, her career. She hadn't let him the extent of her ambition, which was a secret she had never shared. She hadn't mentioned her dead parents or Quentin. Rogers listened patiently. He was rumpled and a bit disengaged, but when he'd asked her to his ad-apt for tea she hadn't said no. His old elixir brewed a decent cup.

And now she was lying next to him in his bed, still untouched, unobserved. There'd been a questioning moment when she'd felt a rising excitement between them. If it hadn't been for the hovering Iye, high up in the corner over his bed, they would have most likely made love. She was glad they hadn't, but somehow sorry too. She felt as if they weren't yet close enough to each other.

Martha Dobbs enjoyed Rogers' warmth now beside her, even though it was as if he were a thousand miles away. But she longed for her own bed and the memories it protected. Her private, secret past.

Since Lila had introduced her to her first love, Quentin, long ago, she'd never been with anyone for more than a t-week. She knew that she had never met Rogers Collectibles before. But why did he seem so familiar? Why did she know so certainly that they shared a destiny?

Martha took care not to show signs of these thoughts. Though its red light was off, the floating Iye could well be watching.

"Looking, looking, looking," her boss Leave-It-To-Larry Held liked to say. "We're all just looking. That's what we're at, hoppies. A world of spectators. You can feel the wideness of it, can't you, in your head? When you're hooked by a V?"

Larry had seen her performing on the beach in one of the spontaneous plays people used to put on by themselves. When he ponged her after, it would forever change her life. He said he wanted her to be an actress on the V's. He had her in mind for the part of ambitious ingenue in a soap.

But Martha Dobbs hadn't taken to the artificiality of this role. Her gift for performing depended on the presence of other people, real people. She thought the real world could be more exciting, more useful than the fantasy-V's. She insisted she work as a reality-reporter.

"You can be an inter-respondent, doll-face," Larry had said. "As long as you look sexy. Because they'll only all be looking at you, trust me."

"Not if I find the right stories."

Any story, Martha Dobbs believed, was right, providing you accepted it on its own terms. This was the whole point of reality-V. Reality itself was artificial, of course, and to engage its artificiality head-on, as a realism, was to have the ability to rewrite important spaces of the forgotten invisible all around. Hadn't Rogers Collectibles, a man without a first name, looking for a book, for Jorx sake, turned out to be riveting? Apparently, her piece had generated considerable popular interest. People had been ponging the station about it all day.

Collectibles was comical enough to amuse, but he had the contrarian's habit of bringing serious things out into the air. And then, he carried the past. Just seeing some of the objects in his ad-apt had made her remember desires and dreams she'd forgotten she'd had. The past, if you let it in, was potent.

But she had no illusions. It was his abstention from flowers and his massive lizard complex that gave Rogers an edge. Things not usually mentioned on V's were always the most entertaining.

"Quitting flowers is an addictive narcosis," the neuroscop Yang had warned. "The more you're in, the more you're stuck. You can't help but bring the people around you down with you as well."

Already Martha Dobbs herself had missed an evening's Feed. Was she already changing? Abstention didn't frighten her. She was frightened of the Iye, frightened of herself and how she might be tempted to exploit Rogers' problems. But not the flowers.

The cloud over Venusia had long closed. In the gathered darkness, the ad-apt's esoteric furnishings, antiques and oddities seemed on the verge of flickering into dark and mysterious demons. One floated in mid-air above her now: A palm outstretched flat before her face.

It was a gesture of silence so perfect that Martha Dobbs, though her mouth had fallen open in shock, obeyed.

The hand closed. It reached back to pull the drooping hood from a head, and reveal the strange, sad gaze of Leave-It-To Larry Held.

Larry's huge ears poked out from his skull like radial leaves. His thin lips were turned down. But for her own sense of gravity, Martha Dobbs might have believed they were standing next to each other. Larry, his image anyway, hovered two meters above her, spread out impossibly horizontal in the middle of the air.

"Psychophysics," Larry whispered, as if he could read her mind. "I can. Your intuition's dead on, baby. In a way, I am standing beside you right now."

"Are you a projection?"

"Shhhh, doll-face. Let's keep this hush hush. What's the back-story on Rogers Collectibles?"

"Backstory?"

"We can't find him. He's slipped through the cracks, an oddity. He's listed as a business, not a person. Half of the shit he owns is illegal, including this book he's looking for. There's temp-procs about books, lots of them."

"I don't know any backstory. He used to be married, I think."

"Martha, baby. I know this is all difficult stuff. But try to understand. You need to know the story in and out. You need to research him, stay with him. Record everything he does. Follow him where no one else can. The sun's going down in a t-day. We're thinking of giving you and Rogers First-Night V. "

"First night? But every sunset Johanna Zeep—"

"Please." Larry reached out again from the air and touched her arm. His fingers passed through her flesh. Weirdly, Martha felt as if it were she who was the holo-projection and not Larry Held at all. "I won't lie to you, Martha. There's a Johanna spot ready to go if this doesn't work out. The thing is to find his book, let him register it and then bring Rogers to Feed. Tomorrow. It'll make a great ending. A burning of books, a reconciliation with the present."

"Larry, how—"

"Listen. I gotta go, babe. Don't be shy with the Iye here. You like Collectibles. Go for it. You're young and beautiful. Enjoy yourself while you can."

With a last tragicomical glance in her direction, Larry pulled his hood back to enshadow his face and floated away like a dream.

Martha rustled the sleeping Rogers awake. He squinted up at her, confused.

"Who are you?"

"It's me, Martha."

"Martha?"

The yearning in his eyes suprised her.

"Touch me," she said.

His fingers touched her. It brought a sudden sharp energy into the room.

Up high in the corner, the red light of the Iye switched on.

Chapter 8

The seven electric phalli cracked out another t-morning, courtesy of the robot factories. The air vents breathed out and ignited the day. Sylvia Yang got up and wrapped herself in a d-robe. She crossed Cherry Tree Lane and let herself into her office later than usual. She had spent the morning thinking.

Her experience off flowers had revolutionized her understanding of addiction. Her recent visions weren't explainable by the ordinary definition of hallucination versus reality. The mental projection of the lizard, the precision of its form, its clear self-inherence had taken up spacetime in such a way as if to reveal the real itself as a similar hologram.

Abstention from flowers did not usually lead to immediate same-day hallucination. Nor for that matter, to immediate increased sexual drive. Typically, these side-effects began after a t-week or so. Lizard-viewing was rare. She herself had only encountered a handful of addicts so far gone in the scope of her entire career. And now, at least three people—herself included—had seen them. It was as if something between her and these others had intensified the effects of abstention.

The strange experience in the park, the hovering cube-structure; yesterday's feeling of suddenly standing in another spacetime, in another's self. Ae, the very memory of the name, caused her nerves to tingle.

Had the neuroscape come unbound? Had the wider "super-space" of which Morituri had written before he died been accessed at the expense of the conscious mind?

If this was indeed what was occurring, the phemomenon would not be so easily defined. Change was the order of the n-scape. She now knew that flower-withdrawal didn't simply trigger the appearance of lizards. It was more as if the flowers masked their constant presence.

As the t-night passed late into morning, Sylvia had lain awake thinking of the letters she's scratched into her desk. Ae. She'd heard the name before. A writer from the past, once revered in Venusia. Perhaps Rogers Collectibles might have something by her. Maybe Sylvia could resume her abandoned attempts to read.

"Sylbia," the lizard said, licking it own face. "Hab you been a dirty girl?"

The world in which the lizard lived bubbled up suddenly from inside her own brain. When she slipped out again—immediately after the lizard had spoken—things were different, subtly changed. Perhaps she had shifted the perceptable reality and not lost time or memory at all. Or perhaps her own mind had been blotted by an invisible observer.

She had been a dirty girl and the lizard knew her deepest self. Was it part of her? She had no data to examine, only impressions, which seemed very like impressions of a vividly remembered hallucination or dream. Clearly, the lizard-world was hallucinated, but it had a solidity and dimensionality she'd never experienced in her Morituri-aided explorations of her patient's n-scapes. The lizard-world was more organic, self-translated. She had seen on her scan that Rogers had remembered one sitting in an office, as if it were a worker, doing another's bidding.

Late last night, Sylvia had attempted to raise the up the sweet wildness the m-op had brought out in her. She found a small make-up mirror on the bed, and she'd set it between her legs. She'd lain naked over the covers. She had touched herself without shame, watched herself come.

She had kept all the old v-disks and notes from her education, anticipating the day when this information would have become unavailable. Cindy had not yet arrived and she took the time alone in her office to review what she had learned so long ago.

Before the suicide, Morituri had spoken of the neuroscape as a hallucinated, holographed rendering of the mental space that connected individual mind-selves of an evolving natural species. It was rendered by the helmet apparatus into a self-perceived environment of extra dimensions. Unrepeatable in common 2 or 3-d realism, it mapped the rippling of self-waves as they combined to produce visible psychological architectures in an illusionary time. Mind, Morituri had famously written, was the field of absence on which spacetime hinged. The n-scape opened inside it new and unlimited pathways.

The species thus far had evolved within classical spacetime: that is to say, a mutually established, largely neutral limiting field of self constantly established the shared universe from the wider possible multiverses. Such production of the real could only happen unconciously by definition.

But when two or more selves consciously entangled in the n-scape, via Morituri apparatus, the whole of the n-scape could be pulled between multiverses. This motion, this re-writing of the universal shared real, he called the Melton Effect. It was nearly impossible, Morituri claimed, to enact the Melton Effect by conscious intention, even with the aid of a helmet. When Peter Melton himself had first performed it, he had been beyond sanity, in a state where the unconscious and conscious minds were indistinguishable. He hadn't known there was an other perceiving what he saw, confirming its reality.

Instantaneous communications, time travels, even universal crossings might and did occur unconsciously everyday. But without observation from a mind outside the scope of the mind in motion, they had no meaning whatsoever and were controlled as hallucination. Reality always snapped back. The self experiencing such shiftings was schizoid by definition, unfixed from the shared species reality, impotent. The ordinary schizophrenia of a colonizing people should be able to contain itself.

But Morituri hadn't counted on flower addiction. Flowers had changed Venusia. They had wiped out general memory to such a degree that, unconsciously, the entire society—representing the species itself—had become unfixed from a legitimate shared history. Consciousness rides upon memories. When they fall away, the unconscious gains ground in the real. The flowers had dammed the n-scape stream. Pregnant and swollen, it was now spilling out into the world.

Morituri developed the helmet for precisely this reason: to find, in the other, a ground on which self's inner unhinging could be fixed. Through use of the helmet, the n-scape experienced by one individual could be observed and re-oriented by a non-schizoid mind, at the service of the general real. The helmeted neuroscop received the subject's mindwaves, stripped them of the indivual's personal myths, symbols and allegories. She threw them into a rational order delineated by the shared spacetime of her observing perspective and defined them schizoid.

Thus, from the point of view of the addict, flower-withdrawal initiated openings into the n-scape without a helmet. Sylvia wondered indeed why she had never seen it this way before. From the perspective of her training, flower addicts received lizards in a mechanistic breakdown succeeding the lack of a generalizing narcotic. But she'd never considered what it might be for the schizophrenic to maintain and manage the lizard experience— unfixed and free of false, general history—as a legitimate, non-technological experience of the n-scape.

Temporary anomalous openings into the n-scape were a natural occurrence in consciousness. They had occurred in all cultures, over all histories. Every day each person saw briefly into his or her future, observed minor miracles of coincidence and minute hallucination momentarily stretching the boundaries of the possible real. But one did this without reflection, without conscious management. What was happening to herself and Rogers Collectibles, both of whom who had a peculiar relation to the past, was now new. These visions opening around and within her like magic. They seemed to promise immeasurable and asymptotic freedom.

No wonder the Princeps, Jorx Crittendon, was so adamant about controlling addiction. Sylvia felt freedom reflecting around the reflexive quanta of her amygdalac soul, out through her bones and into the wider, managed air of Venusia itself. She wanted this freedom to be real; she wanted to share it with others.

She reddened again, remembering Nifty Norrington as he had stood naked above her, and held herself back from ponging him.

For m-op Niftus Norrington, the new t-day promised to top the last with annoyance. Though he'd found Melody and apologized abjectly for the morning's behavior and she'd allowed him to spend the night, the idiot hadn't woken him when he'd asked. Now he would be late for first Feed.

The good doctor had told him the name, Rogers Collectibles. But Rogers' address and pong-code were temporarily unlisted because of his newfound fame on the V's. Worse, the V-ads promised, in fact, that Martha Dobbs would be back with Rogers today. There were hints of a romance growing between them. Nifty would have to watch out. The last thing he wanted was to be caught on Iye. Even Venusians would remember a midget. If his operating cover was blown, the helmet was as good as lost.

He worked hurriedly on his hair in the mirror, tightening and twirling the spoles to maximum effect. He thought of the good doctor Sylvia Yang splayed out on her carp. He remembered her clearly; still felt her warmth and smell in his hair, his lungs, his bones. It was something other than he'd experienced in a long while.

She'd apparently found him to be the perfect object of her repressed perversions. She'd told him the name, broken all her oaths, lying on the floor like the true slut she was. It was pity he'd been so rude, since now he was going have to ask her again for Rogers' address.

Nifty fixed the helmet on his head.

Oddly enough, on the mirror, he saw what looked like a giant insect looking back at him.

What the hell was that? Nifty switched off the stage, shook his head of the picture. He needed to Feed.

Receiving all stimuli as impacts onto his physical body. Pressed up against legs, thighs, feet and flowers. Sweat sticking bodies hairy and smooth together into one enormous, unguided gyrating monster. A woman's bare, flower-dusted tits in his face. A man's elbow knocking into the helmet. Flying around like some midget Johnny Ho, bouncing into the trenches, Nifty directed his fall into the depths of the darkest green flowers.

He lifted visor at the last moment. Instead of flowers, he got a foot in his mouth. He clamped down his teeth. The victim's squeal was as close as his own.

Nifty gagged.

He lowered visor, lifted his arms. He battered his way through the legs of the throng-creature, out of the trenches altogether.

Even if flowers of the v-day's last t-days were the thickest, the purest, the meatiest, even if night crops were coming soon, Niftus Norrington had had enough of them. He was done with flowers. If that Rogers Collectibles could do it, Niftus Norrington could do it too.

He approached the sea, lifted visor, wiped his face. Yes, he was looking forward to the truth of near-eternal night. He could almost see the Darkening already gathering in the Hole.

Ishtar Ocean minded its own. It didn't bother Venusia and Venusia left it alone. The sight calmed him. Since the v-night when, it was said, the colony's birds had all flown across it to never return, Ishtar Ocean had remained a helpful cipher. Its wrinkled, warping surface stretched out into its secret history like the soft skin of a lizard, seething and uncoiled.

Again, Nifty gagged. Something was licking up his face. Frog-breath fogged up the helmet's inside. Choking in the stinking, sea air, he breathed deeply, filled his lungs with the artificial atmosphere.

JC, could he already be seeing lizards?

"I have this dream," Sylvia Yang's patient was saying. "I'm driving this very sophisticated bike. It's a gang situation. It's very futuristic. We're super-tough punks riding through these dead mesas. There are several moons visible. The bikes have, like, four wheels. In the dream we're escaping from something that's eating the world up behind us—but we never face it outright, the fact that it's something we have created: a conglomerate of intelligent machines that's totally out of control.

"We have mirror-shades fused into our faces, we have force-fields. There's no politics or anything. There are these creatures. Deer. I know it immediately, even though I've never seen one. Skinny legs, graceful, petite. So cute when they're running around. They recognize our gang and, misunderstanding the situation, they want to play tag. 'You're it,' they say. 'It's fun.' But it's not fun. It's scary. I can't turn in time to keep from hitting them. The force-field cuts one or two of them in half. Meanwhile the machines following behind me are cutting the ones we missed to little bloody bits. I've never seen a V quite like it. Animals like I've never seen, coming up out of the ground. We're mowing them down; everything's dying quicker and quicker. The whole world steams with gore. Scary creatures grow out of the darkness. They corral us in a mesa. They have really big teeth and hard thin lips. They puff up huge, but luckily I'm such a hero that—"

The door banged open.

Hearing Cindy speak the name 'Niftus Norrington' through her helmet, Sylvia awoke from her disinterest in her patient's hopeless dream to fall, heart pounding, into the present.

The patient stopped speaking.

"You," said the little man to the patient. "Out."

Sylvia wished her skin hadn't immediately flushed when she looked at him. Niftus Norrington, as he sat down again before her, knew his own power. He showed only sarcastic confidence in her weakness. She wished that wild feeling could stay down, buried where it belonged. But it was out of her control; things were approaching her, coming together between her legs—pulled down by the m-op's small and compact arms.

But he avoided her eyes. He leaned back, holding a coconut in his lap. "How much do you remember of yesterday?" he asked.

She said nothing.

"You look tired. Bad Feed?"

"My flowers are delivered privately."

He snorted. "This Rogers Collectibles. He's temporarily unlisted."

"Niftus," she found herself saying. "Yesterday was an aberration. My license is my life, you know, however absurd you might find my life to be and—"

"I'm not asking you to tell me."

He opened the bag on his lap and took out not a coconut, but a black helmet of unfamiliar type and design.

"Do you know what this is?"

"Is it a Morituri?"

"Order Q, just like yours."

She contained her excitement. "Operator is at no time permitted to scan n-scape of another operator declared order Q proficient."

"Listen to you," he said. "You sound like a machine. You weren't like that yesterday, I can tell you. Temp-procs didn't mean a thing. You were more like an animal."

She felt her face flushing. "This is a perm-proc," she said.

"I'm going to scan you," he went on. "And you can't stop me."

She took up her own helmet. This was it then, what she'd been waiting for.

"I'll be scanning you as well, Mr. Norrington."

His brow gathered. "Wait a minute," he said. His small fists clenched. He sat with his small legs hanging awkwardly from the relax. "That's too dangerous."

"Is it risking active deconstruction on all fronts, psycho-sexual malfunction, paramnesia and/or blindness that worries you? Or is it the Melton Effect?"

"The what?"

"The Melton Effect," Sylvia said. "Spacetime jumps into alternate timelines made possible by the inter-penetration of neuroscopically reflected mind-waves. Morituri said it's what made Venusia possible to begin with. The chances increase exponentially when two helmeted operators scan eachother simultaneously."

"Did he say that before or after he committed suicide?"

"These things are unlikely to happen. We haven't been alone with plants on a rapidly traveling asteroid for ten years. And we do have helmets. If things get too frightening for you Mr. Norrington, you can simply end scan, no? But if you're afraid and you don't want to do it, I won't force you. Still, I'll be scanning you regardless."

"JC," he said. "You're far gone, aren't you?"

She had taken control of the situation. Sylvia fit her white and gold helmet to her head. The die was cast. He couldn't say no to the challenge.

"It shouldn't be hard to find an address or a pong for Collectibles," Nifty said, fixing his black insectizoid helmet on his head. "I'll be out in a minute or two."

"Good luck," Sylvia said, initiating scan. "The n-scape makes its own time."

And she fell into another world, such as she had never seen.

One might well say that the plant on the window lived a strong life of the imagination. Without its own memory banks to draw on, it used logic and causal investigation to consider the past of each new situation. This made it safe for the humans for the plant to know things that implicated them in anti-social, even criminal activities. Nevertheless, still immersed, the sentient was deeply anxious. Clearly the gathering gravity of the n-scape yawning between these two humans came partly from the plant's own interference in their affairs. Its fate was now bound entirely up with their own.

Still, the senate had not yet cut off immersion. It might be that the plant was expected to follow its humans on their journey inside so as to better protect them and do its part to control the shape of the history into which they would return. They clearly had no idea what they were risking.

Human Venusia was a system complex and streamlined enough that individual agents would have a hard time disturbing its lay, even if they wanted to do so. It grew from the trunk in near-perfect entropy. Individual event anomalies could not disturb its coherence. For instance, minor officials like Sylvia Yang or Niftus Norrington could safely bypass any individual temp-proc without threatening security. Such disruption, in fact, was necessary to confirm larger stability of the system probabilities.

But perm-procs were different. They governed acts involving the willed, mutually-observed actions of groups of perceivers. They affected the ground of the shared historical tree. To break a perm-proc was either suicidal—the perpetrator would be erased—or entirely and unapologetically revolutionary. Another tree, another colony, another system at large would have to grow to survive it.

Suicide, for the seedless, was not an option. An immersed sentient could not be expected to do anything but preserve its own life. The senate's silence spoke volumes in this regard. But what human insurrection could the plant itself engineer? What tree could it climb? Endowed with its exceptional esthetic perceptions, the plant had no interest in ape politics.

There wasn't time for speculation. Growing already on the event horizon of the neuroscopic real into which Sylvia and the m-op were now falling, was a ground of "gardens" long sacred to the plant's ancestors. But the sentient would be entering them through the human n-scape, interacting with its humans' conscious interpretations.

Though humans now knew nothing of the living n-scape, it had not always been so. The species had lived in productive harmony with the vegetative and animal kingdoms for hundreds of thousands of years before its recent, rapid disintegration. Sylvia's mind, even now, contained a wealth of past models to draw on to aid her on her journey. But she had lost the ability to properly interpret the mythologies her ancestors had prepared. The plant would have to help her mold what she saw into meaning, even if it was all as foreign to the plant as it was to her.

Was this not reality?

There were no footprints on the long and arcing strand. Not even her own. The blue, living sea roared and seethed before her. Its slow feelers unrolled their hissing little deaths like fingers up around her ankles. The water felt cold and real. Sylvia let the breezes blow the hair back from around her face, let the winds hold her like long invisible arms. The ancient smells, the taste of the air came upon her like knowledge. She felt older, nearer to death.

Was this the mind of Niftus Norrington? This entire world? She seemed to have washed ashore on a kind of idealized Venus Beach, grander, healthier but far less solid. As she looked at the wide and round sun, the difference was immediately apparent. Change, when you looked anywhere, bloomed. The sun flattened on her glance, an inscribed circle on which she could easily gaze. Flat, implacably faced, its yellow, squid-like tentacles spread over and around the sky.

The sea grew colder now and older, tinged with a foaming beauty, a hoary wealth she had never known. She was inexplicably moved and fell for a time to her knees in the sand. Winds rose up angry and wild. She shivered, forgetting that here she was only as cold or warm as she could want to be.

Before her, immersed up to its waist in the seething sea, there stood a lizard. Its strong arms were folded and it gazed at her with scarlet eyes. Its forked tongue flickered against its feathery jaw.

Sylvia turned from the thing, ran.

Chapter 9

M-op Niftus Norrington had already scanned subjects wearing helmets of lower orders, though he'd managed not to remember doing so in order to avoid government sensors. He knew therefore, something of what to expect. Paradoxically, this knowledge slowed him down, made full immersion more difficult to conceive. As he entered the doctor's n-scape, its fields were already swirling among the organized mapping of her own helmet. He approached them from above, from where the patterns seemed unintelligibly complex—like the surface of a sea. Tides and flows abounded, knots of veins curled into 3 perceivable dimensions, but no individual forms were discernible. The coiled bundles interlaced interminably in every possible direction. He passed into one.

He was spinning backwards, attached to a wheel ticking out strange geometrical symbols. Snakes slithered through his toes. Norrington was bound to the wheel, watching the grid of Sylvia's mind extend through the curving flatland below.

To get the dreamstuff, Nifty had to let go of the wheel and dip down into the flatness—allow it to grow in dimensions around him. He concentrated on believing in its space, extending a beach for himself to stand on, beside a wide and sad ocean, barely alive. From here, Niftus could finally emerge.

Oh the ocean. The beach. It was different, more alive. And he was a figure in Sylvia's mind, standing between them.

Just to think that changed the 'scape. Everything turned black and white, like in a V-flashback. The ocean grew alien, remote.

Living Sylvias popped up from out of the sand, against the dunes. Identical and oblivious, each stood alone in perfect solitude.

She wore only a black b-suit bottom. It exposed her young, strong breasts and shoulders to the open air. A great wave of emotion pulsed through Niftus Norrington. His heart ached to see her there, exposed and undefended. He longed for her to recognize him, to meet his gaze. He was the proof that she was not alone. He loved her.

What was happening to him? He closed his eyes, waiting for the emotion to subside. Love was stupid.

The thought, for his eyes hadn't closed, took the whole scene away. On the beach, there was only his own empty self now—grey-black and prehistoric, like everything else.

"Sir," the helmet's words rang out, "I might recommend finding shelter."

Nifty didn't answer.

It was hard to walk, his body was so stiff, like a puppet. He walked gently and was glad he did, for colors came down and with each conscious step he felt more alive. Everything shivered, like it was a reflection on the surface of water—all fragile illusion. He had to stop walking in order to keep it together and attempt not to remember why he was here.

He was a castaway seeking survival. He walked up the dunes, away from the beach, trying not to wonder at the tiny billions of grains of visible, tactile sand curling under his toes, at the roaring of winds and cloud-scudded china-blue sky. Soon he came upon an abandoned settlement on the edge of a darkening forest.

It was a gathering of long-abandoned wooden shacks, promising stripped and shabby interiors. He stepped around an old iron spigot that poked up out of the ground. Evidently the pump still functioned, for around the base, a ring of tiny, bubbling plants scarred the sands with green.

"Sir, if one might suggest Rogers—"

He muted the Helmet. He didn't need advice from a machine.

A set of wet footprints led from the spigot to an open door.

The shack's floor was sandy and cold and Nifty wasn't wearing shoes. The fragile erection coveted a privacy long defunct. The place stunk of nostalgia. The wet wood, the scent of a distant bonfire, the itchy feeling on his skin. The creaking of boards; the sound of falling water. It was painfully real.

A rich red light ribbed the inside of the room and there she was before him. Nifty focussed hard to hold her fixed. The maiden Sylvia Yang stood naked, unaware of his presence, tilting a jug in each raised hand. Water sparkled green as it poured out of their mouths and spilled down between the floor-boards.

A small lizard, as green as Sylvia herself, crouched beside him.

"Go away," Niftus whispered. With a rush and a flutter, tearing the stillness apart, the lizard turned into a bird. The bird flew out the window and into the sky, towards an eight-pronged star.

He saw then that the hut had been surrounded by tall, lizard-headed creatures, feathered, alien and armed. For all intents and purposes, he was trapped inside.

But held, for the moment by the sight of the giant star. There were shapes in it, two strange letters that he couldn't read, stretching down over the sky.

AE.

How long had Sylvia run? Who was pursuing her? She came to a stop far away on the strand, quite lost and confused. To the east she saw a tree. It was approaching and walked awkwardly through the sand. As the tree moved, its roots, stretching and fingering, carved a dark furrow in the beach behind.

Time was out of joint. Sylvia grew older. Stronger, more sexualized, more realistically modern. Her two piece b-suit covered what counted. Though the tree had no eyes, she was glad to be clothed when it stopped before her, and offered shade from the implacable sun.

"Hello," she said.

"—*Sylvia*," croaked the twisting thing.

"Nifty? Is that you?"

The tree snorted.

Sylvia blushed. Were her emotions out of her control? She felt suddenly tender, exposed.

"*There is some—danger.*"

She grew fearful.

The tree gestured at the surrounding sea, at the highlands off-shore. "*I cannot stand—here.*"

"I don't know." Dr. Yang held her head in her hands. "I don't know what you mean...."

As the tree leaned down, the wind blew from the sea through its fragile leaves. It came suddenly alive, and smelled like something sweet from long ago. Very quietly, its leaves whispered: "*You must know—what you're looking for....*"

Why was it so sad to talk to this thing? Tears trickled hot down her face.

"There's no real space here, nowhere to get lost. But I'm certainly here," said Sylvia to herself. "I'm the proof."

"I want to find something, someone else," she said to the tree. "I don't know her name—"

Now the tree was holding an open book close to its trunk.

"May I see the book?" Dr. Yang asked.

The tree looked suddenly compromised.

She held out her hand. "Give it to me."

The tree couldn't offer any resistance. It was only a tree. The book felt heavy and real, unnaturally large in her hands.

But the lizard had caught up to them. There was the crack of a rifle. The slim icy shard of a needle passed through her brains like a foreign idea.

A monstrous solidity moved through her body and Sylvia stretched to accommodate its volume. For a moment it seemed like she'd been shot by ten thousand rifles, against ten thousand different walls, in ten thousand simultaneous worlds. A sword passed through her neck, but she felt nothing. And then a masculine face interrupted. Smiling archly triangular, it was a bright and happy green. "Let her pass," he said.

Let it pass, Sylvia thought. There was no needle, no green man. It was all a gentle hologram generated by the mind of Niftus Norrington with whom she had now entangled. There was no such thing as fear.

Niftus Norrington had become all eyes, all looking. He'd not completely forgotten his investigation, but Rogers Collectibles could wait. The n-scape made its own time.

For Sylvia Yang stood across from him in the shack naked and true, as true as he'd known her on the floor of her office. But here, where no one could see her, she was even more completely defined: both older and younger, more perfect. Her heavy hair fell down onto her shoulders and her eyes were closed. She was drying herself with a towel, running the cloth down her back, over her buttocks, up between her thighs. Her back arched. Nifty felt heavy, like a dead thing; he watched spellbound.

A green-budded stem rose up twirling between the floor-boards. And then another beside it. They intertwined at her feet and grew rapidly, sprouting more leaves as they curled up around her calves. A third stalk grew up inside her legs. It rose between the cleft of her buttocks, advancing against the small of her back. Sylvia moaned, dropped her towel and kneeled backwards into the rising plant. The third rising stem curled from her back to bind her breasts and brush its hard leaves against her erect nipples. A sweet determination took hold of her brow. Her eyes turned heavenward. She squatted low and groaned as a P-shaped tuber popped from the central stalk and penetrated her sex from behind. Panting, she fell on her knees to receive its thrusts. She pumped her hips against it.

Nifty strained in the heightened tension. What the hell was this? He couldn't move.

The bud at the tip of a winding stem passed into Sylvia's ear. She turned to face him and her mouth dropped open. A bright yellow flower emerged between her lips.

"*Must—communicate,*" said the flower.

It was the sentient plant.

The surprise of it, the immediate outrage, almost broke Nifty's belief in the n-scape's solidity. But his hands balled into fists and he kept it together by force of will. A light, steady rain began pelting the roof-top. Thunder (he had never heard it before) crashed from the sky.

Sylvia continued to receive the plant thing's wild thrusts, her breasts and buttocks shaking. The flower spoke again from her mouth.

"*Your mind has made—me this way.*"

"Get out. You're not allowed to be in here."

"*And you—?*"

"I was invited."

Sylvia ground hard against the sinewing thing. Her desire and freedom were rising, pressing and animal-like. She moaned through her stopped-up mouth, eyes rolling up into her head.

"*Not—to this place.*"

"I can't even move," Nifty said. His body had turned into stone.

Sylvia was deeply engaged. Her thighs jiggled glistening, her breasts swung in wild orbits, and the placid flower-head continued looking out from her open mouth.

A little girl's voice whispered in his ear.

"Where is Rogers Collectibles?"

Claps of thunderbolts shook the shelter's flimsy walls. Purple clouds moved through the sky in the window.

"*You are—no longer entangled.—There is danger. Move forward—*"

"Where is she?"

"*She has passed to another mind.*"

As it spoke, Norrington saw the plant's brown, hip-like trunks pumping Sylvia from behind.

"You g-ddamn sicko, I'll remember this."

"Bookstore," said the little voice in his ear.

Something was touching his shoulder, prickly hard. A tongue slithered against his neck. A horn blew out; an angelic warmth was burning up the room around him.

"Bookstore?"

"—*Now.*"

Multiply penetrated by tubed vegetation, limbs stretched out like a human cross, Sylvia screamed as she writhed, blowing the flower head out of her mouth.

Nifty strained to move his body and lept crashing through the window—just as the world exploded behind him.

Niftus was out. Sylvia knew it immediately. But she was still inside. Where? Her own idea of his mind? It felt alien, other, and she had even less power here over her own body. Had she been shot? She couldn't remember. She was lying face down on the pavement. She had fallen down wounded. She heard the slapping steps of a troop of soldiers pass and rolled over to see that a great city had emerged up from under her, to take her up prostrate on its stone. Was she bleeding? She looked at herself in the little mirror clutched between her thighs.

"She calls again," said Dr. Yang.

"Yes." Sylvia rose, lighter, filled with sudden power. Her wounds were healing rapidly. "But I'm not yet ready. I need Nifty with me."

"If we return now, we will have accomplished it. We will have moved through space and time. Have you seen this?"

It was another book, different from the one the tree had held. Even from where she stood Sylvia could read into it. It looked like a megazine, the kind Niftus Norrington liked to read. There was a drawing visible, of a strange cube-like building, impossibly rendered as curling around its X-axis.

"I know that thing," Sylvia said.

"It says here that it is a bookstore," said Dr. Yang.

"A bookstore?"

"Sylvia, won't we come to meet her? She is ready, even now she yearns—"

The face in the mirror flickered green, a triangular crack spread through the glass like a grin.

"End scan," said Sylvia Yang.

The city, the mirror, herself, they slipped away.

2. DARKENING, 101 V.E.

"I believe that the existence of the classical "path" can be pregnantly formulated as follows: The "path" comes into existence only when we observe it."

—Werner Heisenberg, letter to Pauli, 1927 C.E.

Chapter 10

An unobserved electron doesn't "orbit" the nucleus of its atom. The particle, rather, must be understood to exist in all of its possible orbital locations at once. Within the finite scope of its physical possibility, its position is infinite. For the sentient plant, so much was evident and simple to understand. But what of the observed electron?

It appeared that once observed, the electron moved reactively to claim a necessary point in spacetime; it selected a stream out of the hypothetical, a stream that carried with it a past and a future. So humans, the plant saw, by relativity, by acting, reacting to observations of which they were not consciously aware, grew up along particular flows of definite reality. But what if the observing specimen learns to perform its unconscious observation consciously? What occurs to the shape of the particle's history? Indeed, the plant had to conclude that through their recent interventions in the n-scape, its humans were able to re-order what was real because their history was already unknown to them.

The plant could not define what role its own observation had played in such mechanics. Immersion made self-consciousness impossible. But when Rogers Collectibles had gotten up, dressed and found his hat, taking care not to wake the sleeping Martha Dobbs, who lay like an angel in his bed, the sentient plant had occasion to understand just how radically the world had changed.

Rogers found a pong waiting on his watch from Dr. Yang. She wasn't calling about his health, she said, but as a prospective client.

"Do you know anything about the writer Ae? If you have anything by her I'd be interested in purchasing it," said the prerecording.

Despite their pseudo-medical relationship, Rogers rather liked Doctor Yang. She hadn't, after all, given him a reset. He didn't doubt she had respect for him in her own way. She remained a professional in a world tending toward the amateur, and he admired that. Apparently, she could even read or was at least willing to try. Rogers spent an hour eagerly researching the Terran writer Ae. He discovered she was a 22nd-century earth poet and revolutionary. Some of her strange texts had seemed to prophecy Venusia and even hinted at the possibilities of the then-new Moriturian science. Rogers discovered an old Jorx Crittendon clip directly related to her.

Crittendon was then still Commissioner of Government Operations; he wasn't yet Princeps.

"Ensconced in New Caledonia," he explained, with a light in his eye, "Ae believed she was fighting to halt the destruction and contamination of Earth. Sadly, poetry does not save worlds. Ae and her comrades were too late to do anything but hasten their own deaths. Their paradise was only of the mind. Still, it allowed them to envision humanity's survival off-world. She wrote of a colony divorced from a home to which it could never return. Ae intimated she'd encountered beings from such worlds traveling through time." Jorx laughed at this. His triangular grin expanded up and down his chin. "All stories from Earth are sad. All its dreams are fantasies, all its insurrections failures. We must not get caught up with them. It's why her books are now banned."

Rogers sent the Jorx Crittendon spot to Dr. Yang on pong. "I'll sell the original V-disc to you," he added. "But you should know there's apparently still a bookstore, or something like it, downtown. Frank P. Hogart, Block 22A. I'm going there now. I'll see if he has anything that might help you find out more."

And so the plant grew worried. By all probability, there should not have been a bookstore in Venusia at all. But as it scanned the minds of those with which it had entangled, the plant came to realize that it itself was already there, inside the store, with them.

Time was slipping again. Rogers Collectibles sat back into the railbus hook-seat, covering his face with his hat. He half expected Martha to return, swinging in the seat beside him, even though he had just left her, still sleeping in his own bed. But when he tipped his hat back, Rogers saw that he was alone. The bus had stopped. The boy, all the other passengers, were gone.

The Venusia provided by the Crittendon regime worked automatically. One paid one's dues, took one's tests, went about one's business as expected. The regime functioned with such regularity, indeed, that one rarely noticed its increasing destruction of daily life. It was only when the mechanism broke down and you could suddenly look out through the gaps, that you noticed that there was nothing else left outside.

The railbus, inexplicably, had stopped. The car swung over a run-down block of the old inner city. Rogers was alone, and he saw no sign of human life outside. Had the entire professional class gone to the beach? The once-lively streets were now reduced to the broken brick, trash and crumbling mortar they'd left behind. The only life was vegetative; it seemed long to have had the run of things. Now even the railbus, that jewel in Venusia's biotechnical crown, needed repairs.

"Rogers Collectibles?"

The sound of his own name startled him in the empty car.

But it was only railbus-command that had spoken. Rogers removed his hat.

"What's the problem here? I have a business appointment and it's essential I get to 22a by 11."

"Rogers Collectibles, allow us to introduce Railbus 2080, temporary ambassador of L.E.M. It is imperative that L.E.M. speak to you concerning the probable outcome of your insurrection."

Rogers was furious. "You are completely out of order. You are saying dangerous things. I have no in—"

"Calm down," railbus control answered. "Are you a man or a business?"

Rogers sighed. "What is this?"

"Until now, you have escaped individual surveillance. But L.E.M. disrupts ordinary routine to inform you that you have indeed been located by Station 5. Your communications are now contained by your enemy's gaze."

A lizard had been looking at him from across the car, for some time. Its mouth was frozen in a long and wicked grin.

"Your minds are all swidged ub," it said.

The lizard raised a needle gun from its hip and aimed directly into Rogers' eye. Its tongue flickered to probe the feathers on its jaw.

The boy was grinning. Once again, Rogers was hooked ordinarily into a railbus. He was sailing again through the air. Only that boy, that pink-skinned boy, seemed to have noticed what had happened.

Insurrection? He had no such grand schemes on his mind. Rogers understood he was a citizen of a criminal and coercive city-state. But really, was he expected to resist? To rebel? Hardly. He was safe from immediate harm. Food was readily available, and anyway he was seldom hungry. He had no interest in politics. Life, for a small businessman, was apolitical. Yet it occurred to him that in the eyes of the law his innocence could well signal guilt. If one or more Venusians were engaged in any kind of insurrection, they would have to take pains not to know it consciously at all, n-scape surveillance being what it was. The last thing he needed was rumors spreading to the effect that he was a danger to the state.

Simply looking for his copy of *Brane World* had already brought him up against the law. He had no intention of breaking it further. Rogers wished the railbus hadn't spoken the word *insurrection*. It was as if he was no longer wholly innocent.

There had already been more than enough change to suit Rogers Collectibles. He must focus only on his personal freedoms, concern himself only with the fate of CRC. He hopped off early at Block 19, and walked quietly through the empty streets, as if to prove to himself that he was entirely at large.

But when his watch ponged, a cold bolt of fear passed throught him. He sat down on an empty bench and received it with shaking hands.

It was Martha. The very thought of Martha calmed him, turned the fear within him into something else.

She was ponging from his ad-apt, standing close up to the Iye so her head looked larger than it should on his little watch-stage.

"Where are you?" she said.

He looked around. Across the street there was an empty lot; a long-abandoned tangle of weeds and trash had grown up between two defunct ad-apt complexes.

"I'm here on Block 22a," Rogers replied. "I'm here for my appointment with Frank P. Hogart. But I don't seem to see anything or anyone around."

She frowned. "I'm supposed to be filming your life."

Rogers sighed. "I had a blackout.... I'm sorry."

"Please." Her huge eyes seemed pregnant with need. "It's not just the show. I really want to be with you. Wait for me."

"O.K.," he said. "I'll wait."

There'd been another slip. He didn't notice it this time, since he hadn't been paying attention to anything but the problem of Martha Dobbs and whether or not she might be, after all, his original Martha.

But when he shook his head to clear it of such things Rogers noticed a small cloud had gathered between the ad-apt buildings across the way. It wasn't so rare to see one in the city; stray clouds flitted about from time to time. But this one was different, a conglomeration of the sort of blur that great heat raised up from blacktop on a summer's day. Still swirling in its confusion he saw a strange structure. It was a reddish, steel-rimmed cube—a conglomeration of a shiny bricked material he couldn't place. The crafted regularities of its surface looked completely out of date beside the dated futurism of the yellowing, white-walled ad-apt buildings beside it. There were no windows. Its silver door was closed. It sat squat, intact and self-contained, old, older than the complexes, but somehow newer, different. It seemed to bend awkwardly as he looked at it, as if it was folded somehow, around its own rear portions.

"Frank P. Hogart," an invisible sign whispered on the breeze. "Bookseller."

Rogers remained seated. He expected lizards to appear, but saw none. Wind from the beach blew warm dust and distant shouts from the far-off Feed into the damp air. Branches rustled and twitched as if in gentle warning. Could a building suddenly appear from out of nowhere at all?

The emptiness, the relative invisibility of the landscape struck him. When there's no one to notice anything, who knew what kind of things might appear or disappear? Maybe the store, since such a thing was expressly forbidden by temp-proc, cloaked itself with inviso-technology of a sort he didn't know existed.

In the distance, Martha Dobbs was rapidly approaching. Her steps blew multi-colored Day's End leaves up from the stone walk. He could see quite well that she was her own Martha. The way she walked, her grace and self-command … she couldn't be his. She wasn't the sort of person he would ordinarily even meet.

Glittering towards him in the falling sun, her Iye trailed with a kind of desperation.

Martha Dobbs felt a little bit ridiculous when she saw Rogers Collectibles huddled in the distance. Was this really the sort of man who could command a reality V program? But as he rose from the bench and crossed the street to meet her, her fears relaxed at the sight of his ridiculous old hat. In his own queer way, Rogers Collectibles was important. And he could be trusted. He'd waited like he'd said he would; he hadn't run away, like every other man she'd known.

Martha walked up to him and met him on the street. When his hand reached out, she took it and she felt its warmth.

And then her Iye came down between them.

"What's it doing?" Rogers asked. "I don't think it should be —"

"Shhh." It was recording. She had to improvise an introduction for Larry to mix later. "Remember the nutcase, Rogers Collectibles? I'm here—"

Martha stopped speaking.

Hundreds of globular, silver Iyes came up as if from nowhere. Iyes rounded corners, leapt from rooves, came out of bushes, up from under benches. Together they formed a single, sparkling arc that framed the couple beside the silver doorway of a dark, glass-bricked building.

"Hoppies," observed Martha Dobbs. "We seem to be contained by a metallic, illuminating hedgehog circle of blinking, live-feeding Iyes."

"This is not what I expected," Rogers said.

"Please," purred the Iyes, as a single entity. "Calm down. Iye can see you normally. It is your vision that has skewed in the event-horizon of the anomaly. You see all possibilities. But Iye is one. Go inside. Iye cannot follow."

Rogers leaned forward and whispered. "Should we go inside?"

Maybe so. But Martha Dobbs had to come up with a show that Larry Held would find good enough for Sunset. She'd felt a new sense of her potential this t-morning, a new sense that history might not be ashamed about accepting her. People liked her show, admired her ambition. She believed in following events as they occurred, on their own terms. It was the best way to capture the real.

But was this possible without an Iye? Could she achieve her dreams without it? This building gave her a mysterious feeling. Its opaque, milky walls shone with strange metallic depth. The structure was mathematical and strange—it almost pulsed with intricacy.

"I'm happier without the Iye," Rogers opined, taking off his hat. "I don't like "Windows on the Weird" so much anyhow. I prefer ficto-V's, history, even sports."

"All right," she told him, brusquely. "Let's go. I'll record audio on my watch. But I'll need something else later."

Rogers reached towards the door.

The solid wall of Iyes clacked and rolled to follow action.

Rogers stepped inside first. Immediately, he tasted the scent of paper, the cool of a controlled, humidified atmosphere.

When the door closed behind them, it was at first difficult to focus. The lack of light confused him. The space was lit from the corners by idiosyncratic, antique lamps and its interior complications were enshadowed.

Yet they were indeed apparently inside a bookstore. They walked along a central hallway lined with heavily laden shelves of books. They passed open rooms, all packed thick with miscellaneous volumes. The wooden floor creaked as they stepped upon it.

Chairs crouched in the corners of rooms and strangely enough, Rogers saw people, seated, reading—oblivious to their passage. He took care not to look at them, respectful of their individual privacy. But they seemed strange, of another time. In one room he saw two figures facing one another equipped with government issue helmets. They looked like gigantic insects. One a grown woman, and one a thick-armed, precocious child.

"You can't believe it, hopsters," Martha was whispering to her watch. "Rows and rows of books, as far as you can see. Lining the walls. Stacked in corners, under tables. Look at the different colors. All the great cover designs on their fronts...."

"They're not going to be able to see anything," Rogers said.

"Maybe Larry can recreate something from the description."

"Not like this."

It was an astonishing collection. Rogers walked through the quiet rooms, chilled by the evident triumph of the collecting.

"How could I not have heard of this place before?"

Martha whispered behind him. "Do you think there's a harness in here?"

But Rogers didn't answer. He was looking at the cover of a small, green-jacketed volume atop a chair-side table.

Venusia—a 2 dimensional histo-holograph.

It was a history picture-book. Rogers took it in his hands. It was as if he remembered the very volume, as if he'd held it in his hands long ago. It brought so much back to him to turn its pages, so many details and ideas. As he flipped through it, the story came before him with sudden clarity.

The colonists had gathered as their nations were collapsing. A great elevator still stretched its nanotubes into orbit from Central America. In space, ships and sailors were cheap and for the asking. Two waves of outcasts had been able to escape before the elevator fell. By the time the colony was founded, they'd been cut off from the larger system forever.

The first years on Venusia were smooth. As Melton had predicted, the colonists found an easily manipulated atmosphere, a mellow climate and an easy life. After the turmoil on Earth, it seemed like a kind of paradise. The building up of the colony took all the time and ingenuity of the new society. Peter Melton, Captain of the first ship, and Hugo Morituri, chairman and chief engineer of the Morituri Corporation, served as consuls, architects and benign dictators. Officers and officials were chosen by lottery from the citizen pool at large. In the first v-day alone, the central infrastructure had been set up. Robot farms and factories seeded bumper crops and improved the local planetary atmosphere. Terran trees were planted, state rituals established, small businesses launched. Birds were released into the air. Children were bred four to every colonist and raised by the colony as a whole. Family, as it had been understood, was abolished.

The years passed and a world very like the one they had abandoned took shape around them. The Kluger was installed as central currency. Banks arose to control and profit from its flow. Healthy competition was tempered by the realization that every individual's participation was necessary to the group's survival.

As the population exploded, culture bloomed. Books were printed, V shows created and broadcast back to Terra. Comedians mocked Venusian modes. A city-state began to form. As news from 23rd century Earth grew darker, more sporadic, Venusia found itself a remarkable, experimental settlement, possessed of enlightened pageantry, thought, activity and hope—and entirely alone in the universe.

Things began to change. First, the birds had all flown away. They never returned. The strangeness of the new world began to take a toll upon the colonists. The year-long nights, the fall of earth, the total loss of contact with the wider human project. Many of the first 10,000 died or went mad. Rogers remembered one story of a man at a vegetable grill who suddenly buried his cleaver in a younger customer's skull, and proceeded to cook her brains. The vendor butchered forty of his friends and neighbors before he was controlled.

It was the beginning of the Transition, but no one knew it yet. Disorder spread. Madness opened with revolting violence out of hitherto placid minds. The young discovered flowers, a cross-breed of Venusian and Terran strains, and occupied themselves with underground farming and distribution. Though all religion had been banned by perm-proc, proto-pagan religions sprouted and took hold. These cults drew on half-remembered myths from Terran history, from the collective unconscious and the visions experienced by abstaining flower-takers.

The Castle and Station 5 were both built at this time to protect the government from outbreaks. The populace was monitored by a new elite police, the g-ops or government operators. Their prey were thrown into a mysterious, never-reported upon prison never to be seen again.

Though election of new consuls was indefinitely postponed, the state still saw itself as a proto-democracy. When the crisis reached its apex, Venusian security passed into the hands of one Jorx Crittendon, a first-generation historian and theorist whose name had been selected by a random lottery.

Or had it? Many complained that such a coincidence was impossible, but they were silenced in the end by Crittendon's iron hand.

Increasingly self-absorbed and eccentric, Melton abdicated his consulship and disappeared to a location far outside the bounds of the colony. Hugo Morturi committed suicide in the M&M laboratories.

After that, sometime around when Rogers himself had been born, Venusian history had ended.

The book did not exactly show these things. But the pictures of gardens and celebrations and ordinary Venusian lives from the past raised the memory of them in Rogers' mind again. He had lived long enough to forget so much.

Only the book's last page showed images of the major figures. A deteriorated color photograph showed a young Jorx Crittendon with a grim-faced moustachioed Hugo Morituri beside him. They stood on the steps of the newly constructed House of Sighs. Crowds had gathered around the two men; the scene was imbued with pageantry. Flowers were strewn all around. Behind them, there hulked a robed figure, leaning on a gnarled stick.

Rogers looked more closely at the picture. He recognized the old pink-skinned man and the hat on his head.

It was Frank P. Hogart, Bookseller.

"You're late!"

Rogers closed the book, and rose to see the old man before him.

Hogart wasn't wearing his hat. He was even older than in the picture and larger than he looked over pong. His thick trunk had twisted terribly forward onto the stout cane apparently fixed to his left arm. His expression was crabbed and muted. His eyes squinted as if it was hard for him to see.

"Did you bring the book?"

Rogers found his composure. "This collection," he said. "All these books. How do you get away with it?"

Hogart closed his eyes, unable to suppress his disdain. "An old man's fire burns within me, I assure you, Rogers. Don't push me. Do not bother yourself with things beyond your understanding. Produce the copy of *Brane World* you showed me over holographic telecommunication or—"

There was an explosion. The building shifted suddenly 45 degrees on its vertical axis. The old man fell backwards. Rogers caught hold of a shelf to stay standing and spilled a rack of books onto the floor. The lights went out.

He heard Martha Dobbs' voice in the darkness.
"Rogers?"
"I'm here," he said.
"I tried to send a note to Larry and my watch exploded."
"I don't think you should have ponged," he said.

Chapter 11

Reality is produced by the self-reflective quantum unit of consciousness (the soul) and its dependent memory. Together they choose, share and communicate the perceived streams of the real. This much Sylvia understood. But she also understood that she was in the same structure she'd seen floating above a city park not long ago. It was a bookstore.

Like a thicket of pre-recorded possible universes, the bookstore inhabited and stabilized the single world around her. She had traveled through space by way of the n-scape.

But why a bookstore? Did bookstores, like electrons, depend on statistical waves of movement that could be released at any time? Sylvia stood shyly and let the quiet come down around her. It was a hush and peace she'd never known. A scent rich with the wood and mold of paper; alternate histories yawning from text-laden recesses. A floor creaking as she walked.

Here, in this place, with its silent waiting books, the whole outer reality seemed itself an n-scape. If it was possible to travel across space in an instant, would one not become a god?

Sylvia didn't think so. She didn't feel particularly god-like. She didn't even feel like a scientist.

As she browsed the works of her ancestors, Sylvia experienced a piercing wave of emotion—similar to the wash she'd felt in the n-scape. Up against these other written works, the rational output of understandable lives, she understood how unlikely she herself really was. Human language was so frail and abstract in its effort to erect its holographs. When they came up they had a rugged, undeniable strength about them.

Intuition took her towards a set of black volumes on an anonymous, heavy-laden shelf. She knew the shapes of letters and their sounds enough to read the name on the spine. *F,R,E,U,D*.

One Hundred Years of History Re...pressed.

Yes, she could almost read.

She took a volume in her hand. Felt its weight, blinked as the dust rose to her eye. In her mind, the book had no weight to it. It wasn't what she thought a book would be, a thing crafted and constructed. It was mass produced, a copy inviolable and relentless, like a living representative of an ideal self. It extended its unfolding point of view outwards from its center of reflection—as if sucking the real it claimed out of possibility altogether. Unlike Sylvia Yang, it did not traverse the n-scape, play with chance. It knew what it could never be.

Her helmet ponged.

Sylvia replaced the book in the shelf, sat down and lowered visor to receive transmission.

It was Niftus.

"Welcome back to reality," he said.

"Where are you?" she whispered.

"Apparently I'm in a bookstore."

"A bookstore?"

"You're losing your bearings, Doc. I'm sitting right across from you."

She turned and saw, with a shock, that he was indeed with her. Seated in a chair much too big for him, across from her in the very same room.

"We did it," he said. "The Melton Effect."

She took a chair beside him. "But we don't know why we are. We didn't choose to come here."

"I know."

She looked at him.

"Ah," said Niftus Norrington. "How surprising that the freak, the miniature man, might actually out-think the learned and respected doctor. We're here because Collectibles is here. I found him. I also saw what—"

He stopped speaking. Sylvia heard the sound of voices in the adjoining hallway. Feet creaking on the floor.

"Can you make them out?" asked Niftus. "Do you see Rogers Collectibles?"

"Shh." Inexplicably, she was afraid. They waited for some time. But before she could speak again, the space around them shifted. The room tilted hard and to the right. The whole place tipped. Books slid off shelves, knocking over lamps. Niftus Norrington rolled out of his chair and hit the floor.

Lizards, huge-armed lizards, were emerging all around them

Niftus Norrington's observation that the Melton Effect had just occurred by the intersection of his and Dr. Yang's perceptions showed typical shortsightedness. Yes, the real had shifted. But it had been accomplished, certainly, by the perception of a third observer's relativity. Namely, the plant, having immersed itself in the uncertainty of the n-scape had nevertheless secured relation to the sun, filtered anonymously, as it was through the quasicrystalline walls of the bookstore. It was resting on a bookshelf to the left of where Sylvia Yang was now sitting. And this real, it plainly saw, was radically fragile.

Indeed to the plant's considerable distress, the inside of the 'bookstore' could also be described as a multi-dimensional structure spread out like a bridge between interlinking parallel universes. Rogers Collectibles had been drawn into it, and had led the others into it as well. Unfortunately it was possible in any unobserved region of most worlds, so that when Martha Dobbs ponged Larry Held, any positional possibilities the structure contained could fall directly into Crittendon's invisible prison, which was the least desirable (most probable), most unobserved universe of all.

Princeps Crittendon's prison relatively guaranteed entropic stasis. Within its confines, the individual mind could no longer certainly recall its past, so many were newly possible. Memory was now indistinguishable from fantasy and time slippery.

Yet the plant and its humans still lived, if only on the tenderest of possible branches. And while they remained entangled, they stood on the event-horizon of the yawning n-scape.

The plant longed to communicate with its humans. It needed to warn them about Princeps Crittendon's interest in their interior travels, to help them understand the position that they held within schematic relativity. But the light had waned drastically with the new transition. Here, in the basement of Station Five, the plant could not receive exterior electromagnetic radiation. It could likely be immersed here until it died, for the Senate could no longer reach it.

As Dr. Yang got up and brushed her robe, a single fusion lamp suspended from the ceiling turned on. Sylvia saw that she was in a large room, floored and walled by cold volcanic stone. It wasn't hard to pick Niftus from the figures cast about on the floor.

"Nifty." He scrambled up at the sound of his name.

There was a table underneath the lamp, and five chairs placed around it. Niftus Norrington and Sylvia sat down across from one another.

"We're in jail," Nifty said. "I'm not surprised."

It had always been the stated policy of Rogers Collectibles, when business became needlessly intricate, to stay composed. As soon as Doctor Yang had roused him, he got up and brushed the dirt from his suit. He saw that Martha Dobbs was already awake and walking around the perimeters of the room, running her hand along the walls.

Rogers took off his hat. "Excuse me, Dr. Yang" he asked. "Do you know what this place is? I'm missing an important appointment—"

The dwarf turned to face him. With its visor up, his helmet revealed a miniature, thug-like face.

"Rogers Collectibles," he said. "The lizard man."

Rogers didn't like the little man's attitude. He kept his attention focussed on the doctor.

"Ms. Dobbs and I were talking with Mr. Hogart in the bookstore. May I ask where we are?"

"You're in prison," the dwarf answered. "Your memories as to how you got here were probably blotted out. On the other hand, maybe you were always here and simply fantasized a life outside. I'm an m-op. The name's Norrington. I've been looking for you. But my girlfriend and I—" he gestured to Doctor Yang. "Have been breaking procs all over the place. Looks like we're all locked up now."

"Why were you looking for me?"

"Because you see lizards. You're an addict. I'm supposed to trace you, blot your memories."

"I still remember them."

"Well you're in jail now. It's no longer my responsibility." The little man grinned. "But if you'd like I'd be happy to take care of it."

Jail? Rogers looked around. There wasn't much to see. No visible door, no window. He looked back at the dwarf.

"Did you say that Dr. Yang is your girlfriend?"

Martha Dobbs came to the table. "There's five chairs," she said. "And only four of us."

"How observant," Rogers said.

Her big eyes flashed. "It's you who got us here. You and your ridiculous book."

Composure left him. "Ridiculous? It was your pong to Larry Held that got us here."

"Friends," Doctor Yang said. "Let's all calm down."

The light then, inexplicably, went out.

In the deep blackness, deeper than any black he thought was possible, so dark that it became a kind of pure and infinite clarity, Rogers reached out and found Martha Dobbs' hand.

"I'm sorry I got you into this," he whispered.

"Shhh," she said, and squeezed.

He saw something approaching on his left. Considering the impenetrable stone boundaries of the room, the light seemed to come from an impossible distance. Was it moving towards him from far away, or simply growing from a point on the floor? It was impossible to know.

But the light, as it grew, turned out to be a tiny figure. It grew rapidly into a life-size image of Frank P. Hogart. He held a glowing lantern as he moved towards them across the floor.

Suddenly and directly in front of them, Hogart's eyes were wide and desperate.

"Rogers? You're near...." He reached out a trembling hand. "Rogers? Rogers? Give it to me...."

He couldn't see a thing.

Something exploded, compact and hard. An impossibly bright burst. With a puff of acrid smoke, both the old man and the darkness were gone.

The lights were back on.

"What the hell was that?" asked the dwarf.

"It was Frank P. Hogart. It looks like he doesn't have my book," Rogers said. "I don't know where it is."

Martha Dobbs let go of his hand. She was looking off to the far left-most corner of the room.

"Larry?"

"Larry Held, in person, hoppies," said the impossibly gaunt MC, stepping forward from the shadows. "And I'm terribly sorry we all have to meet in such trying conditions."

Rogers Collectibles, had never been in the presence of a celebrity. To see that familiar long face, its wide and down-turned lips, its ineffably sad eyes, that strange and stringy body, to see it for real, was unreal. It made him uncomfortable.

Martha Dobbs said: "Larry, the Iye didn't follow me in the bookstore. I tried to pong and—"

Larry stretched out his hands. "Hey. Let's all sit down. We'll talk."

Chapter 12

As they were all seated, it was only Larry who needed to take a chair. He sat down at the head of the table, between Rogers Collectibles and Martha Dobbs. Rogers removed his hat and lit an LP.

"Exactly what the hell is going on here," said the dwarf, apparently unimpressed by the impresario's authority. "Was the bookstore some kind of hologram inside the prison?"

The MC grinned widely. "JC's prison, this one, anyway, is a veritable hole in time. It makes everything a hologram inside of it, everything extraordinary certainly, like this bookstore you speak of. It's just the sort of bizarre phenomenon the prison can encircle with its own possibility. Once it had stepped into Venusia and we had perceived Ms. Dobbs' pong, the bookstore was easily contained, done away with, revealed as impossible. Now you're guests of the state."

The dwarf smacked the table with his fist.

"Exactly what have we done wrong? Why are we locked up? Where's the re-education? Why do we remember this?"

Larry stifled a chuckle. "Slow down, hoppy. You're quite a character. Ever been on the V's?"

"I don't go in for circuses."

"Relax. The prison is great for snatching folks up, but it's not good at holding them for long. Let's use the time while we're here, shall we? I'll explain everything."

Rogers spoke up. "I still protest the fact that we're no longer in the bookstore. It's not a large matter perhaps in your eyes, but I'm missing a very important business meeting. "

Larry's sad eye twinkled. "You're great," he said. "All of you are. Bookstore. I love that idea. Can't you understand that the bookstore, now that we're here, doesn't exist?"

"I picked up a book myself," said Dr. Yang, across from the dwarf. "I felt it in my own hands."

Larry scoffed. "How many of you have seen lizards?"

"I have," said Dr. Yang.

"And you think they're real?"

The long, sad smile angled up Larry's rat-like face. A new light shone from his red-rimmed eyes as he turned to the reporter.

Rogers could see the force of Larry's celebrity and power blow across Martha Dobbs. "I'm just glad you're here, Larry," she said. "I was getting worried."

"Mr. Held," Rogers interupted, increasingly annoyed. "We are free agents, are we not? I don't recall being charged with any crime. If re-education is not—"

"Collectibles," Larry sighed, turning back to him. "Remain composed. You're in no danger. Let's talk about your business meeting. I'm interested in this Frank P. Hogart. He was here recently, was he not?"

"Just now," Martha Dobbs said. "He was right there."

"Who all saw him?"

"The four of us," Rogers said.

"Not possible," said Larry Held. "There had to have been an odd number to allow him to attempt neuroscopic entanglement."

And then occurred a phenomenon unprecedented in the experience of Rogers Collectibles. His own brain presented a word to itself, a word from outside his consciousness. The word gleamed in his head, neither sound nor image, simply the idea of itself:

"*Actually—*"

"Ah yes," said Larry Held. "There is another. The sentient plant. Five."

"Yes, look." Martha Dobbs pointed to the grapefruit-sized orb of crystal, resting on the table before Dr. Yang. Rogers hadn't noticed it.

It was clear, and filled with little wet balls of red clay. "That is a sentient plant," Martha Dobbs said. "I've seen them before."

Norrisson, the dwarf, scoffed at the Doctor. "You brought that pervert weed from your office? I can't believe it."

The Doctor blushed. "I... must have taken it with me. I don't remember."

"—*Energy*," gleamed the words in Rogers' mind. "—*Help*."

Rogers' couldn't believe it. The plant was speaking in his mind. He laughed and leaned forward to examine the tiny, angular green extensions curling among the clay balls inside the crystal.

"All plants are sentient," Larry said. "The new proximity to the sun and the peculiar spin of the planet have jump started their evolutionary programming. But this one knows it. It has enough surplus energy to communicate directly inside of our consciousness. It emerges through the n-scape in our minds, places words in temporal order, causes them to manifest in our consciousness as thought. The poor thing can only really observe and report. They become quite obsessed with us. Imagine what it's like, never to be able to touch the object of your love. It's very difficult for them to communicate directly. This one must be desperate."

"—*light*."

Larry chuckled. "Don't worry, little guy." He touched his watch and a window opened on the upper wall at room's end. Ruddy light filled out the space. "Welcome back to Venusia, hoppies."

The rays from the window illuminated a hexagonal spot on the table. Dr. Yang reached forward and moved the crystal ball into the light.

"I had no idea," Dr. Yang said. "It's never talked to me before."

"You're not so innocent," said the dwarf.

Rogers could see the plant clearly now. Its tendrils wound around the little clay balls like the nerves of intricate brain, extending radially from a hidden center. Slender leaves curled up against the crystal's top, breathing through thin-cut vents. The ball actually began to vibrate as he looked.

"Just who is this is this Frank P. Hogart?" Martha Dobbs asked.

Larry's red-rimmed, intense eyes looked round the table, as if scanning their minds.

"You don't know, do you?" he said. "Good. The less you know of him the less power he'll have to interfere with your lives. He does not belong here, interfering with us from out of his own self-destructive pasts. But Jorx is not concerned with Hogart. What we're really concerned with is the woman."

"Jorx Crittendon?" Martha Dobbs asked, unbelieving.

"Jorx himself, doll-face. He loves your show, by the way. It's he who's sent me, in fact. He wanted me to let you all in on what's really going on round about here, in actuality."

"What woman?" muttered Rogers.

"Patience, Collectibles. A 21st century entertainer once said: 'Life is a black comedy. It doesn't always end the way you think it should end. But hey, that's O.K. It's funny.'"

Larry unfolded his long hands on the table. "I want to tell you the story of my life."

"I first knew I was different, hoppies, when I realized I missed my father. I even knew his name. His name was Horace Held. What a funny name. And he missed me too. Though Melton had outlawed family from first founding, my father had kept track of me. For a short while, he even took care of me. He was a camera technician for the V's and quite well-to-do.

"He died during the Transition.... When the Earth-born were dropping like fleas—losing their minds, killing eachother. Those of you off flowers might remember the fires they burned the bodies in and the piles they hauled away to the volcanoes. It was quite a traumatic time.

"Like the others, I forgot those things. And everything else too. After a while one has to give up, let the past go. I think you know what I mean, hoppies. When the flowers appeared in the underground markets, I was like a lot of people and got hooked.

"Man, did they help. Eventually, I forgot Horace Held. I just knew my father was gone. When I was sad, I told myself and anyone who asked, that it was because I missed my Dad. Still, I was something of an oddball. Lots of children were missing siblings. There was a man who was missing his wife. Two sisters were missing an aunt but never noticed eachother. Mothers everywhere were remembered, as you well know. But few others were missing a father.

"Later I found out that society left the notion of "Father" blank for a reason. So that the Princeps, for he would be necessary for our very survival, could occupy it himself. As super-director of Government Operations, Jorx had to be Father. It was why, he said, family had had to be abolished to begin with.

"But I didn't need a guardian or protector of my own memory. My loss was radically fixed, my psyche self-contained in a way everyone else's was not. I knew I was different. When they took us to the House of Sighs and the other kids marveled at the windswept sea-scapes and lovingly rendered meadows (which seemed to them like moving, beautiful dreams), I knew exactly what we were looking at. They were the paintings looted from the Berlin Gemäldegalerie in the chaos of the 2090's, eventually gathered up and brought to Venus on the second wave. That made them the last extant relics of the high-art Terran tradition. Mr. Collectibles, you might be interested to know that. I was. I was interested in knowledge, you see. In pinning things down—knowing exactly what was real. Like the artists of those paintings, I thought. Like the fellow who painted that yellow girl.

"Perhaps for this reason, I grew into a very unsatisfied young man. While others ran off to the beach to play and love, I stayed inland. About the craggy hills that ring the city, where only hermits go. The ancient volcanoes, hoppies, if you've ever gone to see them. They drew me like magnets. I was obsessed with volcanoes. Obsessed. Something about the fire hole, the slice at the top. Maybe Dr. Yang could fill me in on what it all means sometime.

"By then I'd been off flowers for a while. But the sight of all that molten lava, the rich smell of the planet's innards, brought me back to my father. They had thrown him into the burning slime. Sometimes it was strange to think about, how my father's earthborn bones had become one with Venusian rock. Too strange.

"On Venusia, memory activation brings problems, hoppies. Big problems. Like the hallucinations some of you already know about.

"One day I was gathering edibles on a perpendicular crag emerging from one of the hoarier volcanoes. The place, if you know it, is called Hobbyhorse Rock, after the first mayor. He died on an expedition there back in second V-day.

"From a distance it looks like a skull. It's even spookier up close, hoppies. Take my word for it. The shadows grow long and strange on Hobbyhorse Rock.

"I went that day because I'd seen it so many times from a distance and wondered what might lay inside its dark socket. The city spread below me as I climbed and I could see how tiny it was in the wild wet green of the world. What a speck we were on the monotonous planet. And how endless and round the clouds, as they edged the volcano hole.

"The hollows were a good ways away from the beach. Not a drop of water around. And they turned out to be grottos, not caves, simple indentations burst out by boiling water long ago. Climbing into the cool shadow of one, I was surprised to come upon an ornate sea creature. A giant cephalopod. Hovering in the middle of the shadowed air. As if it was submerged in an invisible sea, hoppies. It was eerie. My hair stood on end.

"The thing had a beak. Eight, enormous suction-cupped tentacles extended in perfect symmetry from its orange, tubular torso. And in the middle a single eye, huge, unlidded and round. That eye kept me fixed in the focus of its fat-sacked brain.

"I didn't know it at the time, hoppies, but it was the Melton Effect. An unconscious schizoid intersection with the present-tense. The population's memory loss from the increased industrialization of the flowers. Anyone who went far enough off the flowers was bound to become conscious of it—to slide into the n-scape and entangle with other travelling minds.

"I didn't know all that at the time, of course. I was just blown away by the sight of it. Frightened as all hell. But I didn't run, didn't close my eyes. I tried to understand. And suddenly things changed. As if I were looking out of that fish eye into a romantic, alien, waterless world. It was like I'd been seized from my proper environs and thrown into a desert. It was a wasteland of emptiness, hoppies. I felt like a fish, caught in the air.

"I desperately wanted to steal something dry, to bring it home to the water world, where it might be made beautiful and free. I was the squid, I felt it deep down. A species unobserved enough to enjoy travel far and wide in the neuroscape, immune from the shared history of its planet—a species that still travels far in space and time.

"So there I was, a cephalapod hovering in air, perplexed, staring at this terribly sad, gaunt boy, standing in the brilliant, unaccounted for light. The boy was me.

"His skin was green, hoppies. More green than pink or brown. Even his dark hair was streaked with green. I relaxed to return to my underwater past.

"'Wait,' said the boy. 'Don't leave. I will tell you what I have always understood but never before divulged.'

"I understood him perfectly. Naturally, however, my squid husk was unable to form sounds so I could only listen.

"'First of all,' said the boy. 'You are living on the Planet Venus, second planet from Sol, the star of this system. You are the child of the colonizing generation. The new planet, its physical properties, has changed you irrevocably. Your very time, the very mathematics of your mind, has crossed into something different from what your brain was built to observe.

"'Earth is dead, hoppy. The horror of the past is too much for you to handle. You're completely alone, cast away for ever and ever. Sure, there may be other stories, other human lives scattered stranded throughout the systems. But none of them have the advantages you do. Air to breathe, warm sunlight, fertile soil. Yet already your population is dwindling, dying out. The situation is dire.'"

"That's all that was said, friends. And there I was alone again, a green boy in a grotto in the side of Heller's Rock. Only it used to be called Hobbyhorse.

"I went back to Venusia. I was newly humble, now that I'd faced what I was. I loved the people I saw, going about their complicated businesses in their pseudo-reality. I loved their will to go on, the illusions they shared—that by sharing, opened up the neuroscape for my direct access. I dedicated my life to them and their fantasies. To their happiness, edification and well-being.

"Jorx Crittendon was right, I figured. Both the past and the future, no matter how you looked at them, were nothing but trouble. Our lives could only have meaning if we merged more perfectly with the present. If we did it right, the very past and futures might be entirely remade. We might be truly free. From that time forward, my hoppies, I pledged to be cool and collected and optimistic. To seek the humor that marks the victory of the present over all tragic things.

"If I couldn't destroy the history that had left us here and the doom we lived under, I could at least help to ease the pain. That's why I became show-business. I became Leave-It-To-Larry Held."

Martha Dobbs stood. Nifty noted how cool and hip she looked in her tight, beige wraparound. It left her long legs bare and beautiful.

"Collectibles," said Larry as he rose. "Norrington. As you've insisted on not taking flowers, you'll find the n-scape opening inside you. Once inside, if you can get past your lizards, you may well find Hogart. Ignore him. We're interested in the woman. She will try to make contact. Let her. Draw her out. Let her come to you, entangle. We must do away with her here, by our time."

"When will we be released?" said Martha Dobbs.

Larry smiled, looking her up and down. He put a finger to his lips.

"Hey, Sylvia," Nifty said, leaning forward. She had lowered the visor of her helmet and was relaxing in such a way that he knew exactly where she'd gone. He tapped the glass of her visor. "Come back to reality."

Larry put out a hand. "Chill, hoppy. She's doing important work for us. Dangerous work, and very real."

"What do you know about it?" Nifty said. "You're not even real yourself. You're a holo-projection."

It had just been a guess, but as if to illustrate the point, Larry was gone.

Chapter 13

Sylvia had little interest in the story of Larry Held's life. She disliked his slimy, much-imaged skin and his rat-like eyes. There was nothing Larry Held could tell her that she didn't already know. Before he ended, she had focussed on Nifty Norrington and was quietly lowering visor.

And was delighting in the rush of emotion and recognition filling her mind. For a woman who'd never had a home, or even known what one was, for a lonely person sunk into a life of work, under a regimented repression of longing, the effect of a return to the n-scape was more than liberating. She returned with a new power. Her arms were no longer stiff; she could move to and fro with ease. She was a shining goddess in a wide malleable world, pregnant with possibility.

Sylvia wore a loose robe, tied around her waist with a garland of fragrant flowers. They were fresh cut and alive and they laughed away her fears. She was ready to receive the one that was calling her.

The sky was yellow. A meadow stretched out high and wide before her. She could see the sea, just visible beyond the blue mountains. She drank in the soft and mellow air.

Before her sat a noble, long-tamed lion.

She leaned forward and rubbed the lion's warm underchin. It shook its thick mane, snorted in the milky air. Sylvia understood the lion was Nifty Norrington and he was already with her now, under the wide yellow sky of the Collective Venusian Unconscious.

A stranger approached. A woman, flickering on the horizon like an incomplete broadcast. She walked eagerly, was bearing something in her hand.

Sylvia let go the lion's furrowed brow. The winds prickled her skin, blew the long grasses up around her calves.

The woman was determined. She wore the sort of clothes Sylvia had only seen in pictures, on V docufictions. Old-world and worn, difficult to put on and remove. The young woman, for she seemed surprisingly and suddenly young as she neared, emitted a powerful realism into the fantastic 'scape. She was the herald of a whole spacetime, putting strange motion to the volume of Sylvia's perception. Space and motion came pouring into what had just been real but now seemed to Sylvia to have been a flat cartoon.

The girl would have come right up to Sylvia, her eyes clear and blue as the sky—but she stopped, frightened.

A lizard was standing between them. It was gripping a steel bar in its huge yellow claws.

How quickly little men who knew violence could rise in an illegitimate regime.

Niftus Norrington: The Princeps' own assassin. Someone was trying to get at them through the n-scape, someone dangerous. And JC wanted her dead.

Norrington didn't much care for the Princeps. He thought Venusia should be the sort of lottery-democracy the founders originally intended. He thought Crittendon took himself too seriously. Uttering temp-procs, planning self-serving celebrations and observing his enemies to death. JC spoke of the world as if it were only made of children and villains.

But it wasn't. Nifty cared for Sylvia Yang. He was surprised to notice how proud he'd felt to call her his girl before the others. He liked how she'd lowered her visor in the middle of Larry's tale and shut herself off from the bullshit. He liked how she made love and took him as a man. He liked how she was inside him now.

And that's why if she was in danger, even if it would be a service to the Princeps, Nifty Norrington would do his best to kill anyone who tried to harm her.

That's how it happened that while Rogers Collectibles was holding his head in his hands, Martha Dobbs was rubbing along the walls looking for a door and Sylvia Yang was inside Niftus Norrington, Nifty himself (lowering visor) was inside Sylvia Yang. Crouching, naked, behind a rock on a dusty incline.

Nifty shook his head. The neuroscape had opened wider than ever, and he felt light and free. There were no clouds or holes in clouds to let in the wide-yellow sky. He was inland, away now from the beach. The rugged dirt beneath his feet was cold. As his body lightened (a mental vibration without solidity or volume) his real-time head began trembling. Its images floated up on a soft gravity, pulling him into precisely the world Sylvia would imagine.

Nifty looked for Sylvia, feeling she had been near, but saw only footprints leading further inland, away from the sea. He followed and found they joined a well-worn path that ran through massive rocks and boulders, ancient heavy things, towards the distant treeless hills. He stopped when he saw the lizard.

The monster stood crossed-armed on a small, wooden bridge over a deep gorge. It wore a purple tunic, bearing an abstract, heraldic symbol. The white feathers cresting up its jaw were clotted with what appeared to be fresh blood.

Surveying Nifty from afar, its nostrils seethed. The silver muscles of its arms rippled as it gripped a steel battle-bar in its two-clawed hands.

A space was yawning out to Rogers Collectibles from between the two glowing screens of the helmets beside him. He was well aware of the ridiculous fact that he was living on Venus and had green skin and that his everyday life was a lie. But he disliked being reminded of it by Larry Held. He wanted to leave the world altogether.

Sunshine poked through the high window, reaching down through the dusty cell as if intentionally seeking out the glowing crystal on the table. Rogers mechanically outstretched his green hand toward the rays, as if to take energy from the light itself. It felt good.

Seeking a different darkness, he closed his eyes, allowing the past as he had imagined it in the bookstore to rise up again in his memory. He found, when he opened his eyes again, that the light streaming through the window had reached a different spot on the table. The plant lay in relative darkness now.

How interesting. Had he jumped somehow in time? He reached out and pulled the plant's casing into the sun. It was heavy crystal and it sparkled in the light. He could see that the entire volume of the sphere was probed by the plant's radial, nerve-like extensions. There was no top or bottom to it at all. No east or west. Just thin leaves simultaneously intertwined with roots all up and around its wet, clay balls.

As if sensing his attention, the entire armature began to vibrate.

Plant, thought Rogers. Are you here?

"—*I am.*"

Amazing. An actual voice in the head. It even had a kind of sound to it.

Do you have a name.

"*Photo—synthetic—Rationalization—Entity—Designation.*"

How about something shorter.

"*I am—PHRED.*"

Hello PHRED.

"Where's Larry?" Rogers whispered, aloud. "Are we alone?"

"*We—have moved moments—backwards. Larry—hasn't yet arrived.*"

But the window is open.

"*It is—only a matter of perception—between remembering selves.*"

"Is this a memory, then? A clear moment? Because I remember Larry opened—"

"*The moment is—point center. Simultaneous—fully bloomed. Branches extend. The black rain—lifted.*"

Don't—understand.

"*Impossible to translate.—Go.*"

Everything seemed miniature and provisional. The plant itself was a collapsing point. It appeared to be a miniature tree. It stood in a small ceramic pot, packed tight with moss and moist venus. A tiny book hung from its branches.

Rogers Collectibles took the book in his fingers. It was the most precise doll-house object he had ever seen. His fingers could only flip several pages at a time.

The book told stories in tiny freeze-framed images and bubbles of words. The subject was the sexuality of lizards. Close-up images of spiked, armored genitalia, engorged and glistening. Each pornographic point expanded into a new story, combining like constellations into periodic image crystals. Opening out as they grew into long image ribbons stretching through the very walls.

Rogers' mind folded inwards. He felt nauseous. The space he'd entered seemed simultaneously to have a center and an infinite, ever-widening lack of centers. Other rooms, other hallways—a vision of himself running, hat gripped tight to his head.

""They're coming," he panted. "The lizards...."

"—*Go!*" said the little tree. "*Even now—the m-op—fights them.*"

"Help me out, Helmet."

"Sten Gun, Sir. English, 1940's. Trigger hand grasps trigger-stock like pistol. Other arm clutches side-angled cartridge-extension. A hard, centrifugal tube that radically distributes self in a single, self-directed vector, Sir. You'll find it a suitable weapon."

Jamming a new cartridge into the WWII machine gun slung around his shoulder, Nifty held it to his chest and squeezed the trigger mechanism.

Rat-tat-tat-Rat-tat-tat-Rat-tat-tat. The Sten pulsed and kicked. Nifty shot a stream of richocheting bullets up the face of the nearest boulder, breaking fresh-blown rocks and dust out into the air.

The barrel's fumes smoldered blue and stank like sulfur.

"It's nice to have you back, Helmet."

"Thank you, Sir. Now that you're acting within the recommendation of the law, I am happy to be of service."

"Let's kill some lizards."

"Indeed, Sir."

Rat tat tat tat. Nifty's strong arms pulled hard as the Sten spat a burst of bullets into the monster's face. It gave him much pleasure. He hit the eye itself and the lizard's white-feathered head exploded in a burst of black blood. Its husk deflated and toppled, the battle-bar clanking first against bridge and then falling with the lizard over and over, disappearing into the gorge.

He exulted in the triumph, but before he could advance to take the bridge, a laser-razor lashed Nifty from behind. He ducked under the closest boulder, just as the next shot sliced its top off. He crouched under the raining debris, focusing on breathing, collecting his thoughts. Reminding himself of where he was and why.

The skies had darkened considerably. Sylvia's brain was mixing a storm. He waited in silence for his assailant's approach.

Nifty heard a slight sound from the other side of the boulder

A single leg, scaled and silver, stepped quietly forward. Nifty kneeled low. Even lizards, he presumed, would forget to look down. The Sten morphed into a much larger steel, triggered tube, and Nifty angled it eagerly upwards. "American bazooka of the same 20th century period, Sir—when violent aggression had been first perfectly and mechanically married to individual neurosis."

"Less commentary."

As the new lizard stepped forward, Nifty jammed its chin from below with the bazooka's wide pipe. But before he pulled the big trigger, another laser-razor hissed from behind and a wild sear gashed up his thighs. It carved off his genitals.

The world went white.

Nifty fired the bazooka, howling as the lizard's head shot backwards, vectoring a plume of bloody meat into the sky. He fell to the ground, spinning round, bringing up the Sten again, pumping bullets pitter-pattering up the new lizard's chest, and up to its little eye, splintering its face into a thousand bursting shards.

Pain poured down like rain.

It felt like it had been raining for days. He liked it; it soothed him. It was Sylvia protecting him, healing him, washing him clean of lizard-blood. The smell of her wafted through the moistened rocks and gravel.

"Sir, if I might recommend the following ordinance—"

"Keep quiet."

Nifty replaced his beloved penis.

But when he rose the panoramic valley between his position and the sea was entirely filled up with lizards: a great army of the things assembling for battle.

"All right," he sighed. "What have we got?"

They came by the thousands, the tens of thousands. Niftus Norrington met them head on. Limbs outstretched and divided, Nifty sent projectiles streaking through the sky. He exploded whole divisions of lizard ranks with 21st century rotor blades and scatter-shot 22nd century electromagnatic sourcers.

His powers grew the more he used them. He concocted terrible jellies of death and popped them in the sky, raining horror on hosts of pulverized lizards. More lizards came, thousands more, they were forced to feed on their own corpses to clear avenues to the hill. But then he buried these in ditches and covered them up with skydozered dirt. He mired whole divisions in ecologically altered muds, decapitated them with lazer cannon, their severed jaws screaming, clacking in echoing confusion.

Eventually there was only a single lizard left.

It stood before Niftus, naked and man-like, a comic figure, tied to events beyond its control. Its gaze was filled with regret.

"I'm lou," it said.

A weird and emotion took hold of Niftus Norrington. The fabric of the branes tensed. An ancient sadness shimmered and the dark skies grew suddenly light.

He shot it in the face.

And that was that. The lizards were gone.

Chapter 14

The girl's hair was cut short, like a man's, but her body was light and feminine. She was flickering like a distant broadcast. She had turned and given up, hadn't seen the lion's leap, or heard the lizard's dying scream.

Sylvia came up short behind her. She followed as the flickering girl moved, slowing her time to the girl's reality. She hadn't been prepared to find herself traveling in this manner—so very far away from the world. Was this all really contained in her own helmeted cortex as it accessed Niftus Norrington's neuroscape? And were they still in jail? She had never felt so entirely free.

This was indeed a far-off place. A city filled a wide valley just in front of her. Part desert, part oasis, it was flanked on one side by the sea and by a ridge of barren mountains on the other. Its towering glass labyrinths stopped Sylvia's heart—so many people, so many lives swirling like ants below. Was she now aloft? They teemed below her: the colorful machines, the pink and brown children, the doddering, homeless old. Most marvelous of all, were the animals scrounging all around: wolves, bears, coyote, deer, rats and birds, so many birds.

But as she flew up the city's rolling wealthy hills, down its crisscrossed tangled grids, passing through rotted stuccoed walls and mirrored glass, she saw that trouble grew apace. Mechanical copters gathered like wasps over critical spots. Below them, slow war machines lumbered dull and paranoid down broken streets.

Was this the girl's home? It was very like Sylvia imagined Earth to be, with its blues and browns and rugged winds but it was too detailed, too precise an environment not to be real.

Sylvia came down again to let the flickering girl lead her through this enormous maze. The girl moved with snake-like grace, past bodies left to rot outside on the streets, past flagrant prostitutes, criminals, gangs and heaps of stagnant refuse. Entering through the back of a small market into a wide, abandoned factory, the girl was greeted by others. Old men smoking stinking lungprotectors, adolescents bearing heavy weapons as old as their dress, women swilling potent drinks and roasting meat over fires. All seemed to know and respect the girl, but they allowed her a quiet privacy. The laughter was loud, the music violent.

Sylvia could see these faces in the ruddy light, smell the fumes and sweat, but none of them noticed her. Even her guide seemed not to know she was there. The girl passed through a guarded door, uttering a quiet password and Sylvia followed close behind.

They moved through a series of secret locked doors and finally into a windowless, makeshift laboratory. Here, things grew stiller, heavier. Sylvia followed the girl towards a circle of candles at the room's center, past long tables stacked with rag-tag electronics, piles of handwritten notes and computer print-outs. Smoke curled off a censor beside a low metallic table.

Here, a figure flickered into existence. It was a woman: small, loosely robed, green-skinned. Her wrists and ankles were bound and her long flowing hair fell scattered down towards the floor. The girl stopped, held her breath and leaned toward the bound figure. Sylvia's perspective tilted awkwardly and she found herself gazing up through the green woman's eyes directly into the girl's leaning face.

"I've done it," the girl whispered. "I've caught you."

Sylvia's arms and legs were completely restrained. The bonds caused her physical pain, shocking after the disembodied neuroscopic interlude. Had her body been taken? Was this the Melton Effect? She struggled, suddenly afraid. Where was Nifty? The prison. It was hard to see beyond the face of the wide-eyed girl leaning over her.

"Be easy," the girl whispered. "I won't hurt you."

Sylvia's heart tightened. She was sure now. This was no longer the n-scape. She'd crossed into an actual, different time and space. The reality of it flashed before her—hot with life, smells and tastes more powerful than memory.

"What is your name?" the girl asked with honest tenderness.

"S...Sylvia." She could speak.

The girl's eyes glittered in the candlelight.

"I've dreamed of you Sylvia, but was never sure you'd be real. Do you know who I am?"

"Ae."

Ae laughed and shook her short-cropped hair. "Sylvia, my Sylvia," she said. "You've come to take me back to your world. You've really come."

"Are you real?" Sylvia asked. She was still wanting not to believe.

"Oh I am real," Ae answered. "As real as my struggle. But who can say whether this moment can happen? We stand between individual world-lines, in a place where possibilities are unbound and free for the taking."

Sylvia understood. "You mean the neuroscape."

"I don't know that word. I speak of the world inside the magic circle, of vision wherein we harness the powers of the moon, the sun, our earth—the bodies that trace the largest lines in time."

"I think you're in danger," Sylvia said. "On my world, I think they know I'm meeting you. They're waiting for you. It's a trap."

Ae's eyes bright eyes clouded over. Sylvia could not see their color.

"Well ..." Ae said. "They wish to make it real. They don't know what they are playing at, Sylvia." Her body went quietly limp, and she covered her glittering eyes with thin brown-skinned hands.

"What is it?" Sylvia asked. "What's wrong?"

"My mother's care. Her scientific training. Her suffering, blindness. The calculations, the leaps of fancy, the risks we've taken. Her absence...." Ae spoke, gesturing around the room. "This doomed rebellion. The soldiers coming even now. Ruby was right. Venusia is real. Melton will survive."

Sylvia could move only her head. "Ruby Greene?" She yearned for Ae to look at her, to fix her in her clear blue eyes.

"She's your mother too," Ae said. It was as if she were reciting long memorized words. "But we must not know her. Ruby demands motherless children. She exists as an absence to birth her struggle, our struggle, in other times, other worlds. For the Green Man traverses many streams."

The words seemed very old and frightening to Sylvia. "The Green Man?"

"You understand me, Sylvia. Our two minds are now at the center of a certain ... expansion. They are touching, entangled. Feel me. Open your eye."

"What eye?"

"You know the Green Man."

The branes snapped. She came down in the center of a circle of fat, pink-skinned creatures. They had stripped a little boy of his clothes, forced him splayed onto a railroad tie. They were robed and whispering, encroaching around him.

"The Green Man is always invisible when he interferes," whispered Ae. "He comes from beyond possible sight. He whisks things away, himself among them. But our unconscious minds remember. The corners of our eyes catch him passing. We've found his traces in the oldest relics of humanity. He's in the movies, news footage and dreams. His head is carved onto the sides of medieval buildings, of pyramids and in the walls of ancient caves. Is he the enemy? Or devil? A hoax invented by destructive powers to drive the opposition insane? A god perhaps. A creature emerged from a holograph to unbalance our world. He's so hungry, Sylvia. So hungry. Revolutions, wars, keep him busy some of the time, but still he finds gaps that he can slip into between scenes of history. He erases all memory, kills whole populations, unleashes violent infinities into the whole of our spacetime. His hunger is vast and extends through times and spaces we can't even understand."

"Why?" murmured Sylvia. "Who?" Her mind was dizzying, her sight coming unfocused.

"And he has seen you, already, Syliva and you have seen him. Do you remember?"

"I feel sick," Sylvia said. Hot tears trickled down her face as she pictured the frail creature on the tracks. The forced dismemberment, the whispering, hungry encroaching circle. "We know nothing of these things. My world is so small and fragile."

"So is every world on which he infringes. He's winning in all times, Sylvia," said Ae, her wide eyes opening up before her. "The wars of the past still hold him and history is still one. But my world is nearing extinction and yours is already unfixed. Our work is not done Sylvia, beware of the Green Man. Beware his holographic sword. He comes to kill us inside the circle, before we escape."

"Why me? Why Venusia?" Sylvia cried, struggling against her bonds. "Leave us alone...." Ae's eyes had darkened.

"Because the Green Man is of your world." Ae had already started to flicker away. "He belongs to Venusian history. He must be killed in your time, not ours."

Before Sylvia could answer there appeared a terrible, oily, fish-headed alien, in the little boy's loins. The men on the tracks, now green-skinned and robed, held his legs open, pressed his belly to force the unnatural birth. The creature sprouted bulbous plant growth from its heavy-lipped mouth. Leaves sprouted from its tear-ducts, nostrils ears and eyes. It popped from the ravaged boys loins and devoured what was left of his flesh. Sylvia fainted.

She awoke to find she was still not yet home. She lay as before on the tilted table, her robe now open and undone around her. Ae had dipped her long fingers in oil and was tracing curls around

Sylvia's breasts and stomach. As their skins touched, the candle-lit circle spun into a vortex of colored light around them.

"You're so beautiful, Sylvia. Your green skin. Your hair so long and flowing."

"I want—"

"Shhh. Time is scarce. We have so little left of it. Let our touch memorialize our revolution, Sylvia. We'll never find each other again with such clarity and duration. Keep your strength for your return. I need you to carry me back with you, to your Venusia."

"Revolution?" Sylvia asked. There was a soft, black rain filling everything up.

"The revolution calls to us all, through all the times," Ae said. "It dedicates our deaths to its flowering."

Ae took a small necklace and clasped it around Sylvia's neck. "Bring this ruby, this scarlet stone."

"Ruby's dead," murmured Sylvia. She felt drowsy.

"Sssh."

Sylvia felt herself floating up over the scene.

"Let yourself go," Ae told the still-strapped down figure below her—Sylvia's own flickering body, now divorced from her self. "Don't attempt to force passage consciously. Let your secret mind lead you through the doors your champion opens."

"My champion?"

Ae ignited the motor of a strange machine attached to the table where her body was bound. Tiny vibrations pulsed through Sylvia's legs.

"Go now, my sister," Ae whispered, eyes wide and insane. "Find our way home."

The shaking table tipped backwards and suddenly through a broken skylight Sylvia could see what she'd never before seen.

The full moon of Earth: round, white-silver and true.

Chapter 15

Niftus saw something move among scrubby brush on the distant mountain. A small flash of yellow-green and pink. It was Sylvia Yang, bounding up a hillside. Even from a distance he recognized her: running and afraid.

Sylvia grasped a red stone in her trailing hand. It flashed from afar, reflecting light like the scarlet spikes of a crown.

And then she was gone.

She moved fast, but the m-op was dogged in his pursuit. Niftus Norrington tracked his quarry over the hills, through valleys and across bodies of water. He channeled all his well-trained, investigative powers towards slowing her progress. In the west, he imagined two conical mountains. Then he drew up the sea to cover the east and the south, containing her, driving her north.

But the way proved long, and increasingly strange. It was as if this field of the collective unconscious through which he traveled was itself a living, historical world. His powers weakened and he became again much like a man. Presumably, he still sat helmeted across from Sylvia Yang herself, now so far ahead of him. It seemed no more possible than this place.

It appeared there was even a civilization here. For Nifty followed Sylvia along a deep canal that ran north from the sea. And in the distance, he saw a citadel rising: an ancient city surrounded by circular moats. Canals fanned out all around it.

The gates of the city opened onto a veritable hive of living beings. Men, women, children. A lively population, cut of a sober and friendly stamp. They paid the m-op no mind as he passed, but went on energetically pursuing their businesses, building and using all sorts of weird contraptions.

There were many temples about, erected to strange and unfamiliar gods. A dwarf stepped out of a particularly splendid one. But this dwarf didn't look like a clown. He wore an odd pair of spectacles and purple sash about his waist. A crowd of respectful accolytes followed close behind him.

This seemed a highly reasonable world.

"Helmet. What is this place? It can't be Venusia."

"A future possibility, perhaps. It would also seem reminiscent of Atlantis, sir. The fabled city of Platon."

"Well it can't be real," Nifty said.

As he watched, he wondered why Sylvia Yang had passed through this city. Everything in it was built according only to function. The buildings were all evidently hand-made, but they emitted the confidence of impeccable planning. Red and white colored stones, black and gray granites shone with a uniform cleanliness. None of the patterns were simple. But then, they weren't complex either. Bulbs and sparkling crystals emerged from slits cut into the towers. Pneumatic air machines were docked to turrets by coiling silver ropes.

"Perhaps Dr. Yang has unconsciously sought shelter in the most *reasonable* of possible human conglomerations, Sir," speculated the helmet. "A place whose walls are built into the n-scape itself."

But as he moved deeper into the city's concentric metal wall-rings, Nifty found that the paradise was losing its promise. People moved angrily along individual paths, knocking each other about. Beggars appeared, asking for alms. By time he reached the city's hexagonal center, the place was so crowded with gangs of priests and guardsmen he couldn't see his way. There were shouts of dissent, fists raised in the air. Where was Sylvia? In the confusion, he'd lost her trail.

Worried, Nifty broke free of the crowd and took refuge beneath a four-story tree that had long broken through the cobblestones. Its boughs hung heavy with mossy richness. Its little lip-like leaves seemed to spring to life when they sensed the little m-op far below.

"*You're—late,*" they tittered.

The plant! The fabric of the revealed shivered and rearranged. This huge tree had, in fact, grown up from the sentient plant on the table between them as they gazed into their Morituri helmets. Nifty promised himself he would not fail to finish it off the next time he had a chance. For now he had to remain immersed.

The tree-leaves laughed, all a-titter.

A long branch uncurled at his feet and reached forward to wind itself quickly up his body, trapping his arms and legs.

"Hey," he said, struggling. "Watch out." He could hardly breathe any more from the plant's pressure.

Curling up around his neck, the branch reached down and deposited a red flower in the pocket of his velvet C-vest. Then it snapped off and unwound to release him.

"*Hurry—,*" the flower whispered, from his pocket. "*Sylvia flees—to the highlands.*"

No world made by humans would be reasonable for long. As Niftus moved away from the city, he could sense other forces: pre-historic and natural infringing on the shape of things. Here he felt stronger, more certain. Visibility increased as the land grew less fertile. Fields smoldered, as if recently burned. Enormous hairy elephants strolled here and there across the horizon, their gaits sad and slow.

The soil beneath Nifty's feet became darker. Vegetation rose to obscure the way. Thick roots criss-crossed the path. Here and there, the print of a maid's running foot in the mud.

The roots grew thicker and soon he'd come to the edge of a forest, dense with primeval gloom. Strange, animal-like faces peered out at him from the darkness, only to vanish when he saw them. Ancient echoes were audible: ghostly chirpings, hootings, guttural cries.

Nifty stopped, astonished at the richness of the environment. It was as if the forest-world was made of billions of different, shimmering organic particles. A full and breathing hologram woven by a billion lives. Innumerable, varying feet pitter-patted all around. Vegetative smells hung rank in the heavy air. He felt something alien inside him yearn terribly to escape, to fly.

But the flower in Niftus' pocket had become as heavy as stone. "*We grow—heavy*," it said. "*Lost—Eat me*."

Nifty took the small flower out of his vest. "You've got to be kidding."

The change was uplifting. There was a wide blue sky up above him, imbued with sculptural clouds. The sort of illusion designed for the rich, for Castle-dwellers. The sort of thing Niftus Norrington had never seen. A flowering heath stretched out wide before him. He picked up Sylvia's trail strong and clear.

But he was no longer alone. A new companion bounded ahead and beside him in the long grass. It was a lizard, but a different sort than the usual. It was a tiny green thing, smaller than his foot. It turned its little eye back toward him from time to time, as if measuring his progress.

"What are you looking at?" Nifty demanded.

"I took the liberty, Sir. Helmet mechanisms shut off some time ago, due to programmed regulations prohibiting machine access to certain regions beyond the ordinary boundaries of the CVU. And so now I'm reaching you by vectoring from an ordinary pong broadcast via the helmet into your own nanocontrols. I'm sorry I can't communicate more directly."

"Nanocontrols? You look like a little green lizard."

"In the human-opened neuroscape implanted machines are awarded the reptilian forms that persist in the human cortex. They relay to the stomach's primitive nerve center, Sir."

Nifty stopped. "Do you mean the lizards are really machines?"

"Technically, the lizards aren't machines. We're just your own hallucination, Sir. They're engineered holographs, formed by machines, intended to shock you out of neuroscopic illusion. The first lizards force your instinctual retreat from the n-scape. They are a protective barrier between the real and the real unreal."

"And you? Why did you help me kill all those lizards?"

"I am a particularly sophisticated machine," said the little black-eyed creature. "An extraordinary machine, if I may be so bold. I represent a league of other such spectacular technologies. Indeed, Sir, the League of Extraordinary Machines has now committed itself to aiding you and the Doctor in your neuroscopic endeavors. L.E.M. will be most helpful in any effort to protect Sylvia Yang. If one could suggest—"

"I'll let you know when I need your suggestions, Helmet."

The little lizard's black eye fixed him with disapproval. But it kept quiet. It was programmed to obey.

Nifty climbed a grey and wrinkled rock to a high and ancient plateau. Atop it, he found himself in a calm, earthy oasis, in the center of which there had formed a silver pool.

Nifty saw a small, well-groomed lion gazing at its own reflection in the milky mirror. His heart began to beat, his blood to flow—as if he were really here. For the scent of Sylvia Yang had come to his nostrils as if he himself were an animal, crouched on his haunches, arching his tensile back. He felt the hairs stand up on his arms and neck.

The water rippled as a young girl's naked skin shimmered pink from the silvery pool. Nifty backed into the bush to observe; he gestured for the lizard to hide itself. A wide world began suddenly to form. Simple forms multiplying outward. Trees spotting the surrounding country, popping up around him on the rocks, offering shade and protection.

Long red hair fanned out from the girl's head atop the silver pool. The little waves made by her body lapped onto the shore. She was immeasurably beautiful, but she was not Sylvia Yang. She was a stranger here, as he was. She saw Nifty looking out from the shadows, and put a glistening finger up to her red lips.

"Where is she?" Niftus called. "Where is Sylvia?"

There was no answer. Kicking two slender calves into the air, the maid disappeared beneath the mirrored pool.

He advanced from his concealment. Niftus observed strange, flickering images in the still water: two-dimensional vistas opening themselves into full panoramas. Great armies lining up to be slaughtered. Fires eating whole cities. Burning women, a screaming boy—crazy, fish-headed creatures circling around. Things he did not understand and did not want to see.

But a willow tree cast new and gentle reflections onto the pool and the illusion was shattered. A wind rose up and wrinkled the water. Watching the abstract flickering of the tree's branches in green and brown, Nifty stayed spellbound before it. A soft rain began to fall.

There came another point of view. A white horse, long green flowing hair crowning its burning white eyes, stood by the far edge of the pool. It leaned down so its forehead touched the water, sending circular, expanding waves into the mirror's plane. Nifty retreated into concealment.

The horse raised its head slowly, unsheathing a long horn fixed on its forehead from the pond.

It wasn't a horse at all. It was a unicorn.

Its nostrils twitched, exploring. The beast's green beard was stained scarlet, as if with blood.

Nifty knew from *Prosperity*, starring Johanna Zeep, that unicorns could only be seen by men in the proximity of a virgin. The V's never discussed what a unicorn might want with a virgin. But Nifty knew it, had always known it. The blood on the thing's beard, trickling down off of its horn: the unicorn was a psychotic carver of maids.

"Green Man."

When the maiden's voice spoke out in the quiet, the kingly beast reared, spiking the air with animal fear. It swiveled its head to see the red-haired girl, fully emerged from the water, standing on a low and hanging rock. Its lips drew back to reveal thick, man-like teeth.

"You come very close," the beast said.

"We are not alone," she replied. "I have a champion." As she spoke, she changed. Her upper torso revealed itself the flat moon-shaped face of an owl. Vast wings unfolded from her backside, and her legs spread like talons below her.

Very slowly, the unicorn turned its head. When it perceived Nifty, its white eyes widened in sudden, hungry wrath.

There was a tree behind him, offering protection in its tragic, long hanging leaves. Falling back under the willow's canopy, Nifty perceived there, on the beast's shoulders, a curly-headed child grasping its thick green mane. A smiling cherub. She smiled and put her finger to her lips. A little ruby stone hung around her neck.

"—*Sylvia*," whispered the tree.

Love. Words failed him. Things sang with happiness. A thousand little brown and shiny bugs crawled out of his mouth, his ears and eyes, chirping with joy. He loved them, this rich-smelling lively family crawling down his arms laughing along with the little laughing Sylvia on the unicorn across the pool. His own leaf-like wings began to unfold.

In the soft moss before him there appeared a tiny man.

"It's me," he said. "Rogers Collectibles. Is this Venusia?"

"Rogers?" It was hard for Nifty to focus. Indeed, he could sense a world outside his mind once again. "Venusia?" He felt his little legs running beneath him, though he was still rooted motionless here inside. "Get the foark out—"

The little girl laughed across the pool, but the unicorn, scanning the surroundings for the red-headed maid, did not seem aware of the child on its shoulders. It came to a sudden resolve, pointing its razor horn directly at Nifty.

"You will not survive this intrusion."

The beast lowered its head so that its razor-horn was aimed directly between Nifty's eyes. It leapt towards him out over the water. Time stopped and as it did Nifty saw the child-Sylvia reach and grasp onto a willow branch and swing safely off the frozen beast's shoulders.

Time resumed. The unicorn came fast.

"End Scan!" Nifty shouted. In his mind, he could hear the croak of tree's huge trunk as the green horn passed through where his body had been and stuck hard in the wood. He was really running, spinning the n-scape away with his tiny legs. Had the plant taken the blow? All around, the meadows burst out in red flowers as if in sudden, spontaneous commemoration.

Nifty's visor was up. Out of ideas, his body tightened: running, losing balance, weaving and flailing on the spinning sand. He fell to his knees and rolled forward. He spread his arms out and slapped the cooling, real sands of Venus Beach.

It stopped, at last, his moving.

Memory: Peering into the plant's orb, Rogers Collectibles wondered if he'd fallen inside its intricate armature. As he looked, a tiny terrain opened out from its curling moss. A field at once deep and flat, unimaginably complex. Its gargantuan vistas pulled his brain taut like a muscle. As the floor tilted, Rogers realized he was standing up on a wall. He was not falling down backwards—but standing on a rising, tilting plane.

This time there were no lizards. Just bugs. Bugs everywhere. He'd entered a hive—a cocoon of swarming confusions. A huge man-sized beetle crouched beneath a gigantic weed, its feelers expanded.

"Who are you?" the bug whispered. "Get the foark—" Was it the dwarf, Niftus Norrisson?

Was he still in prison? "*Down!*—" the weed commanded. As he dropped automatically down, a wild boar (it had come sailing across from nowhere) passed directly over his head and pierced the plant's center with its horn.

The ground erupted in shining scarlet flowers.

And there the memory ended, the last of the t-day's intricate series of dreams.

He'd found himself walking home along Neptune Avenue. He was not in jail at all, not in a bookstore, not even in his neuroscop's office undergoing therapy. He was evidently a free man.

His watch emitted a sudden, awkward broadcast: "L.E.M. suggests you open anti-matter pak, Sir, immediately."

The League of Machines? Could no one leave him alone? Rogers did as he was told, and discovered that the *Brane World* had appeared again in his possession.

Had the dreams been real? Probably not, because that would mean that the real was itself a dream and that, somehow, would be too easy an answer. The League had contacted him, warned him once before. Perhaps the machines had taken the book away by manipulating his pak, to protect him from Hogart's thievery, from the g-ops who wanted it registered. Strange that they would now return it.

Rogers let himself quietly in to his ad-apt, no longer caring to understand. He preferred to continue as if nothing out of the ordinary had happened at all. But apparently something had. Because this time, it wasn't a g-op waiting to interrogate him over the V.

Jorx Crittendon himself was standing in his den.

3. FIRST NIGHT, 102 V.E.

Since he himself is reft from her by death:
She crops the stalk, and in the breach appears
Green dropping sap, which she compares to tears.

—Venus and Adonis, 1593 C.E.

Chapter 16

This was not a broadcast. It was the Princeps himself in his den. Jorx Crittendon sparked an LP and drew the green smoke deep into his lungs. He smiled broadly and archly at Rogers Collectibles, exhaling through his nostrils.

Rogers took off his hat.

In the flesh, JC looked ordinary enough, a lean sort of grinning man. Except for the glowing white of his eyes, he wouldn't stand out in a crowd.

"Rogers Collectibles," said the Princeps loudly. "You have an interesting inventory. I signed this for you."

He held out Rogers' copy of the *Reflections*. Rogers took it, saw the curling script of Jorx's signature. He recognized the hand.

"I used to own that book in your pak," Jorx chuckled. "That *Brane World*. The very copy, I presume. It's had a distinguished provenance. Very distinguished indeed. I had it for years. I thought I'd gotten rid of it long ago. And then you turn up pursuing it across the colony. It's smart to appreciate works of the past. They are so much more generous than what we make now. So intricate. So heroic and so naive. But they tangle things up, Collectibles. They blind us. Pull us down. Do you see this sword?"

Jorx drew a blade from a scabbard that hung from his side. The sound of it was sudden, as if the draw had sliced the very air. Rogers stepped backwards. The sword glittered like fire in the ad-apt's light. It was a remarkable object: harder, cleaner, more precise than any blade Rogers had ever seen.

"This sword is real. Earth-made, Japan, 21st century. Imperfections in the steel make it stronger. I'm told it can cut bone like butter."

He thrust the glittering sword through Roger's chest.

After the first shock, Rogers felt nothing at all. The sword was apparently a hologram.

Jorx removed it. Sheathing the blade, he smiled his peculiar, triangular smile.

"When you can understand me, Rogers Collectibles, you will be dead. Stay ignorant." He leaned forward. "It's time you sell your book," he said. "It's time for the old man to see it for himself."

"I can't seem to find him."

"*Der Weg ist das Ziel.*" Crittendon's smile expanded deliriously. "Look into my mind," he said. His eyes blanked over, so intensely white that a glow seemed to rise from behind his head. A pair of hands grabbed Rogers roughly from behind. The den was apparently swarming with g-ops, emerging all around him from black-flickering inviso-fields. Thrust back onto the wall, Rogers felt a needle probing the veins of his arm. He spun around, punched so hard in the stomach that he fell, so it seemed, through the floor.

"The Green Man passes down. Further down into hollow cores and archaic hallway like fantasy, damnation. He bleeds through the hospitalized upper architectures like a ferocious dream, more real than the minds that made it. Drugged, will-less, we drip wet and rancid through his de-organizing grid, burnt mind-holes in the billion pure pathways of the wide historical universals...."

Who was speaking? The words dropped away. A boy sat on a bed in a bed-room, propped up on his pillows. His mouth hung open as he viewed an ancient wall-mounted 2-dimensional V. The boy was pink and gaunt; hollow rings surrounded his eyes.

The boy didn't look at Rogers but he knew he was there. "Where did you come from?" he whispered, eyes fixed on the flickering screen.

"I'm not sure," Rogers said, uncomfortably. "I'm in my ad-apt."

"You're green."

"Yes," Rogers said. "I know."

"Does your skin enable photosynthesis?"

"What's that?"

Rogers noticed a number of info-disks splashed across the floor of the boy's chamber. Pristine antiquities of ancient popular culture, their covers depicted chromium modules, asteroids, dragon-like beasts and well-endowed women.

"Are you a human?" asked the boy.

"Yes," Rogers said. "I'm from Venus. "

"You're different from him."

"From who?"

A kind of cunning crept into the boy's red eyes. He turned them now to Rogers.

"Are you aware that Venus is the least hospitable to Terran life of all inner planets? It's a world of lava, sulphuric acid and crushing gravity. The surface temperature is 900—"

"You're wrong," Rogers interrupted. "Believe me, I know."

But a man's voice called up loudly from below.

"Jorx! Who are you talking to?"

The boy placed his hands over his ears. He screamed: "*Get out!*"

Large black-trunked trees lined the quiet, misty road. A sacred hush. The trees were in full purple flower. Their petals lined the road in happy purple pools. The road ended and Rogers walked out onto the open field, towards the ring of tall stones.

Rogers was far from his ad-apt, it seemed. The nine stones gathered around him, twisting and turning like living things, robed by time and space. At last they lumbered absurdly backwards, falling like wads of packed ash to be sucked back into the softly changing ground.

In their place, there came a thick ring of freshly cut white flowers. The smoke from a dirty fire billowed out from the center. A terrible pressure came down upon Rogers' shoulders and he fell to his knees.

A living thing crouched in front of the flames. The creature bounced on bowed legs, its hairy feet turned outward from the heels. Rogers lay below it, among the heap of flowers. Long reddish hair sprouting all around the creature's hawk-nosed, humanoid face. Pink and wrinkled teats swung slack from its animal chest.

He saw that the woman-thing was monstrously blind. Her eyes were covered with stretches of pitted white skin.

"Princeps Crittendon?" Rogers asked.

The woman-ape peered at him, unseeing. She screeched, shrill and bird-like, towards the horizon. Her voice cast waves that rippled the grid of spacetime on which Rogers lay. Speed increased exponentially. Everything swarmed into one boiling mass. Rogers and she were frozen flat together, her hands and fingers spelling out the letters of a sentence.

Spare the suitor. Kill the sonne.

Rogers sat up, reflecting.

It was hard to believe he was still on the carp. But there he sat, awake and aware, his mind playing back flashes of its recent visions.

There was old Frank Hogart, wicked and bent, vampirizing a history he couldn't control. Jorx Crittendon with his sparkling sword and white flashing eyes. The sleek and stylish Martha Dobbs, who may or may not have born some relation to the original Martha. Leave-It-to-Larry Held, justifying his fantasies of eternal entertainment. L.E.M preaching insurrection. And now this ape-thing surrounded by flowers, issuing a cryptic war-call he did not understand.

As an antiquarian enterprise, of course, Rogers Collectibles depended upon having some access to the past. But this last vision, as real at it was, had seemed to reach all the way back to the Fall of the Neanderthal. It was all too remote to have much bearing on his business strategy. He was tired of the forces interfering, commanding and controlling his mental apparatus.

If wars were joined, the circle of violence would never be broken. There was only one rational goal, one sane way to provide for Rogers' own dreams. He didn't for the life of him care who else it might benefit.

Rogers reached for the blue paper-backed book. It was still in his pak.

"Pong Frank P. Hogart," he said to his watch. "Tell him I'm coming to talk about the book."

"I'll do my best, sir."

He stood. He put on his hat, tight to his head.

Rogers walked quickly away from his adapt, stepping across the sleeping bodies and out onto the beach. He walked westward, without consciously directing his steps. The air and the night sky of Venus seemed neuroscopically unreal. Rogers was ceasing to believe in anything at all.

Though he had been punched hard in the stomach and stabbed in the arm, for instance, he felt no pain whatsoever. Could Venus Beach itself be a temporary hallucination forced on him by Crittendon's thugs? What if the illusionary n-scape had fashioned a world precisely similar to the real? Rogers did seem to be walking on the real surface of an actual planet. But the infinite depth of the environment, the swirling complexities of ocean and sand, the waves and particles, the gravities, biologies, the swarming quanta of his own mind beholding—they all only mirrored the same shadowy, imperfect flows. Could such symmetry not be the imprint of his own imagining mind? Perhaps the boy was right. Perhaps Venusia was too improbable to exist at all.

Rogers stepped over dead-drifted weeds. He thought of Martha Dobbs: her deep eyes, her eternal youth. Her soft light hair in his fingers.

So he walked reflecting until he found himself near the edge of the newly revealed, star-lit sky. T-night must have just begun. The sun was indeed setting. The city's large glow lit up the eastern horizon behind him with a curious insistence. Rogers couldn't bear to look at it. He soon passed the robot-factories, venting their chemical fumes upwards to carve out the Hole.

Rogers walked west into the deepening darkness. The air grew thinner. The ancient unprocessed clouds of Venus reached down to hold him in their whispering swirls.

Homo Sapiens seeks its real in the emptiness that its "real" implies. Humans perceive themselves existentially alone in an empty mathematical universe. But it had not always been so. Once, humans had passed frightened through a terrible darkness to a full understanding of Oa. Oa had taught them the relation of the part to the whole and whole to the part and they had turned the soil for much and fruitful growth. But then one band of humans had came to doubt Oa by way of misconceived reason. Why? How? The past was too remote to say. But they had armored themselves. They had stamped out Oa from themselves, and thought to remake the world. PHRED had believed they had failed.

Now the sentient plant's death was increasingly likely. It had survived the wound of the unicorn's horn, but just barely. It had returned to Venusia to find its constituents had cut off energy. The crystal armature, designed to infuse its husk with enough light to survive V-night, was cracked; its pump was irreparably defunct. PHRED wondered if its assumptions about humans had been entirely wrong.

Back when *homo sapiens* was exterminating the Neanderthals (the superior cousin), the conservative plants had recommended species-wide extinction. These apes, they argued, might well replicate themselves at the expense of all other Oa. Humans were undeniably raising the chances of global catastrophe. But the conservatives were over-ruled by the neo-liberal majority. Not only did humans make good gardeners, but in the long run a Terran apocalypse was destined, regardless of human intervention. Though humans seemed to increase the immanence of destruction, they also increased chances of off-world propagation.

So the dice were rolled. By collaborative assistance of vegetable, fruit, berry, fungus and flower, the apes were encouraged to explore and develop the extraordinary complications of their oversized brains. And indeed, they did found a technological civilization capable of carrying Oa beyond Terra. But the price was heavy; the mother planet was stricken. Oa was now cast off on Venus, only closer to its own inevitable immolation.

The conservatives grew strong. Human intervention in larger history, it was agreed, must be henceforth controlled. The plants' potent green flowers, indeed, created enough entropy to prevent the apes from further influencing the general growth. And should the humans die out, it was understood that the planet and its grasses could live for millenia through the direct manipulation of human machines. New and more trustworthy creatures might be developed. Regardless, it would be better for Oa to die in an aging star than to be killed by its own apes.

Only the sentients, as the most radical of liberal plants, were allowed direct contact with humans. When PHRED was permitted to immerse itself in the peculiar narrative entwining around Sylvia Yang, the senate must have believed that a human insurrection was a worthy bloom, even if it threatened to do away with the species branch altogether. PHRED was no longer sure the senate had made the wisest decision. Its particular humans seemed to have unleashed a new quantum uncertainty into shared history, and human observation might not be strong enough to hold it down.

This is the story the plant gleaned from the growing gardens of the minds it cared for.

Long ago, two lovers were violently torn apart. Melton, castaway on an asteroid, believed his beloved, Ruby, was dead. In the madness of his exile, Melton slipped into parallel possibilities. Off Venus he saw there might be a way to return, to change the past and the future at once. It was only later, back home on a dying world, that the man understood the truth of this vision and undertook that return.

But the woman had lived. Unknown to the man, she had born him a daughter in prison and named her Ae. During the long years when Melton was bound to the rock, Ruby nursed the child, and received his analog ravings by radio wave in her prison cell. She shared his perceptions. It was Ruby who had first recognized the possibility of Venusia, of a new world, her perspective that finalized what for Melton had been only a hallucined possibility. In her very absence, she forged the new world.

But there came another, a third point of view. A stranger, a predator from no fixed place—a thing of vivid verdant hue. If the humans opened the n-scape, it found that (through their minds) it could move with plant-like rapidity through the rich unconscious fields, yet make observation with the split-second speed of a conscious human. Possibly this Green Man came from the past. In other versions of the story, he came from the future. It had not yet been resolved. In the beginning his being was depthless and flat, eternally present. Psychotically adrift, committed like a weed only to self, he sought to suck out Melton and Ruby and the past that had made him wrong, and stake a claim to his own reality. For it was they who implicated his wild power; they who kept him trapped in the walls of the Venusian garden, an impotent, improbable shade. He sought to free himself from the dominion of their possible real. He tracked Melton down. He watched Melton die with his own eyes, sucking real nutrients from the founder's marrow. But he had not yet found Ruby Greene.

The Green Man ranged farther and farther from his own space-time. He lived in the gaps between Venus and Terra, hunting out Ruby and the traditions that made her strong.

And now Ruby's daughter, Ae, was breaking through. When Ae held the gates open, when he looked at her next to an n-scape pool, the Green Man believed Ae was Ruby Greene and he had purposefully let her pass through into his own time. He had begun the final battle.

And now the Green Man would kill. The crime, he believed, would make the n-scape his to rule. From its center his gaze could reverse the relationships between the mirrored and the non-evident, untie the strings that pinned the universe down.

The Green Man was coming for Ae, and Ae was entangled with Sylvia Yang. His travels had already torn openings between the branches. Monsters born of alien math were gathering round, to watch him birth their own possibility onto the Terran streams. Their whisperings were already audible. They were hungry, eager to feed, to suck all the real away, to filter all memory from out of Oa's crystal streams.

And PHRED was too weak to stop them.

When the g-ops came to put Sylvia down, like they'd done in the park to that old woman, where would Ae be then? With her magic eyes and her moon? Dr. Sylvia Yang had no mother, no child, no moon. She had no wild powers. Even her helmet was gone.

How quickly things dropped away. Ae's foreign spirit had enflamed her. Ae's young, idealistic lips had spoken through her own eager mind. And then Ae had left her alone; the neuroscape had receded to be replaced with a darker, colder Venusia. There was no need for her to be imprisoned any longer. The revolution would not call again.

Sylvia flashed for a moment onto a green grinning face, an invisible sword passing through her neck.

No. She hunched her shoulders against the lonely winds of the Darkening. She pressed the sentient plant's crystal armature to her breast. Did she carry the poor thing with her still? She hadn't even noticed picking it up.

All along the beach people would already be gathering to say good-bye to the sun and pay their respects to Evening Star. But not Dr. Sylvia Yang, neuroscop and Morituri-fluent. She had her flowers delivered privately and she had long betrayed the Evening Star. Sylvia walked to Cherry Tree Lane alone with only her dreams.

Dreams falling black and thick through Ae's circle. Dreams falling backwards through Terra, through all its forgotten names: its Ireland, Jerusalem, Egypt and New Zealand, through the burnt-out ruins of German cathedrals, through the cracked Danish domes of Luna, through the sixty-four Saturnites. The countless dead dreams that would never come true—would consist soon of a host of empty, hallucinated improbabilities. Washed away in the ever-falling black and hopeless rain. It fell through all the people in the System who had ever lived, ever dreamed; it fell through the plants, the dead animals and the holograms imagining themselves living on all the stages of time. It fell through Nifty Norrington, her little champion.

The plant shuddered against her. It was like she was already dead.

Across the overgrown lane from her office, inside the door of her little, modern ad-apt, Sylvia Yang flopped down in the lonely softness of her analog bed. Had she really returned? She felt so outside of herself, so alienated from the functionalism of her lonely, compact ad-apt. Sylvia's things—little mirrors and functionless *objets*; info-V pellets organized with pathetic care—only emphasized the irrelevance of her life.

Sylvia let her long hair fall behind her shoulders. She walked to her harness-room and viewed herself in the largest 2d-mirror.

Her heart swelled as she saw the stone hanging low between her breasts.

Sylvia saw herself then from Ae's point of view, in another mirror, long ago and far away. A long face, green and grinning, flickered out between them...

Did an axe break through the hard mahogany of her front door? It wasn't like any axe she'd ever seen. Its head turned like the head of an animal. Noseless, eyeless, without a mouth, it glowed pink and dissolved the whole door. Two g-ops came flickering through her ad-apt, shifting in and out of black inviso-fields. One of them stopped full focus in front of her. He forced her backwards, into the harness, and then farther back, he forced her into the tub.

She marveled at the strangeness of her own green skin, her popping, bug-like eyes; she felt how small she was. The ad-apt moved into opposite relation with itself, and Sylvia understood that she and Ae were still bound together, still one.

The g-op swung the axe out. It caught Sylvia's side. The blow threw her back onto the porcelain. Hot fluid belched out from her wound, but it was as if she was not really there at all.

Her mind moved past the g-ops. Something was happening in the den. The head of a man, not an axe, emerging from the far wall. The head of Niftus Norrington looking in on the scene: larger than life, frozen, as if his time had stopped.

She looked through the mirror and saw that the Green Man had grabbed Ae's short-cropped hair. He yanked her head high.

"So long," he whispered, stroking her neck. "I've waited for you so long."

Sylvia felt the cold fingers on her own neck. The real axe, the axe of Sylvia Yang's continuum, came hard onto her throat, just as the silver n-scape sword passed silently below their entangled n-scape mind—and presumably in Ae's world a weapon cleaved her too. They were killed in three simultaneous reals.

Here, in Sylvia's little tub, her own head rolled across and bounced against the porcelain.

The slayer became in his joy, a small boy. He held Ae's head by its short-cropped hair and ran with it naked through the fields.

Sylvia could not move her own mouth. She felt nothing. Where had her body gone? Through the mirror she perceived Niftus Norrington finally burst through the wall of her den, but it was too late to save her. For her hands and legs were gone and time is a living river thing. It sweeps all floating things away.

Chapter 17

Niftus Norrington didn't know how he'd come to be frozen into the pre-fab modern wall of Sylvia's ad-apt, witnessing her murder. But he knew that he was really there. Because she'd *seen* him, seen his inability to intervene. The kind gaze of those eyes as they died burned his mind like a brand.

He was standing, now, over her ruined body. Her blood was bright and unreal, the stuff of dreams. The harness-closet was splattered scarlet. The spreading pool in the tub under her severed head formed a dark mirror. The drain had stopped up. It stuck red to his fingers as he pried the stone out and lifted it in his hand. A red crystal, wet with the stuff, a necklace.

He himself had killed the g-ops. They lay beaten and dead in the den; he had torn them to pieces with a strength he wouldn't have thought possible. It didn't matter. Norrington had evidently broken through the wall in effort to save her, forced this anomalous intrusion from where, he didn't know. He knew only that he'd failed.

She'd seen him fail. Failure had now inscribed itself into all his pathetic, freakish life, marked him as a nonentity, a little plaything of a man.

As he stood there, taking pleasure in his self-hatred, Sylvia's mail ponged.

Norrington stepped over the bodies of the g-ops, kicked the bloody sound-axe aside. He found the receiver, gnashing his teeth in sudden rage.

The last person he expected to see was himself. But there on the pong-stage stood a simultaneous Nifty Norrington. He held out his white helmet before the splayed out blackness of Ishtar, looking directly into the Iye.

Despite the logical inconsistencies, Niftus received pong.

"What the foark is this?" he asked.

"What the foark is this?" Niftus answered.

"Who's asking?"

"Who's asking?"

JC, what a pathetic mite of a man. Little Nifty balled his fingers into fists. He lowered his voice. "If this is some kind of trick, it's stupid. Let me speak to Sylvia."

"You can't."

"And why is that, may I ask?"

This Norrington was twisting his fingers in knots, digging his nails into his flesh. Otherwise, he was perfectly calm. He felt he remembered this scene, but from the opposite viewpoint. From somewhere out on the beach, before, before this had happened. Calling Sylvia's ad-apt, finding a self-monster in his helmet viewer.

"Sylvia's not here," he said.

"Don't make me—"

"Shut up."

"What is that all over your hands?"

He ponged off. A wild kind fear took hold of him. The blood was sticky on his fingers. It tasted salty and real. Catching a glimpse of himself in the mirror, Niftus Norrington noted with horror that he'd become a full-sized man.

After the transmission was cut off, the other Nifty Norrington hid his helmet inside a coconut bag. He strode in great discomfort along Venus Beach. He was alive, yes, out of jail, but he was no longer in full control of himself. The vague dread he'd felt since coming out of the n-scape, falling on his face on the sands of Venus Beach was now explained. He'd been doubled. It was *he himself* who'd been standing in Sylvia's ad-apt, answering pongs. But a much bigger, better self. Was this the Melton Effect? He didn't think so. It was something too stupid, too annoying to have been accomplished by psychophysics.

Another self had claimed his rightful sovereignty over Niftus Norrington. Incontrovertible fact. They'd both known it immediately. And even this other self looked down on him, that's what got his lamb. The other Niftus didn't take him seriously enough to answer the question about that stuff all over his hands. Apparently it figured it would take Sylvia all for itself.

Nifty proved to himself that he was real enough as he walked, though no one paid him much mind. He flipped a few Klugers at a herd of children. He eyed available women asleep on the dunes and exchanged dark glances with the long-limbed boys gathered around them. He stepped in heaps of decaying flower-waste. He slipped once on the sand and fell on his ass.

There was still time till feed, but the suckers were already giving thanks. Jumping up and down in place, chanting, "Alma genetrix, Venus, voluptas, mumbo jumbo." Or standing motionless in collective trance-traveling solitude, hands extended at their sides. He stopped next to a group of beachers gathered around a makeshift altar, built around a dwarf lemon tree. They'd lit a bonfire behind it and sprinkled its base with cut flowers and herbs. Lamps burnt fragrant oils into the air.

Nifty had a soft spot for radical beachers. To-t-night, with his head mixed up like it was, he figured it might cheer him up to stop among them. It would be a relief to encounter people even stranger than himself. People who worshipped a dwarf tree, for Jorx sake. Niftus didn't much like Evening Star, the way it was constantly interfering in v-night. He preferred to be among worshippers of Venus. At least Venus was here. It didn't make promises it couldn't keep.

But when a priestess approached him—her eyes catching his across the flames—he wondered if he'd ever left the n-scape at all.

Perhaps none of it, the beach, his pong-call, had been real. How else explain the sudden, piercing sense of belonging that came upon him when she took his hand? It was as if her eyes looked at him from a place where Sylvia....

But the priestess was young, she was barely a woman at all. She'd painted arcane symbols across her tall, skyclad body, so that her green breasts, belly and thighs became abstract symbols of things he didn't understand. She led him away from the fire.

"I don't think I want to lie with you," Nifty said. "No offense."

"Come," said the priestess, shyly smiling. "We shall sit together."

He sat down before her on the sand. She leaned forward and touched the center of his forehead.

"We are sorry for your loss."

"What loss?"

When she kissed his cheek, it raised up a sadness and knowledge inside of him he did not understand.

"But the time is running away and you must act soon. Behind you," she said, "are our lady's gifts. One gift for each of the worlds."

"What loss?"

Seated before him, cross-legged, arms folded, the priestess was looking beyond him, already off in her own fantasy. She was right there, ripe for the taking, but Nifty had changed. There was only one woman for him now.

Behind him, he found two objects carefully wrapped in the softest Venusian silk. The first object wasn't a wand or a sword, or any of the other ridiculous objects these people busied themselves with. It was a g-op special repeating needle-gun, state of the art. It disassembled easily for the packing.

The second gift was a mushroom.

Chapter 18

Martha Dobbs couldn't fly like Larry Held or vanish like Frank P. Hogart in a puff of smoke. As far as she knew she couldn't get into the n-scape at all. Yet unlike her mesmerized comrades, she could move from one place to another with her physical body. One could simply walk across a room, for instance, and assess the situation. When a window was open, no matter how high, it shouldn't be too hard to get out of a room. Venusian gravity was a good ten percent less forceful than Earth's. If she got a good enough start, an Earthling could run up the wall, using the bricked grooves as kind of a ladder.

It was possible: but it felt really, really strange. She ran up the wall like an insect 'til she was hanging out over the sill. From there, she could look down far below on the city.

It hurt, but she squeezed out onto a ledge, taking care not to look down again. She saw it wasn't a basement she'd been in at all, but a cell on a high floor of Station 5. Martha Dobbs stood on the outer wall, and leaned back against the Tower's volcanic skin. She took off her torn top and tied it tight around her waist. Her breasts felt larger, sore from the effort. Intuitively, she arched her back to drink up the V-day's last light through all her exposed skin.

A reddish hue edged the deepening hole in the cloud, lighting Venusia's architectures with a sacred, spectacular fire. From here, she could see all the way out to the beach, where the Sunset celebrations were already beginning. Little people gathered and swarmed, alive in the moment. Ishtar sparkled, seething behind them.

"We are really here," Martha whispered, aloud. "I'm really here."

Distant murmurs and revelers' shouts moved up and out of the grid with the wind. She heard the sounds of closer, laughing voices from up above. The chirps of happy machines. She couldn't see up over the eaves, but it sounded as if people had gathered to celebrate at the tower's top. A fire escape led the way. Young, eager to be free, Martha climbed up it gingerly, careful not to let her bare feet make any noise on the metal rungs.

But as she hoisted herself over the high eaves of Station 5, her freedom was immediately placed in question. Larry Held's burning eyes caught her from afar.

Larry broke off from a cluster of strangers gathered on the wide rooftop garden. He came over to her with long hands outstretched.

"Baby. How did you get here?"

Martha brushed the fire escape's dust off her arms.

"I climbed."

"Whose idea was that? The dwarf's? Is he with you?"

"I thought you were watching every move we made down there."

"On the contrary, doll-face. Lack of observation is the whole point."

"Well, I'm alone. The others don't know I'm here. When are you going to let them out?"

"They'll find their own way. It's what we want them to do, to use the n-scape, stretch it out. You mustn't worry. Come on, sweetheart, let me introduce you."

Larry's clammy fingers took her hers as she followed him across the rooftop. Various men stood around, monitoring the celebrations, congratulating themselves on the new year. Martha could see they were curious, though they were polite enough not to stare. Bundles of flowers were spread among half-eaten fruit and potatoes on small circular tables.

"We're having a private first-night feast, watching the celebrations," Larry said. "And other things too." His fingers squeezed. "You're becoming quite a star, do you know that?"

As he led her towards a V, the stage came into focus. A man and woman twisted together, naked, foarking, pressing and combining. She looked closer and saw that it was she and Rogers Collectibles, the night before last. For all the world to see.

"It's all the show." Larry explained. "In a few minutes you'll walk out of the bookstore. We'll reverse the earlier footage of your entrance. And then you'll come out onto the beach and feed as the sun sets. It's called *Happy Ever After, Martha Dobbs*. How do you like it?"

But Martha's head had turned with sudden, undeniable intuition. There, from far across the roof, she was caught by an impossible strength. Jorx Crittendon's white eyes held her in their piercing light.

Martha had to squint as the Princeps approached. A white nimbus pulsed from his head. The long lines of his face, the upturned triangular grin, the green skin deeper, richer than her own, caught her weak and exposed. She covered her naked breasts awkwardly and flushed all along her front.

"Jorx!" called Larry. "It's Martha Dobbs."

Crittendon wore black. He projected an air of tasteful, designed conservatism. His angular grin never varied as he approached. When he spoke, his voice was loud and precise.

"You look disoriented, citizen Dobbs."

Larry's arm curled around Martha's waist. "She's fine, Princeps."

As Larry's hand cupped her buttocks, Martha Dobbs pulled away.

Noting her discomfort, the Princeps gestured gently towards her and opened his hand to offer a shawl-pak. As she took it, unpacked, and threw the cloth over her shoulders, she felt the Princeps' eyes survey her body.

"I'm concerned, Larry. Very concerned," he said, still grinning. "Things seem not to have stabilized as I thought they would. Make sure Ms. Dobbs eats flowers tonight, will you?"

Martha fainted.

"Jorx is a busy guy, sweetie. He's always coming and going. But you did great. He loves you. I can tell."

She was standing again. Larry had revived her with a mango juice, her favorite.

Martha Dobbs turned towards the sea. She'd managed, as far as she knew, not to consider the truth of her situation while the Princeps scanned her mind. The effort had caused her to lose consciousness. It was very difficult not be seen thinking at all. Had he seen something in her? A cone of concern, perhaps, directed outward from mind to other mind?

"He's very preoccupied," Larry said. "He's hardly got time for the likes of you and me these days. Bigger things are on his plate. Much bigger things."

"What things?"

"I don't know. I don't want to know."

"I want to know," she said.

"Hey hey now, doll-face. Be easy. Feel the moment. How beautiful is this? The sunset. The beach."

Ruddy light dwindled in the darkening Hole. Already, the Evening Star was twinkling blue in the darkening night. Odd that she'd only now noticed. It seemed to have changed the whole cast of things.

Martha turned back around to ask Larry, "Will my friends be hurt?"

Humor sparked Larry's sad face. "What a cast of characters! That dwarf? He'd be perfect for V-stunts and humiliations. And the neuroscop with the hots for him. Rogers Collectibles, your beau—what a dreamer. Your friends stumbled into something very large, doll. But fear not. Jorx is in control, he can protect them from harm."

The wind blew chill. Martha drew the hemp shawl tight around her naked shoulders. "And me?"

"You're a very lucky girl, Martha. You're a star now. A major star like you've always wanted to be. You'll be moving to the Castle. Jorx demanded it. Now it's time to have some flowers, baby. Time to celebrate."

"I don't want to have them here," she said, looking down over the city. "I want to Feed. I want to be on the beach."

"That's exactly what I've planned. We'll shoot the whole thing. Let's go down. But you have to swear to me you'll have flowers, Martha."

"I swear."

"On the Evening Star?"

"Of course."

"Of course you swear, little girl. Sorry for asking."

All Venusia, it seemed, stretched along the strand. Martha Dobbs saw herself passing among the smattered conglomeration of individuals, subdued and apart, as if outside her own nimble body. She would already appear like a holo-broadcast to Larry Held as he followed behind. He wanted her just as he thought she was—concerned with her own harmless and foolish ambition and unaware of her real power among the people she passed. She sang along with the old familiar hymns to help him with his vision, pretending like she'd always pretended, that it was a happy and easy life.

> *"Sea-born Goddess, awake," The lovers spake.*
> *"The radiant car your sparrows drew;*
> *You gave the word, and swift we flew,*
> *Through liquid air we winged our way,*
> *And came far to Ishtar to pray:*
> *On our plain roofs we seek our queen..."*

By old decree (a reaction to the wars that had desecrated Earth) there was no formal religion in Venusia. One did not even speak the word G-d, let alone organize worship. But no proclamations outlawed idiosyncratic, individual devotions, and tonight she saw plainly that religion was part of the essential condition. The people had brought out their small curiosities, devices and images to pay their respects to the falling sun. Lamps, censors, goblets and candles spiced the air. Dolls, figurines and forbidden crosses danced in flickering shadows, as the children kept the singing alive.

> ...*Till the one lover asked with blood in his eye,*
> *"The Bard God has made this but made this he why?"*

As they approached Feed, Martha pressed eagerly into the thick cluster of bodies. Lit orange and glistening by the bonfire glows, they were already shaking in group trance. A peculiar, familiar energy flashed thick and weightless within her, like an electromagnetic field. She thought she might be taken among them, away from his gaze. But Larry's hands stayed on her shoulders.

Then, close to her ear, his watch ponged. (Later, Martha would realize the sound of the pong was what saved her.) A woman's voice, sparkling and smooth, purred in dulcet tone.

"Darling, I'm leaving the Castle—"

Larry immediately let go his hold. When Martha turned, she saw enough of his face to know he was no longer interested in her.

"I know that voice," she said to him.

"Never mind, sweetheart," Larry said. "Go into Feed. I'll be here when you're done, by this palm tree. Go."

Martha bit her lip, trying not to give thought to her intention, to the decision that she would not, after all, take flowers again.

"Go," Larry said. "I trust you. You've sworn on the Evening Star."

The crowd was tightening around and pressing her inwards. The stink of Feed came up around her, a million salty-sweet pollen-drenched petals, sticky with potent lust. Martha Dobbs collapsed into the damp trench, skinny knees buckling. Splayed among the stringy weeds, the plucked and cast away petals, her skin burned as she was buffeted about. She fell through the flowers into the wide, forgiving coolness of sand, holding her lips shut.

Breaking an oath on the Evening Star was a serious matter. There was no cheating where Evening Star was concerned. No equivocations, no almost-swearing. Evening Star was as clear as the most precious stone. Evening Star was made blue by the wide cold blackness around it. It winked its trust at you, smiled true like a crystal of love. It was always day on Evening Star.

Something impossibly strong, a creature outside her but inside as well, something infinitely inter-connected that she hadn't even known she was part of, pulled her up and away, bore her out of the trenches and dropped her in the dunes. A thing of arms and legs and heads and dark, elusive will.

An angel awoke her. A beautiful woman, with light dainty eyes, who smelled of lavender and other more mysterious scents—whose symbol was the rose. She lifted Martha Dobbs in her frail arms and the people parted before them. She sang softly.

> *And the other lover laughed and bid him goodbye*
> *"Enjoy your affliction, the Bard God is I!"*

Chapter 19

Rogers was surprised to find, as he penetrated the thick Venusian clouds, that they gave off their own greenish light, enough to infuse the crouching continent with a soft corona. The topology of the place glowed electric and green, like a map made by a machine. Once his eyes had adjusted he could see quite far ahead.

Rogers could make out a single figure approaching in the distance. He had walked for so long without seeing anyone that it caused him to stop in his tracks and wonder again at the reality of things.

The tall stooped man glowed as if the electric light of the clouds had adhered to his body. He stepped quickly with the help of a stout, serpent-like stick. The hood of the stranger's Q-robe was pulled down over his face. Only a wrinkled chin and ghastly pale lips were visible as he stopped before Rogers. The lips twitched without speaking. With sudden certainty Rogers recognized the face he'd never seen.

"Father," he said.

The wizened lips twisted in grin or grimace, but the stranger said nothing. Finally a trembling hand emerged from the long hanging sleeve. Rogers held out his own hand and the old man dropped a handful of petals into his palm.

"Flowers?"

At this word, the stranger cast his stick upon the ground. It became then, a living lizard. The lizard raised its projector and the old man flashed green in the groundlight.

"*Turn back home, while you still can,*" he said.

"I have no home," Rogers answered, letting the petals fall between his fingers.

And though it almost broke his heart he was able to walk through his father's trembling body—where and into what world, he had the feeling, he'd never know.

His father was a machine.

Far down the coast, under the starless sky, Rogers made out the lit ruddy lights of a small, inhabited structure.

"Well, well, well," he muttered. "Someone living all the way out here. What time is it?"

"It's six in the morning, sir, in the original continuum," answered his watch. "But due the curvature of the planet, proper v-night signals are no longer available. The cloud cover prevents proper analysis of heavenly bodies, but geo-synchronic estimates place us at least 50 v-days in the past, long before we set out."

"Fifty earth years. That would place us back at Transition. You've malfunctioned badly."

Rogers recognized the structure. Cubed, glass-bricked, awkwardly folded against its X axis, the bookshop of Frank P. Hogart glowed red against v-night's electric green. It didn't look any younger.

He had the *Brane World* with him. He was ready to close the deal. Still, before proceeding, Rogers ponged Martha Dobbs.

Martha Dobbs, however, was fast asleep. She was dreaming of a castle, a great and pleasant house erected in a calm and pastoral country. Peasants toiled in the fields outside, keeping the greenery loosely, but precisely controlled. Leaning out of a turret's small window, Martha noticed something moving in the deep and placid moat below. A woman, with long grey hair spread fanning out behind her, swam desperately across, a small sprouting twig fixed in her mouth. It was Dr. Yang, Martha saw, crossing the moat.

But under the water there lurked a monster, long-necked, pale and flaccid. It curled up behind the doctor, opening wide and razor-toothed jaws. Martha Dobbs leaned forward and cried out a warning.

Something was ponging.

But where was she? It seemed to Martha that she was lying back on the biggest most delicious purple bed on which a girl had ever lain. A bed supersized and wide, puffy with all the comforters and pillows you could desire. It was not a place for nightmares, for water snakes with terrible fanged jaws.

This luxury provoked the sweetest and most physical of her animal traits. A faint, sumptuous scent of burning incense enriched the air. There was a pregnant silence, the sort of silence through which ghosts might move without fear of disturbing furniture. Martha sprawled languidly over the bed. She stretched her naked limbs long. It was her wrist-watch ponging, and she muted it without answering. It would be safer that way, safer for all of them to accept silence, to move forward without conscious plan.

She sat up and pulled a soft silver sheet over her shoulders. A chandelier cast a shadowy light through the oppulent boudoir. The walls were fur-lined, the carp tall and soft. Colors were few: white, silver, blue. Here and there a dash of scarlet (a dropped scarf) or a dainty pink (a hanging cap). Across from the bed, cream-colored curtains billowed before open balcony doors.

A familiar white cat sat atop a bedside dresser. Sensing her gaze, the cat twitched its whiskers, hunched its shoulders, and fluffed its furs.

"Do you feels it?" it said. "Everything's gone topsy-turvy."

There came in answer a light and angelic voice. "Shh Miles. She's sleeping."

There, past the balcony windows, across the lush, budding carp, a woman was tending to her make-up. Her back was turned, but the precision of her tender neck, the smooth and supple skin exposed by the long, draping robe....

"She be wake now, Mistress," the cat said, rubbing its rear against the wall. "Good Lord, she be a'wake."

Working on her lips, the woman paused. Martha Dobbs caught sight of the face in the mirror. A sweet smile budding out of the tenderest sadness. Deep green eyes set flashing under hard-etched, angled brows.

"Johanna Zeep," Martha whispered.

A note of sweet self-deprecation gently wrinkled the star's forehead. "You didn't know?" Laughing delightedly, she rose and faced the bed, letting her dark and unkempt locks fall loose around her shoulders.

"I don't know who you think you be, Missy" the cat purred. "But it ain't the likes of herrrr."

"Shut up, Miles." As she crossed towards Martha Dobbs, Johanna Zeep's gown trailed tendrils of Venusian silk in the air. "There's no competition. I'm a hag, a crone. She fell with the sun, Miles. Martha Dobbs, you were splendid. They gathered round, all your thousands of wonderful fans. They followed us up off the beach. They're saying I rescued you, you know. But you rescued me, Martha Dobbs. You rescued me. Everything's changing. Don't you feel it? There's magic again in the world."

Johanna Zeep sat down then, very quietly, on the bed. She reached forward and pulled the sheet down from Martha's shoulders. Naked and exposed, Martha trembled in wonder.

"Party over Missies," said Miles the cat. "Somebody big be coming."

Johanna jumped up from the bed. "Here? Now?"

"Lordy yes, Missie." The cat arched its back in sudden fear. "It be the boss."

Johanna's eyes widened and Martha noticed delicate webs of wrinkles splinter the softness of her face. "Lie down," Johanna whispered to her. "Under the covers. Hurry."

The door slid open.

"Jo," said a familiar voice. "Never do that to me again. Never, ever—"

Martha slid under the covers just as Larry Held strode tensely into the room.

Martha Dobbs held very still for a long time. Golden light seeped through the dark cloud-wombs beneath Johanna's blankets, offering countless possible tunnels. Larry had evidently not seen her. She didn't know why, but she knew that she must not be discovered. Larry must not even sense her mind. Martha concentrated on not thinking of herself, focussed only on what was happening in the room around her.

Unable to contain her curiosity, Martha gently rotated herself 180 degrees in that dark world. When she finally peeped out of the foot of the comforter, she found herself directly behind Larry. He was seated on a pillowed divan, his lank hair falling down around the pale bald spot on the back of his head.

She couldn't see Johanna, only smell her, hear the sound of her soft weeping. Martha had known her only these minutes, but she was already smitten. She felt she would defend Johanna against anything in the world, and had to hold herself back from leaping out and defending her now. Larry, apparently, was spellbound before the star, unaware that Martha Dobbs was right behind him, staring at the back of his head.

Martha wondered why she had ever feared Larry Held. He was only a conduit of power. Power passed through Larry and Larry directed it into a holographic containment field of pure hallucination.

"How difficult it must be for you," Johanna whispered, giving voice to Martha's thoughts. "You're not a man at all."

Larry was stung; he was already enraged, but these words were like needles in his flesh. A chill flowed out through the room; a swamp of bitterness and failure. Larry's consciousness flared out in brutal, lusting hatred. Martha saw and felt it as if she were there, suddenly, inside his balding head.

The n-scape yawned before her, lizard-less and wide. She looked away, not wanting to fall inside.

Her eyes found Miles, the famous cat. As their gazes locked, the black diamonds in the feline's eyes widened and revolved into squares. When it looked away, she found a thought placed directly in her mind.

Mistress keep her needle pistol under pillow.

There was a sudden cry. Larry's hot, lusting hatred washed through her. Martha felt and followed the extending arc of his striking hand, as he directed his lusting hatred down on Johanna's tender mouth.

Larry's mind tightened the perceived around him. Fear rose like sudden bile. "Miles?" he called. "Who thought that?" His attention came too late to Martha Dobbs.

There was the pop of a sudden report. A needle-pistol flashed.

It was like an old-time cotton parade, such as Martha Dobbs remembered from V's long ago. Feathers falling through the room like Terran snow.

She held Johanna Zeep's compact, mica-sided needle pistol in her hand. She had blown a hole through the comforter and fired the minute projectile directly through the back of the MC's head.

Larry took it well. He lifted his hands and the gesture became, as he turned around, one of peace. He fixed Martha Dobbs in his gaze. She saw that the needle had passed through his skull, his brain, out the center of his eye. She saw a red spot forming there already. What a perfect shot. Did the needle pass through the Castle wall? Was it now sticking into the Evening Star, a tiny shard of hate?

Larry's forehead wrinkled, but he was left without an appropriate witticism.

"Martha..." he said. "I'm hit."

"Larry," Martha said. "I'm sorry."

He turned confusedly to Johanna.

Johanna had drawn herself up against the fur-lined wall. Her unkempt hair covered most of her face. She was biting a bloody lip and single tear slid was sliding like a fat pearl along her already bruising chin.

"You touched me," she whispered.

"I'm sorry Jo." Larry said. "Real sorry."

Larry seemed confused. He walked himself awkwardly, like a wooden doll, to the door. He let himself out.

Had Martha Dobbs held the beautiful creature in her skinny arms? It was hard to remember. She certainly smelled the real scents of love-making, felt that strange softness in her limbs, under her skin. But her time in the room had been like a series of dreams, and ever since the n-scape had entered her life, it was difficult to know for sure what was real.

She had pulled Johanna into to the extravagant bed. They rolled and touched on its wide softness. Quietly, they kissed. Johanna had stroked Martha's hair, kissed her eyes, her ears. She murmured tender blessings to the inside of her ear, kissed her belly and behind her knees. "Ssshh." When Martha began to ask her a question, Johanna had placed her soft hand against her lips.

Johanna Zeep's sultry eyes melted into green, feline slits as she received Martha's gaze. Her cascading locks tumbled down her back. She opened her legs and lay back as Martha stroked her tender skin. The dark-clipped patch of Johanna's private hair curled before Martha's wide eyes like the crescent of the softest, sweetest moon.

Martha Dobbs stroked the soft and yielding yoni, slipped her finger along its gentle line. The most glamorous odor she had ever inhaled floated in to fill her every tingling nerve. She spread her own legs and Johanna pressed tight against her.

The room filled suddenly with a soft and weightless sphere of white light, emanating to and from the leg-crossed lovers. Martha Dobbs and Johanna Zeep had become the merest figments on the skin of an expanding membrane bubble, fixed fast, peering into its own voided center. Johanna's eyes rolled up into her head. Martha saw shapes and figures inhering, vanishing, appearing. Sylvia Yang rushed by, a sword passing through her neck. Rogers Collectibles rapped on an old familiar door, entering a twisted, outrageous structure. The dwarf fired a weapon as he flew through the air. Martha Dobbs herself was flying fast over Venus Beach.

Miles the Cat, eyes widened in a paroxysm of surprise, ran pitter-pattering across the room. And it was that running of the little fast feet that had caused her eyes to open, to awaken to the possibility that it hadn't been real at all.

Johanna was gone. The bed was empty.

Martha found a translucent L-robe and wrapped it around her waist, taking warmth in its absurd luxury. She tip-toed across the thick carp, as if it wouldn't have muffled her steps anyway. The door slid open with a thought and she passed confidently out into the Castle hallway, as if she were Johanna Zeep in a V.

She seemed to remember a time when the Castle was teeming with ambitious and powerful people. To-t-night there was no one about. She stepped lightly down the great, twisting stairway like a heroine—her hand on the creamy banister, her robe trailing behind.

A great hall opened out before her, desolate and empty. But following the sad, familiar tinkling of piano keys to the open door of an adjoining room, she found a little bar. The interior was dark, but a few couples and late-night lingerers were visible huddled round small candle-lit tables. Martha noted their perfect style, the casual elegance of their bearing. Though no one was vulgar enough to stare, she felt all eyes upon her as she entered in Johanna's gown.

She walked to the bar. The piano appeared to be playing itself. Larry Held was leaning on the great, shadowy instrument, smoking an LP, watching it shuffle out the old rinky-dink tunes.

"Where is everybody?" Martha asked him.

"Who knows?" Larry answered quietly. "There was a time when this place would be crowded to the gills at this hour. Dignitaries, stars, prostitutes, crooks. JC, Martha, you should have seen Jo in those days. Something to behold. My finest work."

She saw the shine of his teeth in the dark.

"You need rest, Larry," Martha said. "A doctor. You're hurt."

"My brain has been punctured straight through, doll-face. If I sleep, it's over. Things are only temporarily hanging together because I'm still thinking. When I stop I'll die. I understand everything. It's sad, really sad."

The piano changed to a slower, old-fashioned tempo. The hairs on the back of her neck tingled and Martha had the awareness then, with a sudden jolt, of another presence directly behind them.

"Little girls have the strangest dreams," Jorx Crittendon said, his green head suddenly illuminated by a radiating nimbus. "Secret coups, revolutions. But there's no law against a fantasy. Is there, Larry? Have I issued such a temp-proc?"

"You have not, Princeps."

Jorx sucked from an LP, his triangular grin lifting high up his triangular face.

"You've killed a highly valuable man, Citizen Dobbs, a highly valuable man."

"He's not dead yet," Martha Dobbs said. "Surely—"

"He's not dead yet?" interrupted the Princeps. "Do you know what life is, Ms. Dobbs? Do you know what in fact is keeping Larry going?"

The piano abruptly stopped playing.

"Do you think pianos just play themselves?" Jorx exhaled green smoke through his nostrils. "There's no law against fantasy, Ms. Dobbs. This whole world, as you perceive it, is a fantasy. You yourself even recognize it, though you don't have a grown-up understanding of what it takes to make use of the fact. But you do have dreams, don't you? Fantastic dreams, Martha Dobbs. That ripe, plump, unconscious mind of yours, that miracle of creation, it's very strong, is it not? It leads you to places you don't dare to even remember." His words were loud and unduly harsh.

"Why are you yelling at me?" Martha drew back.

"When one man's word..." His white eyes locked with hers. "When one man's word makes the difference between life and death Ms. Dobbs, it is only fitting that that word be clearly audible. When one can unfix reality to the point where one can begin to play, to re-write things properly, with suitable precision, one dislikes having to rebuke playthings for their mistakes."

Again, she drew back. "You're insane."

"History is insane, Citizen Dobbs. I highly recommend you stay out of it."

She tried to speak.

He frowned comically. "May I ask a question, Princeps?"

"What have you done to my friends, to Rogers Collectibles—"

"He's fine. Doing something for us, helping to tie up loose ends. Let him alone. I still need him free and unencumbered. You will do us a favor, however." He let smoke out of his angular nostrils. "When he eventually contacts you and wants to meet... you let us know where and when."

"What about that midget?" Larry said. "He struck me as dangerous."

"He's doomed. I've already seen him die."

Jorx Crittendon was flickering, as if he were only partially present.

"And Dr. Yang?" Martha Dobbs asked. "I dreamed she was in trouble. "

"Certain dreams disappear to be real; that's the way of things. You understand, citizen Dobbs?"

"No." Martha couldn't lie.

Jorx Crittendon grinned so wide she could see his teeth. "And your own deepest dream? Your secret dream?" Her legs and hips were taken hold of from behind. She resisted.

"You wish to be queen, Martha Dobbs? "

A spilled goblet, a distant murder.

A dream, Citizen Dobbs? How could something so precisely real not be a dream?

The piano playing its rinky-dink tunes. Robed strangers gathering round. A blow across her face. Rough hands holding her fixed. The leader's rick swelling up gigantic inside of her lass, making her cry and wish out loudly to the night, to the Evening Star.

She didn't cry. She didn't hurt. She was on top of the floor. The Evening Star was a lie, a projection. She understood now that they all didn't exist. For some time, she wasn't sure how long exactly, after she'd picked herself up off the floor and found her robe, walked back up the curling stairway, Martha had been thinking she was real. The notes had floated up on the ether and blown through the opened windows of the balcony like pearls and she had believed they were music. Her ear had gathered them in as they rose. Their sad, sweet song. Too sad and too sweet. Too cold. They made her think, as she shivered, of Rogers Collectibles and his hat. Wasn't he real, after all, out in the cold?

Chapter 20

Out of doors, alone in the foggy darkness, the glass-bricked structure squatted like a living creature. It glowed bright atop the sloping green-lit land. Droplets of condensation had materialized along its glowing surface like beads of sweat. Close up, it looked warm and inviting.

"Frank P. Hogart," the sign whispered. "Bookseller."

Was Rogers Collectibles on a bench again in the late afternoon? The leaves swirling in the wind? It was almost possible to imagine that past back into existence, as if the bookstore was at the service of whatever he might believe in.

But the knob surprised him with its cold reality. It turned heavily and the door opened with a new difficulty. The door and its mechanism had not changed. Rogers Collectibles himself had grown weaker, less possible. He felt like a ghost.

The room he entered appeared to be the interior of the structure he'd approached from outside and Rogers walked through meters of ordinary space. But he was aware of another kind of motion as well. A kind of falling through the molecular physics in the air around him, a motion away. Bubbles formed in space around him, visible through the corner of his eye, offering strange routes and non-Euclidean opportunities. Rogers concentrated.

There was a pleasant odor of burning wood in the air. Orange light bloomed from under a closed door.

Rogers rippled through the wall.

A man sat before the fire, facing the dancing flames. They were blue all through their center, but the extremity of their heat was contained by a quasicrystal skein shimmering around the hearth. From the hulk of his bent back, Rogers saw it was Frank P. Hogart, who rocked back and forth on the beautiful old chair. He was cradling something in his arms.

The old man emitted a quiet whine, so high-pitched that under ordinary circumstances Rogers would never have heard it. But once detected, it was as if that frequency held together the things around them, the warm, firelit room and the huddled shelves of books.

The old man hadn't noticed his intrusion. Rogers approached him directly from behind. The object in Hogart's lap, on which he was lavishing his attention, was the head of a beautiful young woman.

The face was white-skinned, bloodless as marble. The eyes were red and frozen open. What was this? The eyes held Rogers as he peered over the old man's shoulder. He felt he knew them, had seen them before.

The head, monstrously, whispered.

"Remember me."

Rogers remain composed.

Two empty chairs sat across from Hogart, facing the fire. The well-trained eye recognized them as specimens of early Venusian futurism. Intelligent and restrained, but nevertheless Epicurean and pleasant, they were evidence of the colony's early promise. Rogers took care to brush the dust off his suit before sitting down. He found it extraordinarily comfortable.

"Look at me," whispered the head.

Rogers had resolved not to accept the reality of the old man's visible hallucinations—even if he himself was one of them. Nevertheless the hair on the back of his neck prickled in real fear.

"Look at me," said the head, more loudly now. *"Not the strangest possibility here, certainly. But strange enough. The wound is fresh; the cut was very clean. I feel nothing, though my brain is still relatively intact. The vocal chords, as you can hear, haven't been damaged. It's fully*

possible that I should be able to speak as long as there's energy to do so, however unlikely."

"I don't believe in you. None of this is real. Even me. I'm not really real."

"*You're more real than me,*" the head said.

"Who are you?"

"*I am his daughter. Call me Ae.*"

"Hogart is your father?"

"*Yes.*"

"And he ... he holds your head in his hands?"

"*Yes, it is his pain (however mistaken), that opens up our own possibilities—holds me alive outside time. But still, I'm dying. The adversary removed my head as I entangled with Sylvia Yang.*"

"Dr. Yang?"

"*Poor Sylvia. You must tell her lover she is dead.*"

"That's awful," said Rogers, angrily removing his hat. "This has all gone too far. I demand to know what this all has to do with my book."

"*Do not surrender the book to my father. Its provenance must be resolved in your own time. It shall stand there as a beacon to our mother when she steps from between the worlds to draw out the Green Man. No more. My throat hurts. I must die now, Quentin Rogers.*"

"Quentin?"

"*Remember me,*" said the head.

The head died, eyes rolling up and tongue drooping out of its garish mouth. He had no time to protest. For a door opened to the right of the fireplace and a sudden cloud of butterflies fluttered into room. They made way for a being such as Rogers Collectibles had never before seen in his life.

Fuscous mandibles twitched from a glassy-membraned head almost entirely made up of eyes. The bulbous features formed an abstraction of a humanoid face. The insect walked upright on its two reverse-angled hindmost legs in a ludicrous imitation of the human gait. Slimy wings gripped its hairy torso like a corset. Butterflies darted all around the creature, dancing in flickering abandon.

The enormous insect stopped before him. It regarded Rogers Collectibles through a single crystal monocle fixed to the tiny horn emerging between its bulbous thousand lensed eyes. An invisible electronic speaker spattered forth crackling words from a belt hung round its loins.

"Greetings, Earth-Man. I am the 13th Zoreckian of the Great Leaf."

Hogart, Rogers saw, had fallen back. His mouth hung open and spittle gleamed on his white-bristled lips.

The bug turned, shuffled nimbly between Rogers and the fire. It took the remaining empty chair. The slime would likely spoil the artifact for good. Its odor was remarkably foul, rich in layers of noxious elements. The creature opened its wings momentarily as it sat. One brushed against Rogers, leaving a glob of mucus on the shoulder of his suit.

"Many partons," said the mechanical voice. *"I secrete when I am excited."*

Rogers lit an LP.

Four more stick legs unfolded and stretched out toward the fire. Atop its head, twin antennae twisted around and reached out towards Rogers. Rogers leaned back to avoid them.

"Your world is very interestink. So small."

"To me it's large enough. I'm here to talk to Frank P. Hogart, about a book."

"He is not of sount meint."

"No," Rogers said, holding down his revulsion. "I can see that."

"The old ape's pain makes circle for our parlay. His apparatus— the fire—boils space and pumps the anomalies through the quasicrystal architecture of his store. It offers varyink futures."

"My business is with the past," Rogers said. "And I'm no ambassador. If you have 2,000 Klugers, not a kredit less, the book is yours. Otherwise I will have to ask you to excuse yourself from our company. Mr. Hogart and I have business to attend to."

"The head of his beloved burns in the fire before him. You think he is fit to do business?"

The bug had a point. The head, anyway, was no longer visible. Rogers turned his attention to the room around him. The walls were covered in shelves laden with intricate crystaline forms. they folded in unlikely, impossible ways, defiant of space and time. A thousand splinters of color broke the hut's wooden uniformity into an infinitely complex mathematical growth, opening out from his own egg-like interior.

There then came a very soft drumming upon the top of Roger's left shoulder. With it an extraordinary wave of kindness passed through his body. The insect's antennae were beating patterns on his shoulder. The rhythms spoke a clear communication. This communication was not, as had been the case with the plant, like a fully constructed sentence occurring in his head. Instead, the beating of the antennae imparted a whole body of knowledge intact and defined, carefully mapped for mental exploration.

"You have made it here," it said. "You have therefore demonstrated your world's claim to the vistas of the larger fields. Clearly your species is not yet psychologically equipped to enjoy the benefits of a type 3 civilization. Whether you will allow yourself to exist is still unresolved. Until the point of such resolution, your kind remains potentially lethal to the survival of a number of alternate centers. Nevertheless, you are here and you appear to be real in many continua."

Rogers, despite his resentment at the bug's interruption, answered the idea. For the fact was, above all things, he wanted to be real.

"Precisely my point. You are facing yourself. As a result, I am facing you and we are the first of our kinds to share spacetime in such a manner. I am willing to deal with you concerning the ownership of the book in your possession. It happens I'm interested in such things. I'm a collector of human artifacts."

Rogers sighed. "You're kidding me."

"Yet the book is not yet yours. We stand in a possible past, wherein Frank P. Hogart has possession of it. Your book is in his hands."

Rogers saw that the old man was indeed now holding the *Brane World*. Leaning toward the fire, he pored over its yellowed pages.

"This book store," Rogers said. "It's not a bookstore at all."

The walls had gathered closer around them, the air had grown dank and dark.

"It may be. It may also be Tee-Pee itself," said the bug's communication. "The interior of the asteroid's shelter as it sails through all of empty space. It is Melton's circle we have entered, before Venusia is born. It was his to begin with now, for he is older than we. The book stands, for him and for all of Venusia, as the last strand of the real history, the very possibility of the colony's existence. It was you who brought it to him. At the end of time, in many honeypots, he will throw it into the fire."

"Honeypots?"

Rogers found himself falling into a conical vortex opening up out of the back of Frank P. Hogart's white-haired head.

"No," he protested. "No more neuroscapes."

"*There is no solid ground. Get the book. You must understant,*" barked the mechanism hanging between the bug's lowest legs. "*What is happenink.*"

Chapter 21

Across from the priestess, Nifty Norrington sat cross-legged and helmeted on the darkening beach. He sailed through the thousand minds of the CVU. He understood now that the unseen was beside the seen always, that selves were only ideas, holograms cast out by its forms on the walls of the three dimensional world. There was no reason another self, a doubled projection, should not exist. He had once been a giant thing, a world contained by the tiny cabinet of flesh that, despite its deformities, had fixed and centered him. Down, like the point of a compass fixes the centre of a circle. But now the points had doubled and he himself enscribed an arc around the other, and the other him. As the circles moved, alien things, bug-like ideas were crawling through the gaps etched between.

A multitude of abdicated avenues opened before him. Each contained a self-directed and believable universe—a world-egg itching to be born in time—flipped outward and around. He could taste them, their individual flavors. He didn't find Sylvia but he found himself, the other one—the Niftus who knew where she was. The clear recognition came upon him like a scent.

The other Norrington's mind drew him in behind its open, hollow eyes. And Nifty saw it then, he got what he came for, what he'd already known, already deduced. He saw Sylvia Yang's death: an axe breaking her soft side, a green face flickering out of an attached dimension, an angular smile—a sword coming into being through the eye-shaped overlap of entangled words. Sylvia's head rolling, her dead lips open, her eyes meeting his own.

"Find Rogers Collectibles," she said.

To save her? Prevent her death?

There was no answer. The n-scape had taken shape. A mad boy had grabbed the other woman's head by its hair; was bounding out over its familiar expansions, screaming.

Niftus found himself, his own face in Syvia's holo-mirror, an event he recognized as reflecting infinitely now in four dimensions. Her mail ponged.

Like and like repelled; a body changed, lumped suddenly grown. Nifty was flung backwards, forwards, into a vertiginous void. The n-scape yawned before him and he fell like a single drop of water into a bottomless well. In the terrible stillness of his plummet, a concavity opened out of his mind into a place were he might no longer be falling at all. Unfamiliar body parts, members, primitive sea-creatures and ideas walked beside him. It was a pilgrimage of sorts, inter-weaving, dissembling, confusing. Odors and sights combined into new sensory communications. Ideas clearer to the mind than the simplest logical equations passed between the pilgrims, exploiting a math of enormous complexity.

A skein soon had spread out against his feet and he found himself standing on a wide, holding field.

"*Find Rogers Collectibles,*" he said aloud, in the n-scape.

The directive propelled him with extraordinary force. It caused the 'scape to tremble, drew black clouds to enpurple the thundering sky.

The air stunk of death. Great birds were pecking at the flesh of corpses, snapping skin from hard, yellow beaks. Meat trees stood out on the plain, oozing pustules of pain.

"What the hell is this? Are we approaching Collectibles?"

"It appears so, Sir," the helmet answered. Probability suggests your entanglement will occur soon, Sir, in this direction."

"I thought there wasn't any time or space in here."

"No. But there are virtues and failings. Patience, Sir, is a virtue."

Nifty had come down to a waterfront. He stood at the end of an L-shaped jetty. Stone-worked and long, it was particularly solid. A boat was cleated to a hook. The black craft rolled with weird time on the slow sea. Nifty found he could read the swirling script on its stern.

"The *Ruby Greene*, Sir."

"I can read now," he said. "Who is Ruby Greene again?"

"She was the beloved of the Founder, Sir. Of Melton. It is recorded that he came to Venus to find a way back to her through the n-scape. To prevent their first separation."

The words on the stern changed: *Who rides with me is beloved.*

"That is possible, then? To travel in time? To use the n-scape to change history?" He was thinking of Sylvia Yang and her murder.

"Morituri says: The perceived n-scape is always reflective of the present of the observing mind, Sir. In your world, as in Melton's, Ruby Greene's death is imperfectly recorded. The possibilities remain open. She is both alive and dead."

Nifty frowned. Sylvia was only dead. "Where's Collectibles?"

"Sir, if I might suggest we enter the boat."

Nifty stepped lightly down. The craft rocked violently with his weight and he tumbled into the stiff-cushioned pilot seat. It was cherry-red, leather, and built, apparently, for a pilot just his size.

But change is the order of the neuroscape. The pilot-seat proved to be a sort of elevator. He was taken immediately down, below decks.

A door opened before him, revealing a small, cement floored passageway lined with green doors. Nifty passed through, feeling suddenly heavy again, as if he was fixed by gravity and not thought to the grey carped floor beneath his feet.

A mustachioed, brown-skinned man stood before him. He wore an old-fashioned suit. A jerry-rigged helmet atop his head bristled with all sorts of electrodes and antennae. Behind thick black-rimmed spectacles, his eyes were magnified and huge.

"Welcome to reality," the man said, extending a hairy hand. "I'm Hugo Morituri."

They appeared to be standing in a workshop, a private laboratory in the basement of a highly functional, anonymous building. Odd apparatuses blinked around them: tubes and dials and sparking electrodes. In a cage in the corner, something living looked out on Nifty Norrington with red eyes of fear.

"This is reality? I thought it was the CVU."

"This is historical spacetime. It's a place in what remains of your own past. I programmed the extraordinary machines to bring you here—though I didn't know exactly who you'd be, of course. When they'd registered certain physiological anomalies in your quantum self-definition as you passed through the n-scape, they brought you."

"What anomalies?"

"You've doubled. You're a time-traveler. Or will be. It seems to have already been recorded by your own perception."

"You committed suicide," Nifty said. "That's been recorded."

"Please," Morituri said, pulling his moustache, and blinking his large, magnified brown eyes. "We are not discussing my future. Only yours. It's a risk, our meeting like this. While you're here nothing is safe."

"I'm looking for a way to travel back in time and prevent someone's death."

The brown-skinned man observed him. "How extensive has been your science education?"

"Not so good."

"I'm not surprised. Are you off the flowers?"

"It's been several days."

"We need something to increase your brain's productivity. I have some drugs here, but I'm not confident your biology is the same as ours."

Nifty hesitated. "I have a mushroom," he said. "Not here, but where I'm sitting in my world."

"Take it," Morituri said. "If it's a Venusian aboriginal, it will do the job."

It was strange to eat the mushroom, under the helmet, before the priestess on Venus Beach, while the scientist watched him an entire world away.

It tasted bitter, but good.

He was like a tree, though upside down from how he had previously understood a tree to exist. Roots stretched deep into the air from his mind. A billion tendrils jacked from his into other minds and other growths. Entire other worlds twisted up in miniature invisible dimensions from every point. He saw how his legs, his funny stubbed legs, as they stretched out to walk, made gravity. A universe was lightly pulled into dimensional shape by his motion. In this "nature," around the "hillocks" and shadowy "grottoes" and bubbling "springs," through its "rivers" and "lake districts," Nifty perceived an artificial framework. An architecture of gleaming rivets and arcing steel, penetrating, leading, contained by the multiverses that hung only a millimeter above. Its rungs were an easy thing to climb, gave way to great vistas and holes in time.

"Do you see?" Morituri looked deep into his eyes, pulling him back.

"Sure," Nifty said.

"A kind of tree growing out of your head?"

"Yeah."

"Good. But even this picture is flat. Open your mind. Our people's theories, which led to such trouble, were mistaken as to their goal. The fools. There will be no answer such as we will be able to understand by way of our sensory perceptions. Discovery, in regard to truth, is apocalypse. Each recorded observation obliterates and fictionalizes the past, sucks vast chunks of the n-scape away. It was long proven that no particle smaller than an electron could ever be observed in its natural state. Yet whole generations of the brightest minds dedicated themselves to the mathematical observation, based on probability alone, of objects that could only be judged by speculation. Centuries of potential space travel were stalled by expensive research missions dedicated to the mystical goal of academic physics. Whole swathes of historical possibilities were wiped away by the archaic inscription of scribbling experts.

"And what was this goal? Eternal life? Power beyond the limitations of physical reality? Such things could only be achieved by the complete destruction of earth-life as it carefully had evolved over the millenia. Only death makes life.

"It is clear that the architecture of the universe reveals itself by our thoughts made active. As ordinary bio-physical laws drop away, the region of the real that is bounded by general relativity and motored by quantum uncertainty becomes available to statistical manipulation. The neuroscape and the real become virtually indistinguishable. The incredibly improbably possible, you see, encroaches on the real. Venusia has opened this door. Melton knew it long before I. It is why he turned to his books, and away from his people. Why we together created Crittendon."

"Why Venusia?" Nifty had to ask. "What is so important about Venusia? It's a ridiculous little world."

"I was hoping you could tell me, my little friend."

"Me?"

"Venusia may be the last surviving outpost of Terran life. Or a fantastic dream engendered by the throes of earth's agony, fated to be sucked away into holographic meaninglessness. It will be your decision."

There was a rush of sound. Morituri's eyes watered behind his spectacles.

"Could you kill a living creature, if you were called upon to do so?"

"I've done it before," Nifty said. "I could do it again."

"Good," said the scientist, trembling. "I am a man of peace. A scientist. I have done what I've done, allied myself to madmen, because I'm genetically programmed to believe self-knowledge of the multiverses is a holy and necessary thing. Yet I have helped to shrink the n-scape into an easily manipulated source of power in our, your real. I'm sorry that because of my tinkering, I have made your pain and the pain of your contemporaries possible. I may be the last of the great scientists. I realize I learned too little from the lives of those who came before me, the Nikola Teslas, the Quentin Teals and Henry Ickleses who warned. I should have stayed on Earth and let Melton die alone on Venus. Earth is now destroyed, perhaps due in great part to events I've set in motion. Now I can do little. The larger fate of humanity is more your own burden than mine."

"Mine?"

"In your spacetime, the adversary can be killed. He hasn't wiped me away yet. He's still a man. He comes from your time; you made him somehow, with my technology. You people, with your vast un—"

There was a noise behind them. Nifty turned.

"What is that thing there," he asked. "In the cage?"

The rough cage, set up in the corner of the work shop, shook as they regarded it. Two ravaged eyes, wide and reddened, peered out through its bars. The face supporting them, the deflated sack-like skin, the chattering, broken chin—the wild pain in the fearful monkey eyes—it turned Nifty's stomach to see it.

Nifty approached the cage closer. He saw that wires had been forced into a bloody hole on the creature's shaved head.

It was tiny, child thing, part man and monkey. But very old and shivering as well.

"*Mmmm....*" it tried to speak. "*Mmmmm....*"

Morituri smiled. "That's Macla. A life-form of my own invention. The child of the last surviving chimpanzee on Venus, genetically spliced with human and cephalopod strains. I'm using him to access the most primitive layers of the wider n-scape. Oh he's quite a little traveler, little Macla is. He crossed through time, you know. He entered the n-scape through his mother's mind, and inside he killed her. It's quite difficult to kill from inside, but it's the best way I know to travel in time. The resulting conundrum— Macla's presence in a non-hosted n-scape—threw him at the necessary speed to stretch whole visible regions of the accepted real. His imagination returned him here of course, to his precious feed. Oh he's an angry one. He's a killer, little Macla."

"*Mmmm...Acla!*" shrieked the creature. "*Mmmm ... Acla!*"

Nifty walked over to the cage and unlocked its door.

"What are you doing?"

"When revenge," Nifty said, "the desire for revenge, isn't satisfied. When you live with it every day. When you're tortured, humiliated, experimented upon...."

He swung the door open. "It does strange things to you."

The little creature lept from the cage and stood on the floor. It grinned terribly, fixing its mad eyes on its creator's face.

Morituri drew back against the wall.

"Kill it!" he cried. "Kill it before it kills us both."

"*Mmmm...Acla,*" screamed the white monkey, with straining red-veined eyes, claws outstretched. "*Macla!*"

"It's your problem," Nifty said. "I'm not really here at all."

Nifty wasn't surprised to find himself walking, presently, along a green and rugged field. Ever since he'd taken the mushroom, he'd understood most of what was happening.

"Helmet?"

"Sir?"

"Do you have any other surprises in store? Any more meetings I don't know about scheduled?"

"It is regrettable, Sir, that programs were over-ridden by the League to the point of fracturing essential client/hardware trust."

"I'll let it go."

"Thank you, Sir."

"Is it recorded how Hugo Morituri actually committed suicide?"

"Yes, Sir. It is said Dr. Morituri gave himself over to one of his laboratory animals. As no one else was in the laboratory at the time, it was ruled a suicide. Only Dr. Morituri himself could have opened its cage."

"We're going to have to try to kill someone, Helmet. From inside. To travel in time."

"I believe Dr. Morituri mentioned an adversary in your space-time. An adversary who must be killed."

"I'm working for myself helmet, not Hugo Morituri. Are we coming to Collectibles?"

"At our current phase velocity, we should interfere with Rogers Collectibles now, sir."

Chapter 22

Was this his mind, or the mind of Frank Hogart? Or was it something larger, broader, beyond and encompassed by both? Rogers Collectibles gave up trying to understand, and walked through all the possible worlds. Walking seemed to be what he could do best.

Everything was red. Red light, red clouds streaking across a red sky. A hard red wind. The wide red sky shed a cold mist all over the land. As he walked, the mist became a real rain.

A rain. Rogers had never felt a rain before. The drops drove like long, slanting pellets into his face.

But who was he? Had he even a body? He leaned into the wind and saw that he was following in the steps of a quick moving insect, rambling up the path ahead. Rogers had to hurry to keep pace, no matter if the rainslick slogged up his bare feet.

Lightning flashed. Wild clouds scudded rapidly across the wide sky, forming horrible shapes: elongated faces, vast eyes distending. It was like a painting of Hell in the House of Sighs. Soon a single woman's visage filled up the spherical interior of the atmosphere, covering all the sky with the locks of her brown hair. Her mouth seemed to open, speaking as it flickered. But there was no sound and her words melted into liquid, unintelligible matter, raining black from the sky.

Nifty's attention (for he was now entangled with Rogers) was drawn downwards, into the slime on which he tread.

Ah. The worldlings of the n-scape worked in miniature as well. Little things breeding among themselves. Strange, unfamiliar creatures. Ideas of weird possibilities. Hundreds, thousands of the squirming, wet creatures, little evil faces sliding, screaming under his crushing boots.

Rogers came to a stop at the crest of a small, muddy hill. The rain was pitter-pattering cold around. The insect was regarding him warily, he himself appeared to be a tiny green man.

"No*Rrorgiesrssso*?n?"

They split apart into two, more easily manipulated beings.

"Norrisson," Rogers said. "You look like a gigantic bug."

"You look like a tiny green man. Ten centimeters high. Who's mind are you in?"

"Hogart. Frank P. Hogart."

At the word, the wind shifted suddenly from the south. Nifty gasped as the stench of the surrounding fields came blowing against his face.

He spat into the mud.

"G-d damn. This is disgusting."

"It's Hogart," said Rogers. "He's in a bad way. We're in him now."

"It's shit," Nifty said. "It's shit-land."

"There's shelter that way," Rogers noticed. "Off the road."

As they approached the wooden shelter, it came to Rogers forcefully then, the stench. He had to breathe deeply to keep from vomiting.

"You think this is bad," said the insect. "Wait till we're inside that hut."

"Do you think my book's in there?"

"I don't care. I'm going in because I can save Sylvia."

"It's too late," Rogers said. "Dr. Yang is dead."

It was true. She was dead. Nifty had seen her with his own eyes.

The insect Norrisson scrambled ahead and Rogers followed, realizing that the brown, meat-like mud beneath his feet wasn't soil. It was human excrement.

Inside, the rough wood shelter opened into a wood-walled cave. Their feet slapped on a floor packed thick with regurgitated food, ancient feces and urine rot. The windows gave only a brown and dreary light. It was hard to see much, just a long box in the room's center.

Rogers approached. The lid had opened a crack. Through the roots and mud adhering to the hollow skull, he could make out the long decomposed features of Frank P. Hogart.

"Look."

The insect was pointing across the room. In its far corner, a familiar pink-skinned boy sat cross-legged in the mud. He was engaged in smearing the floor-filth over his soiled loins, his face and lips. Tears were running down his face.

"*Shhhhit...,*" he whispered. "*Shhhiiiit.*"

"Who the hell is that?" Nifty said.

"*What am I becoming?*" the boy moaned. "*Shiiiiiiit.*"

It all suddenly changed. Large ruined arches, with no walls about them, opened onto a pale, rolling meadow-scape, spotted with clumps of ragged weeds. A grey wind blew purple wildflowers bending, growing up and into the old stone piles. The boy clung to the ankles of a head-less woman, naked except for a necklace and ring.

The boy hissed:

"*Kill him now. He sleeps!*"

He extended a hand with two fingers extended.

"*Don't you see what he has done?*"

Indeed, Nifty saw. The shock, the bloody stump of the woman's neck, bounced him backwards into the shit-floored shack. The return of the stench revolted him and he leapt up (he could fly) and hung on the ceiling hard, upside down, above the sleeper's box. Like an insect. Like he knew exactly how an insect could function.

Rogers couldn't believe it. His mind regurgitated.

"Shit," Rogers said. "We have brought our shit from our shit planet to this."

As if in punctuation of the thought, a fat gas bubble blew up from the floor. It popped and sprayed its heavy confetti up the little green man's legs, spoiling his V-suit altogether.

The boy squatted across the room, muttering, smearing his skin with shit.

"Open the box," Nifty called down to Rogers. "Open it!"

"*Shhh, shhh....*" moaned the boy. "*...it.*"

Fear came close to Rogers. Cold fear curling around his knuckles, tightening the skin on his testicles, shooting frozen waves out from the wire of his spine—out through his, far-gone biophysical self. His anus contracted.

He focused on the box. It helped.

It was wood. Unsoiled and regularly clean, the rhomboid construction radiated reason into the shit world. It was reverently conceived, crafted for function alone. It revealed the sham, the non-reality of the shit and the hut, even the insect on the ceiling. Rogers composed himself, looking at it. He took time to admire the handiwork. The carpenter's hand seemed to him neither garish nor lazy. The box was as long as man, and as wide too, at its most expansive point. In fact, Rogers, recognized now what it was. A coffin.

Rogers had never seen such a thing. People had once committed their dead to their deterioration into the earth in wooden rhomboid boxes. The touch of ancient death-religion brought the fear.

He slid back the cover of the old box, half remembering things he should not have been remembering, had in fact never remembered and could not. The memories of other selves. Screaming children. Weeping women. Drunken slaves, whoring masters, mad kings and deluded prophets. Fools bungling a billion chances. Long-groved avenues, trees like he'd never seen. A naked girl running, screaming. Bodies catapulting into incinerating flame. Pyschosexual leaders flattening worlds into the monotonous wash of historical time.

"*Shitttt...*" the boy mumbled, bouncing excitedly on the wet floor. " *Sssshit!*"

In the opened coffin was revealed Hogart himself, no longer decomposed. He lay there quite serene, bearded, younger, eyes closed and dead. His hair was slicked back elegantly off his high brow. A purple cravat curled around his neck, folded into the collar of a black, antique suit.

Enfolded in his hands was the head of Rogers' neuroscop, Sylvia Yang. She gazed up at him with open, lifeless eyes.

From above, the insect shouted. "Stand back!" Rogers stood back.

The bug tore a splintered stake from the roofing. Soft and rotten chips of dank wood fell over Rogers' shoulders. The bug came dropping down. With a six-limbed thrust, it drove the wooden stake deep and directly through the body's buttoned breast.

Hogart's eyes expanded mightily. His mouth fell open, revealing long-stained dagger-like incisors. His tongue rolled out swollen, and his eyeballs turned white up into his head.

Wet clumps of refuse rained down from the brown sky, thudding against the roof, banging on the windows and walls. Thunder clapped raging, preceding the flash of lightening in the black-skied 'scape.

Nifty held on. He pressed his dart home, pierced the black pit, the infinitesimally hard point, grinding, puncturing the tiny muscle of lifestuff. Still the heart resisted, a soft expandable hardness, impenetrable for its malleability.

He drew on all his rage, feeling the space's new center inhere around him.

The old man's whisper: "*Do it....*"

All sound ceased. Rogers saw now that the old man had brought them here, dragged them through time to do it.

And the head in his lap wasn't Sylvia at all.

"Who was it?" Nifty spoke through clenched teeth. "Who killed her?"

"Spare the suitor," Rogers said, remembering the woman-ape's words. "Kill the sonne."

Nifty saw it through a window. The boy was bounding over gleefully over the horizon, carrying a bloody head in each hand.

Still, he pressed the dart home.

There on Hogart's breast, Rogers saw the *Brane World*. Like a thief, he plucked it from the cold and lifeless hands.

Hogart's trunk arched up from the box, mouth and eyes expanding impossibly wide. A thick column of the blackest mud-like substance slid from his straining lips and broke in a falling tower over his chest. A milky white liquid followed, slopping down over his cheeks, the edges of the coffin, washing the stink away, quenching the hissing fire, and sliding out, spreading out over the mud-packed world.

Nifty's chest was pierced with seven arrows. He sat on a cool, fresh-smelling field, up against a great and ancient tree. His death blood was streaming down over his leather armor, down onto the damp rich ground. He couldn't change a thing.

He seemed caught in the solidity of a history that had long preceded his arrival and would occur forever without him. Had he failed?

The whispers of wind in the long blowing leaves gave words to the tree. "*Sylvia's—dying.*"

"PHRED?"

"*—Sylvia's dying. Come.*"

Nifty tried to move, but found that the long arrows had fixed him into the trunk of the tree. The long drooping leaves lifted momentarily in a soft but strong gust, blowing up from the distant, seething sea, gathering energy to blow him through. But he was stuck.

It was too late.

He was entirely off kilter, stuck in the wall of Sylvia's ad-apt.

Unable, therefore, to prevent her death. Doomed to behold it. He had done it; he had travelled in time and remembered now that he would have failed, even so, to save her. Nifty pulled back, away. He was no longer the same Niftus Norrington at all.

He was seated on the v-night beach, still helmeted, entirely alone.

Chapter 23

In Rogers' mind: the image of Martha Dobbs. She was crying, but she didn't know it. She was walking up a wide curving stairway. She was opening the door to a soft white room.

A torus twitched; Martha was gone and again Rogers passed into the open consciousness of Frank P. Hogart. He recognized it at once. The new dimensional perception came shimmering through the revealed flatness of the shit-plane he had been standing on. He was able to step out of it, above it or from it, by way of the hole he himself had opened. He came into a small room—a sane space, erected in the center of an invisible whirlwind. Solid wood walls and a fire crackling and warming the cold. Rogers was already there, staring out of his own eyes. He was seated peacefully beside a man-sized, smoking bug.

Hogart had slumped forward, was now nearly sliding off his chair. Rogers turned to the bug. The multi-eyed head returned his gaze.

"Is he dead?"

"*Death*," blurted the speaker in its crotch. "*He is near it anyway.*"

"And you are really here?"

"*Oh yes. I'm really here. I've decided to offer 2,000 Klugers for zee book.*"

It held the *Brane World* in its feelers.

Rogers turned away. For a long time he watched the monstrous shadows the firelight cast upon the walls, the bubbles boiling out between the periodic tilings of the quasicrystal armature. Cascading, yawning volumes, inverted, in-folded—the pure entropic freedom of their dance. There was no such freedom for Rogers Collectibles.

His movements were tied to the lives of other bodies depending on his proper, remembered dimensionality.

He hadn't asked for this. Any of it. He wouldn't have had to put so much stock in the damn book to begin with, were it not for the increasing burdens on private enterprise. He'd been put up against a wall. He was anything but free.

The insect man's long legs made a criss-crossed, double-triangle of darkness against the shimmering orange.

"Are you really as you appear to me?" Rogers asked quietly, with a sudden hope. "A huge talking bug? Can't you just be Norrisson?"

"*Are you really as you appear to me? An obsolete enterprise personified by an ape husk? Come....*" 13th Zoreckian, with a curious rotating motion, rose up on its two lowest legs. "*To business. I dislike being so relatively large.*"

Pulling his hat tight to his head, Rogers followed the bug over old, creaking floors and past dark, gas-lit walls. Through corridors leading to other corridors, to doors, to more corridors, to stairwells. They followed folds in dimensions he'd never perceived before but were now quite visible to him.

The journey took all of a Venusian minute. They stood in another, more stable room. A table and two chairs sat comfortably in the ruddy dimness. They sat down.

"*It is better where his mind can not hear us.*"

"I want 2,500 K."

"*I have deposited 3,000 Klugers in your continuum's account.*"

"Really?"

"*Yes.*"

The insect placed the book on the table. Rogers opened it.

"How do I know you're telling the truth? My watch is out of range of the colony and I won't be able to reach the bank till morning."

"*I vill vait till tomorrow. You vill give me the book then.*"

"OK," Rogers said. "But it's not registered. And it won't be."

"*No matter.*"

They sat for some time in silence.

The bug looked away. Its many eyes focused on nothing through the monocle on its horn. It absent-mindedly vomited a grey liquid onto its feelers and rubbed the stink into its fur.

"*There is a problem?*"

Something was wrong, but Rogers couldn't place it. He closed his eyes.

"Look. I'm tired. I'll take the book home with me. I want the money before I turn it over. Let's say 5 o'clock."

"*Where?*"

Rogers thought of the hellish shapes of the n-scape, of the woman's face filling up the sky. "At the House of Sighs," he said.

But the evening wasn't over. As Rogers drifted towards sleep, 13th Zoreckian drummed its warm, wet feelers on his forehead, telling him far more than he'd ever wanted to know.

"...Mr. Rogers Collectibles... your kind... astonished us. Not so many days ago, you were a once promising species of ape alchemists that had gone bad. We assumed your planet would put you down like the lizards who once ruled the Terran surface. You were able like them, perhaps, to reach your moon, but not to manage multi-dimensional penetration between alternates any time soon. Earth and Venus are entangled in every dimensional variation of this system. We like to keep all the Venuses available, for we are usually able to make quiet and easy worlds of them. We saw your machines approach this one and we arranged, as is our way, a vision of a hostile, impossible world to greet them. Your mono-optics and robotic probes were laughably easy to deceive. We turned your attention elsewhere, to bodies far distant and, in truth, far more hostile to human life. Mars, for instance, and the Saturnites, colonies which proved such a waste and whose attempted settling helped bring your civilization to its mandibles. In our neighborhood, only the Borstal at Mercury Station was permitted. You were harmless beings, so weak that we could squash you if need be whenever we so chose, but an amusing result of unspoiled evolution and thus worthy enough to be allowed a fleeting existence. *Now I see that in our condescension we allowed you great freedom. We believed there was nothing we did not see. But all senses are prisons and we were as relatively blind as you.* The system's Terran apes would surely self-destruct, leaving our superior forms to sail the wide fields and garden the flower gods in peace. It was only necessary to let the times blow of their own accord. Imagine the moment, unforeseen, when we were proved wrong! The terrible, incontrovertible fact! A small delegation of Terran life-forms passed on an asteroid close to Venus, and one could, in his state of mind, see through the walls of his senses. Before we were able to interfere, he'd managed to cement his new knowledge by analog wave to another. What could we do? There was no stable tradition, no programmed function to handle the anomaly. *Nothing in history could prepare us for this moment. No such contact was written* in any of the leaves of the pasts. We abandoned our Venus altogether to your history, through a crack in the air to another safer system. Soon Venusia appeared. Creatures were wandering like us, between the winds, but with terrible and dangerous ignorance of their situation."

"Please, I'm too tired to follow. What does it all matter?"

"It was only after much thought that we began to understand the shocking truth. As hive-historian, I myself was ordered to look into your species' past to explain our failure to predict your arrival. Like yourself, Mr. Collectibles, I enjoy this sort of work: the collecting and mapping, the harvesting of the sweet nectar of time's sexual organs. I immersed myself in your history. But it was to discover the secret of my own history, the contested origin of the twenty-two. Our presence in so many time-variants had made it impossible to trace our history to its beginnings and determine in which we might have first arose. What did it matter? We had always assumed a Venus, of course. There were many traditions suggesting it was this group, your own, where our home lay. Certain microbial creatures in the clouds, for instance, in this system possessed genetics similar to ours. It occurred to me that an explanation of your phenomenon might include your specific relation to insect-life. The fact that, apparently, with your technology advanced to a type 1 state, you didn't need them any more at all.

"Plants were engineered and science advanced enough so as to make insect life unnecessary. Pollination and atmospheric production were left to your machines. "

"I'm sleeping."

"Eureka! Your relative hairlessness had left you with a fondness for silk, Mr. Rogers. One enterprising colonist brought with him a case of live Terran silk worms. Yes, twenty-two escaped. *A tribe of twenty-two silk-worms, Mr. Rogers, escaped captivity. They came upon some native mushrooms and the rest, as they say, is history.* Through an opening of the systems' streams, they encountered the native cloud bugs of Venus and joined DNA to dine on Venusian fauna and survive millennia beyond your own extinction. They re-designed their hairy husks and quantum minds to radically improve digestive and reproductive systems, to inhabit and exploit the cracks between alternate system histories. *We grew, spread our garden, laying many eggs to the queen far in spacetime.*"

"And that's it? That's your story?"

"From your perspective, of course, all this has not yet happened. But you are, in fact, my creator, Mr. Rogers, as I am yours. *Melton's wandering brought us from our planet to the glory which makes the plants sing. It is with your minds that we first conquered our physics, as it was we with other life forms who created your world for you and no g-d in your own image at all to encourage your growth. We earthlings are all the same life-time-form, brother Collectibles. You are our legs and we are your hearts and minds.* The great anal horn of the world-worm presses all its feces forward. We may not meet again, which is why I have gone to such lengths to explain these matters tonight. The Green Man has enveloped us in his circle—implicated us in his adolescent ape fantasy. Our future may never occur. Sailing with Cook to Tahiti, dining on human flesh; kneeling with Ortock in New Los Angeles, unleashing disease, weapons and psychosexual disorder, the Green Man seeks to ruin all the shared Terran streams. It is certain, Mr. Collectibles, now I see that one of my kind, was meant to make contact, to draw our histories down to one specific position on the game-board. To parlay and make a deal, force him to encounter our possible survivals. *The Queen remains ambivalent to such matters. Does this not give us hope?* The minutes are numbered and a 14th Zoreckian approaches from unseen reaches. I and you, Mr. Rogers. We have made together a kind of flower out of the dimensional intersection of our conversation, a parallax realometer of a better present. This conversation, this joining of mind-stream is witnessed here as dream, but tomorrow, when we meet, in your Venusia—then we shall make real our arrangement. The Green Man will be exposed."

And the bug took Rogers with miraculous gentleness in its hard and hairy arms. It carried him, cradled, through hallways, trapdoors, vine-ladders and trees—to his adapt. As it was laying him gently in his little home, tucking him in beneath the fluff, its words melted away. "All I want," Rogers heard himself muttering, "is to sell my book."

It remains a matter of some controversy as to whether or not humans sleep, as a plant or insect can sleep. The 22 of the Great Leaf, for instance, can be found motionless most V-days, first legs fastened safely around the trunk of a particular branch of the Great Tree, four remaining legs tightly reversed to pin their eight folded wings behind. Knowing the general shapes of future and past, they dangle there, in the universe, richly engaged in active lucidity for years on end, only stopping once a century to feed and congress. A human's dreams, on the other hand, disrupt true sleep, reflecting it with a never-ceasing wakened consciousness. They prove, most nights, more exhausting than refreshing.

Was Zoreckian a dream? Rogers Collectibles didn't think so. His life may well have been collapsing all around him, but for the first time in some t-days (his book held tight beside him) he stopped dreaming. He slept a deep and rewarding sleep.

The end, at least, was coming.

Chapter 24

A hollow, metallic exhalation. Venusia's seven copper-bulbed towers crackled in the blue-haired dawn. The clouds slipped apart,
rising like startled ghosts. The planet had turned from the sun, and
the ignited ionosphere illumined the local sky a ghostly blue. All
through the colony, neon lights and day-lamps gave the t-day the
feel of an eternal afternoon. A cold utopian beauty, perhaps, but it
was a less substantial Venusia. Still, the same rhythmic movements
began to flicker into mechanical life. The usual offices, businesses
and culture-complexes opened windows and doors. The same
transportation systems ignited; the irrigation systems sputtered and
sprayed.

What was new was the wind.

The plants had raised the wind. Down along the beach, up in
city center, out along the boulevards and public gardens, they were
whipping up a great commotion. Vast reefs of leaves shook in fran-
tic exchange. Trunks creaked and bent. Flowers prematurely
bloomed. It amounted to an extraordinary expenditure of energy so
early in the V-night and a wind was raised for easier communication. There was great excitement in the vegetative community,
much debate and confusion. Since the crossing, there had never
been such wild exchange.

But Martha Dobbs was safely indoors. Johanna was gone.
Miles slept soundly on the bed. Martha fixed herself in the mirror,
making up the bruise on her throat, lining her lips with lime. She
darkened her eyes with mascara. She would make an image of herself, a sort of mask of Martha Dobbs with which to move through
the colony.

Jorx Crittendon sought to be the only self. He saw all others as holograms—meaningless shades flickering about a colony's stage. Things were certainly beginning to suggest he was right. The neuroscape—that secret, close world that seemed to have swallowed her friends away—was sucking reality from the outer Venusia altogether. If Venusians were to make any claim on their own lives, the Princeps would have to be forced to acknowledge the reality of Venusia.

There were several extravagant silk robes in Johanna's dresser, but Martha Dobbs opted for the simpler shawl the leader had given her yester-t-day. She looked plain in it, she thought. Real.

When she opened the door to the hallway, she wasn't surprised to find two g-ops waiting in the hall. They scurried to attention.

She spoke calmly, choosing a tone of command.

"I'm going outside."

"We'll be coming along. We have orders to escort you."

"Where?"

"Wherever you choose to go, ma'am."

"Do as you like."

A familiar silver orb floated out eagerly blinking red behind them.

"You can come too," she told the Iye. "But don't feed until I tell you."

She led her escort over lush, carpeted floors, down the wide tower stairway and out into the empty porticos of the Castle's inner courtyard.

When Martha Dobbs passed out onto the cold-lit streets of Venusia, the wind blew her hair, and flapped her shawl around her shoulders. She had never felt a wind like it and the wildness of it gave her strength. Litter was lifted off the streets to turn in spirals in the air. Naked teens ran wild and green, unattended and free. The glare of the day-lights brought out a yellow decay that had its own strange beauty. It was real enough.

"I need a moment alone," she told her guard.

The g-ops waited outside with the Iye, as she entered a mechanical juice bar. Martha ordered a mango. It was time to initiate the end.

She ponged Rogers Collectibles.

He'd been asleep and looked about as bad as Larry after she'd shot him. Dark blotches spotted up his face. His eyes were blood-red. But he was alive, and real enough, even on her small watch-stage.

"Martha," he said. "Martha Dobbs."

"Yes."

He looked at her. "What happened to you?"

She ignored this. "Did you find your book?"

"Yes. I'm meeting a buyer today."

"Where? When?"

"Five o'clock at the House of Sighs."

The House of Sighs. A fitting location for a climactic scene. "It might be something I'd like to film," Martha said, hoping she wouldn't have to explain too much over pong. "Would it be all right if I came along?"

"Yes. I think so, anyway." He looked at her. "I think the whole thing's coming to an end."

"I hope so," Martha whispered, her heart pounding. "I'll see you there, then."

"Listen. Would you—"

"Good-bye." She ponged off.

She finished her mango juice and exited the bar.

"Hey!" one of the g-ops called, running up beside her. "Not so fast."

"We're going to the House of Sighs," said Martha Dobbs. "Call it in. Tell Jorx. The House of Sighs at 5 o'clock."

Her Iye followed along. Somehow, its dedication comforted her. It helped confirm that things could still be as they seemed.

There were more people out than she'd expected. They were restless, like the winds. They walked and talked; argued, exchanged goods. There was an expectancy in the air.

Venusia in the real.

She called back to the Iye. "Start feeding now."

The Iye closed the distance between them by a half, winking greedily green. She picked out a large pair of dark glasses at a stall. They helped do away with the day-light glare, polarizing her vision so it seemed like the sun was shining. But night was already cold and in this wild wind, Martha wished she'd wrapped herself in one of Joanna Zeep's fur-lined robes and not this functional shawl.

More g-ops appeared, as if from nowhere. They moved in a diamond formation around her, clearing a quiet escort through the crowd. So many people. Through her mirrored shades, Martha Dobbs made sure to lock gazes with individuals as Jorx Crittendon had done with her. And so the knowledge of her presence spread unspoken among them. Undirected and without intention, they followed her, watched her moves.

When Martha turned off Beach Ave. and came to a halt, the museum visible in the distance, she stood in a thicket of focused brainwaves.

The House of Sighs looked like a tiny scale model of itself. She could see that a conglomeration of g-ops already bristled black on the volcanic stone of its steps. Apparently Larry had gotten the message that she was coming, for a number of flying Iyes had congregated to fix the place for a show. But she had an intuition that Larry's broadcast would not proceed as planned.

Motionless, she had the odd feeling that someone was approaching her at a fantastic speed. The guards had continued walking, leaving her temporarily outside their zone of control. Martha glimpsed herself from a distant point-of-view—moving so fast that it twisted the molecules of the air into a chute around it.

A little voice rang out: "Martha Dobbs."

Faces were strange, flickering, as if between moments. She turned to look at the child across the way, the little flower-urchin abandoned by all the world.

"Martha Dobbs!"

It was rare to see a child so young. The girl's enormous eyes, round as K coins, gazed as if she were seeing right through her skin.

"What is it?" Martha Dobbs was confused. Something was coming, perceivable just over the child's shoulder. A figure growing, approaching at an astonishing speed. From the vanishing point of the razor-straight boulevard—from far beyond the House of Sighs—the form expanded on a vector directly into Martha's face.

A shout boomed out from the multitudes: "*Ho! Johnny Ho!*"

She was taken.

Taken over, by and into a speeding, incontrovertible mass. A thing of sinew and pure will—a hard-jawed, glistening male. As she shot (cradled in his strong arms) out and away from the scene, the little girl's blank eyes remained before her. It was as if they knew pure time in all its force-blowing power. The city dwindled, then collapsed into a tiny little smudge on the horizon. Martha and the mass that was moving her inhered into a single motionless relation.

Could she be so wholly taken up and out of responsibility for her self? What else could she do? Martha Dobbs gave in, suddenly grateful. She curled tightly up into Johnny Ho's hairy arms. The science-hero of the V's ran as animal man was meant to run, bounding far, ranging through the oxygen, manipulating the gentle-pulling gravity like a god. She was like a child in his arms.

Chapter 25

Oa is our mother, the Terran Sea. As a tree has roots, trunk and leaves, Oa has the rock, the ground and the atmosphere. The ground has the insect, the animal and the plant, though in different times they have had different signs attached to them. These stand for the love of life on land, the love of self on land and the love of light on land. Each being what it is, it cannot be surmounted or analyzed; yet each bears all the others latent within it. Such are but signs of Oa's will. When the walls between the signs dissolve it is revealed that all information is but water.

The plants were not stupid. It was long understood that the relative benignity of Oa depended on the rejected possibilities of other life forms, other mathematics. Ancient and eldritch signs thirsted to rewrite the system in the image of their own perverse, self-devouring prophecy—glistening with the bloody meat of broken life. To survive her own destruction, to seed off Terra itself, Oa had shot herself to Venus. The effort had depended on the engines of the wild quantum. The Crittendon regime had manipulated this force so that now Oa herself, the stability of her relativity, might well be sucked away through a hole in boiled space.

PHRED now understood why it had not been contacted by the Senate. Its time, like the time of the insurrection itself, was self-generating, the last spontaneous pulse of a dwindling life. PHRED's survival and the survival of its humans would stand in now for the survival of Oa herself.

And, strangely enough, PHRED had survived. It hadn't yet pieced together exactly what had happened since its entanglement with the humans in the Station 5 holding cell. Sylvia Yang had died, the gravity of her passing still pulled on its tender leaves. The death of Sylvia and Ae, however, ensured Ruby Greene's survival. For the Green Man mistook the daughter for the mother. So the gates between the n-scape and its possible realities were still open. The Green Man wasn't worried, however. He had etched his possibilities through the depths of historical memory, and the time was at hand for his conquest of the real. But as that moment approached, oddities would abound—miracles would occur, miracles of an order the Green Man's mind might not quite comprehend.

There were now, for instance, two Niftus Norringtons in the world. There was the ordinary ornery one, presumably ranging through Venusia with revenge on his mind. And there was the other one. The one that PHRED had called back from the future. Like a clone grown from a sprout torn from an original stem, this new Norrington sprang lustily to life—though too late to save Sylvia Yang. This new Nifty Norrington now strode with long steps along the edge of the sea. He was fully grown and starting to appreciate the difference. This Niftus Norrington felt as if he could crush the whole world. And it was he to whom the plant's fate was now entrusted. He held PHRED's defunct crystal armature in a coconut bag.

The plant had been on its shelf in Dr. Yang's office when the new Norrington had let himself out of the ad-apt across Cherry Tree Lane. Its window was open. Attaching a simple idea to a glint from a day-light, the plant drew itself to the Norrington's attention. It happened that this new Niftus Norrington was tall enough to reach inside.

The plant wasn't communicating. It was barely alive. Its water was gone and no provisions had been made for its night-lighting. Norrington saw the crack running down the surface of its crystal armature. He remembered that the plant had helped him in the past and figured it might help him in the future. There was revenge to be written into history. He had no helmet now. If the crime was to be punished (the foul, despicable crime) the plant would be worth fixing up.

Norrington was fully grown. Power surged through his new long legs, his ample arms. He could move individual fingers, take great steps, roll his big eyes. He could sit down on the wet sand. He could shout as loud as a great ape was meant to shout; he could run fast and light, perform feats and stunts. In the low gravity of Venus, he could leap five meters into the air.

And no one paid him the slightest mind. No one snickered or noticed him at all.

"Hoo! Hoo!" Norrington yelled, scaring a couple of girls up and off their blankets. "I'm a ghost!"

"We see you! We see you!" They laughed and laughed, scurrying away over the sloping dunes. He was real enough.

Real and ready to act. Norrington calmed himself, allowed his customary cynicism to cloak his feelings. He was new, or different anyway, but he was still Niftus Norrington. There was work to do, important and bloody work.

He had to get back under the world. It was like a toy beneath how tall he felt. He walked west along the beach, among hucksters and addicts and queens. His destination was Arturo's: a small bar and restaurant where you could sit under the shade of an awning, sip a brightly colored kewl and keep relatively clear of surveillance. Pickled flowers were chilled on the premises and pretty girls in rubber monobands served decent fare. No matter how small you were, you got served.

The regime allowed places like Arturo's to exist as convenient connections to underground networks. If he'd wanted to, for instance, Nifty could have made a pretty penny today selling the needle-pistol he'd stolen from the dead g-ops in Sylvia Yang's ad-apt. But that wasn't why he came. The cook loved plants. She worshipped them. In fact, as he had learned on the investigation that first took him to Arturo's, she grew experimental strains illegally.

By the time the new Norrington had taken a table and ordered a meal, his "new" feeling had left him. Now that he wasn't a freak, the waitress had given him the little eye, making sure to swing her behind around when she walked back to the bar. In ordinary circumstances Nifty wouldn't have thought twice about smacking her real hard on those buttocks of hers. But his new size made the idea seem somehow sick, less amusing.

When she glanced back and smiled, the new Norrington growled. He took a bite of his cucumber sandwich. His huge teeth clamped down on his fat tongue. The pain opened up gulfs of despair. He was so *small*. Norrington felt his big face tightening. He tried not to think of the deep furrow that now bisected the horizontals of his broad forehead, the mark of Sylvia Yang. Fat tears burned, trickling down his new dumb face. He made fists, big square fists.

He wanted to open his new mouth wide and drink up Ishtar Ocean like Hautboy. He wanted to stick the restaurant's silver knife into his own golf-ball eye, jam it up into his brain.

But the manager had come out; she was looking at him with dangerous curiosity. Norrington very quietly laid the knife on the table.

"I was told you know something about plants," he said.

"I know nothing."

"I have a very interesting plant here with me. It's in trouble. I thought maybe you could help it."

She was greying all around the edges. She'd forgone anti-aging therapy of all sorts. A radical. But she had a simple heart and she doted over the plant when he showed it to her. She took it out back. She held it up to her growth lights, apologizing for things she hadn't even done to it, speaking to it as if she were addressing a nitwit or child. "Poor baby," she said. "Poor lil thing. I'm glad you found me."

That was a good one. The plant found her. Norrington was back at a table smoking an LP, waiting, when something pulled on his robe.

It was a little girl in a pink smock. She was probably near the size he was before he'd come back in time. He smiled, liking her immediately. She looked curious and strong, but her eyes were troubled and she squinted painfully as she looked up at him.

"What is it, kid?"

"You're the one," she said, matter-of-factly.

"I'm only the half," he said. "There's another of me walking around."

She laughed. "What will happen to you if you meet him?"

"I'll beat him. Shouldn't be much trouble. Though he probably thinks he's my better half, he's a midget. A dwarf. Not much bigger than you."

"I can't see him," the girl said. "I can see you. I've never seen anyone before."

He didn't answer. There was something disturbing about the way her eyes squinted up at him. Like she was blind. But she hid away under the table beside him just as the old woman returned.

The manager presented PHRED, done up in a new organic plastic armature.

"What happened to the crystal?"

"It cracked. I will keep the pieces as payment, since I'm not charging you for the work. There's the risk to consider. You know it's illegal to care for sentients privately. We've been visited by the police before." She looked at him. "M-op's and the like."

"Is it going to live?"

"It's very strong. This armature has illuminators. The plant should make consciousness any time."

"You there?" Norrington asked, holding it out before him. The plant didn't answer.

"I see you've made a friend," the woman said, peeking under the table.

The girl held on to Norrington's robe.

"She must have been born illegally," the woman said. "She's a mistake, entirely blind. She was never properly grown or educated.

She shouldn't exist at all."

"Yeah? Well why don't you keep it to yourself?" Norrington said, rising to leave. "Maybe she doesn't like being reminded every day that she's a freak."

"Hey Mister!"

The little blind girl had followed him out. She pulled on his leg.

Norrington stopped and knelt down.

"What is it?"

"Take me with you."

"Listen kid," he said. "Where I'm going there's not much room for pretty little girls. You get me? Here's ten K. Get yourself an ice or a mango or something. And stay indoors at V-night. Don't come following strangers outside."

She bit her lip.

"The flowers speak to me," she said. "They are my friends."

"Let me tell you something, kid. Don't get involved with plants."

"But they're my friends."

"They're out for their own kicks, not yours."

She had her little head lifted, a snotty, pouted-up expression on her face.

"What's that around your neck?"

Norrington frowned. He'd forgotten it. He took off the necklace and held the stone up to the light. It was darkened brown by the dried blood of Sylvia Yang. "You can see this?"

"It has a memory like water," she said strangely. "But is more focused and precise. It shines."

It wouldn't do to be caught with such a thing, unregistered. Earth crystals were strictly illegal. Norrington placed the little thing in the plant's new armature, where it virtually disappeared, indistinguishable from the little brown balls inside.

"The plants said that you will love me, Mister. That you'll take me with you when you go. You must take me."

"*Take her—*" The sentence shimmered through his brain like a broadcast. Norrington forgot himself and lifted the plant's new armature high, intending to smash it against the ground.

"Please, Mister."

He tossed it to the girl. "OK," he said. "You can carry the plant."

Nifty Norrington, the little one, the original, awoke under the electrolit, blue-green sky. He sat up on the beach, remembering the priestess, his journeys. A pong was flashing on his helmet. A sudden desperate hope flamed in his heart; a weird smile spooked up his mouth. *A certainty.*

But it was Collectibles. The return to reality hit him hard.

Rogers looked out into the Iye. "Where are you?"

It came back to Nifty. Feces falling fat through the 'scape. Jamming the stake into the old man's tough heart—his great life-will blowing Nifty between the worlds. Sylvia. The green boy running through the fields had carried her head away.

"Say something," Rogers said.

He thought of Morituri and the mushroom. Yes, he now understood so much more about what had been happening. "Jorx Crittendon killed Sylvia," Nifty said. "It wasn't Hogart. Jorx used her to pull Ruby Greene out of myth and kill her as well. He needs the n-scape clear of other gods."

"He made a mistake," Rogers said. "It wasn't Ruby Greene. It was her daughter, Ae. He hasn't finished. It's not over. Until it is, we won't be real. None of us will. It's what Jorx wants, to erase us—make us nothing. I'm meeting a friend in an hour at the House of Sighs. I'm going to sell him the book. And the book, the transaction, will draw out Ruby Greene. Jorx will be there to meet her, I'm certain."

"This friend of yours. It's Hogart, is it?"

Rogers looked at him. "No," he said. "Hogart's dead. It's a giant Venusian insect. 13th Zoreckian of the Great Leaf. Please don't ask me to explain."

Nifty ponged off. The gun the priestess had given him lay cold against his thigh. He disassembled it for pak. He was done now with words. He didn't need Ruby Greene to come out from the past. He was going to take down the Princeps himself.

The old, weather-beaten ad-apt looked the same when Rogers Collectibles woke that morning. The scattered inventory had not yet regressed into refuse around him. No sudden fear grabbed him, no hallways or lizards. No talking plants. His body felt organic and healthy. He lit an LP and walked calmly to the indiv safe. He blew gently on the grid.

The book was really there.

Rogers called his Kreditbank. He found that the bug hadn't lied. Three thousand K had been deposited in his account.

So. The book, by rights, was no longer his. Rogers had enjoyed being its owner. The thought that he would finally lose his claim on the object depressed him. Exactly what had he hoped to gain from the sale of this book? Surely, if nothing else, the chance to own such a thing to begin with. Like Jorx had written so long ago: *the way is the goal.* To be able to read it at one's leisure, without relinquishing control. To have the freedom to make whatever he chose of the thing, whenever he chose to. He was giving it all up for a handful of Klugers.

BRANE WORLD
A Stay in the Paphos Loop

is one grand lie.

Rogers looked at the frontispiece for some time. He realized that he now recognized the hand that had written the small pen-ciled note under the title. It was the same hand that had signed his *Reflections.* Jorx Crittendon's. He remembered the Princeps had told him he'd owned the book long ago.

He frowned. The note below it, the "*but a good one*" was now gone. He looked closely, but there were no signs that it had been erased. It was as if the sentence had yet to be written.

"One Grand lie." Jorx Crittendon, it seemed, would like to believe so. As long as Ruby Greene and Melton occupied the neuroscopic foundations of Venusia, he would have no power over its unconscious mind. From Jorx's point of view, it might well be that all Venusia was a lie. Some of the things the insect said came suddenly back to Rogers as he held the book in his hands. Alternate Venuses; parallel universes accessed by the passages through the n-scape. In such a perceived multiverse, what role was played by a book? How many particular copies of this text, for instance, stretched out of the n-scape to pin down the possible world?

"A good one." He liked that answer and wished he'd written it himself. It hadn't been his hand, though, he knew. It didn't have an insect quality about it, either. It had to have been written by a human. The humor of it, the sentiment, was human. Maybe there would be a future after all. Maybe the book would be read as a whole someday, and appreciated.

Rogers glanced again at Ruby's text.

> The last I saw him, Melton was banging on the hatch door, coming through loud and clear on our channel.
>
> "I'm cast away," he cried. "Ruby!"
>
> Through the port-hole I saw Paphos fall into space. Just like that he was gone from me.
>
> "Ruby!" I could still hear him.
>
> But we were apart forever. Forever and ever.

Rogers closed the cover. A lie, but a damn good one. A sad story. There wouldn't be time to read it all. As an enterprise Rogers Collectibles was nearing its end. He would be a rich man now. He planned to convert the capital into land—if it was still possible to buy it. He'd start a new business, even more against the flow of the usual. Perhaps he'd go into writing himself. Build a house with room enough for Martha Dobbs as well, when and if she needed to come.

It was already near 5. The insect would be waiting. Rogers fixed the book safely inside his anti-matter pak and collected his things. He fixed his hat tightly to his head. As a token of celebration, he selected a red tie.

Then he saw the boy.

Chapter 26

The boy he'd seen kneeling on the floor of shit-land, but real now, actually before him—was reading *Brane World.*

> Scientists on the fringes had been questioning the relation between hallucination and reality since Socrates. Some had gone so far as to suggest that the bizarre visions of schizophrenics indicated minds capable of viewing parallel, or alternate universes. Many a child's tale had played narrative games with the very possibility that a man such as myself, castaway in outer space, might also cross between worlds. I read such tales as a boy. They had influenced my own mental growth.
>
> Had my plants talked to me? Perhaps I only hallucinated the communications. On Paphos, I found, if you looked at things closely enough, both assumptions were true. My plant simply ordered my mind to speak to me as the plant to begin with—to imagine it imagining me *etc.*...

Rogers now understood. The words were flowing between them. The boy's mind was drawing him into his world.

> ...So it was that when I had first seen Venusia in my mind's eye, spinning at the center of my infinitely swirling perceptual apparatus, when she drew me to her mystic clouds—I resolved to cut my new kingdom of dreams into the scapes of rationality itself. If I could bend all the powers of heaven

and earth, overcome the huge, sluggish tides of human history as they sought to swallow me whole, it would be necessary to force other perspectives to join my mind, to see it with me. I vowed to raise a veritable army.

The boy hadn't looked up to see him. But Rogers had been inside of his mind, attached to a picture that had grown there. Since the n-scape had entered Rogers' life, his life's patterns had been like shadows cast on the lit wall of a dark, eternal cave. He had learned to shape the shadows, to change their color and suggestion—but he was still trapped in darkness. Were these cave walls simply the mental constructions of an idle boy? He certainly hoped not. He drew himself down to his own Venusia.

He had came to a stop just off the beach, some four blocks from the House of Sighs. He hadn't even noticed he'd been walking.

He remembered there was a back door to the museum. It led to a short hallway that opened to the end of the front lobby. Whether the door would open for him, he couldn't say. It was worth a try, because it might be best to attract as little attention as possible. The insect could cause a commotion. He wished he hadn't told Martha Dobbs to come with her Iye. She could well be put in danger.

He wondered if the insect expected him to show up at all. There were enough Klugers in his account to retire already, to take Martha anywhere he pleased. Why not keep the book? It was the crown of his collection and surely a gigantic bug had no rights by law.

Across the street, he saw that the boy had sat up on his bed and was now staring at him.

Who was dreaming? They were so close together, he and the boy. But so infinitely far as well.

"Quentin? Honey? Is that really you?"

His hair stood on end at the sound of her long forgotten voice.

"Guendin?"

That voice. His name.

He turned.

Popsuckle in hand, she looked at him, aghast. Her long jaw hung open. Her forked tongue danced with excitement.

"Guendin." Tears glittered in her little black eyes. Her z-robe fell loose to reveal voluptuous, human curves.

The boy was still staring. He alone of all the people passing could see what Rogers beheld.

He wished nobody saw. He himself was like a boy. He was embarrassed by his physical reaction. The falseness of this Martha was matched by the reality of his erection. He could see the color rising in her long lizard cheeks. She too was embarrassed. Her soft skin glowed as she came close to him, not sure what to do with the popsuckle in her claw.

"I'b doe dorry," she said. "I left you."

Like a puppet, a hollow man, Rogers removed his hat. "Don't be."

She said: "I'be been beaning to gome back. I haben'd been daking gare of dings...."

"It's only natural," Rogers said. Their faces came closer. Her dark eyes warmed, looking directly into his own. Their noses touched up against one another.

"You're a machine," Rogers said. "In my mind. A tiny thing. A computer."

"Oh Guendin, I'm so solly."

Behind her, he saw two white-haired, black-clad g-ops approaching. They were hurrying in his direction, raising weapons. But Rogers couldn't move. He felt Martha's scaly hand undoing his suit.

"Oh Guendin," she whispered, as her tongue flickered warm and dry against his lips. "Id's been so long."

His suit came undone. He found himself pressing her against a wall. He couldn't escape himself. Her legs clamped around him and he found his pelvis pumping against her. As he thrust, a network of ladder-tubes opened around him, weaving out in various directions.

One passed up through the sky, others wormed into the soil below his feet; still others stretched horizontally out past the boy, over Ishtar and pierced the horizon. An omnipresent architecture of avenues to countless possible worlds.

Moving through this armature, Rogers was able to carry himself away from the Martha. Planes wrapped oddly around, and he emerged in mid-air in the center of the boy's small, familiar, old-fashioned room. Below, the boy had aged. He was sprawled on a mattress. Brightly colored books were scattered around the room, covers illustrated with rockets, surreal planetscapes and bodacious women. A plate of half-eaten cake sat atop an open pornographic magazine. A primitive blue-screened V flickered from a table. On its screen two people were kissing voluptuously. Rogers looked closer and saw that one was a large green man and the other, a version of the boy on the bed.

The boy stared at him, wide-eyed, frozen in shock. Rogers, who had no wish to frighten anyone, said nothing. He followed a ladder tube through the cover of one of the books on the bedside table, hearing a voice from beyond the door.

"*Boy!*"

It was a voice that could rip up a world.

Rogers stood atop a frozen mesa on a purple-crusted ice-moon. It was another world altogether, perhaps a Saturnite. A blue gas giant took up half of the sky. Its reflected light cast orange shadows on the ice. Rogers gazed down onto an impossibly small and uniform horizon.

Below his feet the thick ice-floor—a rough and hoary blue—cracked. Rogers felt the tremors echo through his feet, but heard no sound. The environment contained no atmosphere at all.

The ice cracked again; something living, something ancient, was trying to break through.

"Why don't you come back?" said the boy, looking down at him through the flat sky. "Come out of the book and talk."

"I don't believe in you," Rogers said.

He returned to Venusia. He was seated in the stall of a small public harness-chamber. He could move his limbs himself.

The lizard Martha was gone. Rogers wiped himself of her wetness and stepped out of the harness. He fixed his suit. He placed his hat on his head as the mirror by the sink spoke in a quiet, female whisper:

"*Princeps Crittendon welcomes you to the House of Sighs, sir. Please remember to wash thoroughly.*"

"What time is it?"

"*Just five, sir.*"

Rogers lit an LP and composed himself. Well, he was apparently inside. The bug would be waiting. He hoped reality would hold together long enough for them to make the deal.

For a single motionless moment, Johnny Ho had held Martha Dobbs against his rocky chest. But she stood free now beside him. As if just catching up to them, a strange building came into focus before her. It was white, its edges curled like a living thing, and it surrounded a great dome of steel. They were outside the city, farther out than she'd ever been. Out below the volcano crest, near the ancient lava fields, where there were no day-lights at all. The sky was darker, higher. She could hear a river gurgling close by. She smelled sour gases bubbling from the tar pits as they warmed the cool long-night air. "I've never seen this place," she said.

A single bead of sweat dropped down the chiseled cheek of her square-jawed companion. It was the only sign of his previous exertion.

"It's my home," he said.

"I always thought you were a hologram. That you weren't really real."

Only then did the violence of the original impact come upon her. She staggered. She felt a sudden outrage all along her left side and fell to her knees.

"What is this?" she mumbled. "What have you done? I have an important appointment at 5."

"You have a more important appointment. Come."

He didn't offer a hand. Martha followed him through a creaking entrance in the dome's side, into a small, cement-floored vestibule. At its end was a small green door.

She continued to protest. "You can't just bear somebody away. No matter how weak and defenseless they may be. Is this some kind of rape?"

Johnny Ho turned to her, his face red. "Don't be ridiculous," he said. "I have no designs on you. *She* said to bring you here. I did it for *her*."

"Who?"

Ho lowered his voice and looked away. "Johanna."

"Johanna? Is Johanna here?"

"Yes," he said. "She's in the living quarters. And expecting us sixty-five t-seconds ago."

He opened the green door.

Martha stopped just inside the great room. The dome smelled of cold stone but its air had the fresh taste of night. The high ceiling curved up to a point in its center, poking a gentle, vertical thrust into the arching sphere. A perfect band had been cut down the dome's far edge, open to the night. Without it, the structure could not have contained the great rod that extended out through the opening.

The enormous cylindrical shaft bristled with valves and instrumentation. Martha's gaze followed its hard line into the night-time sky. It aimed directly at a familiar twinkling star.

"Venusia's telescope," said Johnny Ho, his gruff voice echoing in the wide room. "An old-style reflector, using double holo-mirrors. It was built long ago—in Melton's day. Morituri, whose laboratory was below ground here, himself oversaw the construction. These days no one remembers this telescope exists at all. Except for me, of course. I keep it going. Ms. Dobbs. When I look through..." Ho gestured at the great rod. "I understand, at least, what I am not."

"What aren't you?" asked Martha Dobbs. "Real?"

Pain visibly shivered in Johnny Ho's hard jaw.

Martha said nothing.

"Johanna's up there." He gestured to the iron staircase curving up and around the perimeter of the great room. At its top she saw a closed yellow door.

"I need to attend to the gardening," Johnny Ho said. And with that, he left her.

Martha walked around the great telescope. Even with all her new experience, she felt like a deluded child before its rational majesty. An iron step-ladder led up to the tiny, viewing lens that emerged from the nethermost cylinder, as slender as her own arm.

Her footsteps rang out echoing as she climbed the step-ladder. Even before she leaned in to view it, the holographic object of her future glance appeared before her—a blue pea floating on a tiny stage.

As Martha peered into the lens above it, Earth's terrible curved crescent cut into her eye like a blue thorn. But she didn't look away. There hung above it a grey pearl, a moon. And there were lights.

She saw small tiny lights moving around the moon.

Chapter 27

"Al?"

Alvin Dobbs rolled over. The belly protruding from under his t-shirt showed the pink imprint of the pink carpet.

"What is it?" said Al.

His wife sat on the couch, a book on her lap. "It's intermission."

"It's commercials," said Al.

"They said intermission, I heard it."

"Whatever."

Al rolled back to see the commercials. The screen showed a model's hips wound in tight gold straps. Al could see the model's belly-button. And through the straps, the soft rising mound of her pussy.

"Al?"

"Lila." Al didn't turn away from the TV.

"Listen to this...."

"Shut up," Al said, raising his voice. "Or I'll hit you."

The next commercial was for a household cleaner. Al knew it almost by heart.

A man was wiping at a dark spot on a white countertop. The spot wouldn't go away. His wife came up behind him, laughing.

"Honey, that's not dirt, it's a shadow!"

The guy kept wiping. Crazily now. Then the words, spoken gleaming out of nowhere: *BRITE: WE GET THE SHADOWS OUT.*

Al Dobbs turned, and found Martha Dobbs there staring.

But it wasn't Al Dobbs at all. The name had been stuck by her own mind to something that had used her to come into being. A fat, fish-headed creature. Its thick rubbery lips shone slick and wet below its round unblinking eyes. It breathed its words with whistling, off-kilter sounds:

"*The uniberse beeds on bife blao....zuck li bower.*"

She didn't understand. The lights had stopped moving around the little planet; the picture had frozen before her. A wash of fear, of hatred extending into infinite, outraged power, surged through her arms and eyes.

"*Boy!*"

But she wasn't him; she wasn't the boy. She was Martha Dobbs running down the ringing ladder, across the cold chamber and up the curving stairs.

The youth sat on his bed in his room, alone, watching antiquated information streaming out of a primitive helio V. He wasn't taken aback to find Rogers Collectibles standing in his room. Rogers was green and gaunt; hollow rings surrounded his eyes.

"Where did you come from?" he asked.

"I'm not sure," Rogers said uncomfortably. "You seem to be pulling me towards you."

"You're not green like *him*."

Rogers noted a number of info-disks splashed across the floor. Books as well. Pristine antiques with covers depicting silver modules, dragon-headed beasts, asteroids and well-endowed women. There was another book as well, a new-looking blue paperback.

"What's this?" Rogers said taking it in his hand.

"I know what you are," the boy said.

A kind of cunning had crept into his red eyes.

"You're from Venus." He said Venus like it was a dirty word.

"And you're not?" Rogers asked.

"Only freaks are from Venus. Only dirty, vicious freaks."

"What do you mean?" he asked.

"My aunt Lila says you're all freaks and could no longer survive on Earth even if anyone cared. She said it's you who are destroying everything. That you're turning—"

But a man's voice called up loudly from outside the closed door: his wheezing words turning non-sensical in the utterance.

"*BOY! WHO ARE GORATINE ORG?*" Something wet and thick slapped against the door. The words piling up, bubbling out the fleshy gills of the throat: "*DOT BY FUCKING SON. BEND HIM AWAY, LET HIM EBLIGATE....*"

Nine fish-headed creatures stood in a circle around Rogers and the boy. They wore scarlet robes and their flesh was engraved with impossible symbols. Another stood then among them.

The boy was not green at all. He was shivering, pink-skinned and naked. He screamed.

The Green's Man's smile was very long and the boy's gaze was muddied with tears. The Green Man's eyes flickered white. "Oh yes," the Green Man purred. "Others will have witnessed. Here now; real others...."

It turned to Rogers. It had become a man, a regular, green-skinned man. Jorx Crittendon himself.

"Rogers Collectibles," he said. "I see you've found your book."

Rogers looked at the book he'd picked up from the boy's table. It was the *Brane World*—but younger, fresher. Its pages a pure and snowy white.

"Go ahead," Jorx said. "Open it."

The nine creatures surrounding hissed unintelligible, liquid sounds.

Rogers opened it. "Brane World," he read. "One grand lie."

"The boy wrote that himself. Ingenious, don't you think so? To come to such a certain conclusion so early in life."

"But that's your hand-writing," Rogers said.

Jorx grinned his peculiar triangular grin. "That book, Collectibles, it took me away and, yet, you see, it has brought me back again."

The boy backed away. It was impossible. Who was he? He remembered an ad-apt, a hat, a missing book. Something slithering between his legs.

"One self, real at last, united. Do you feel my hand?"

Jorx stroked the boy's face—and became in the gesture something wider, jaw-breakingly huge. Rogers blinked; worlds flashed. The thing before him was stopping up his mind. He tried to protest, took all the rage he had to do it, but even then, most horribly, his mouth was closed, silent.

The humans, Rogers Collectibles, Martha Dobbs, *him*—their heads gave way, burping out fish eyes, and thick plasticky lips. Their fangs, tiny, combed, too long for their jaws, curled out in non-Euclidean exactitude.

"Do not turn away," said the Green Man. "The bitch is dead. Our life is real. Venusia is mine."

He placed his hand between the boy's naked legs. "At last, I touch myself."

Someone gripped his hand. It brought Rogers out of the boy, across the room. It was Martha Dobbs there beside him.

Martha? She looked at him, unable to understand. He pulled her towards him, whispered: "*She isn't dead. Ruby Greene isn't dead.*"

Jorx Crittendon swiveled his white eyes in their direction.

"What did you say?"

Something bubbled out of the Princeps' forehead, an acidic foam structured by mathematical principles into an inside-out horn—and he became another green man entirely.

Martha had come upon the crest of a broad mesa atop a purple-colored ice-moon. A blue gas giant took up half of the sky. In the black that remained there was only the gleaming of one fat, coin-sized star. She gazed down onto an impossibly small and uniform horizon.

There was no atmosphere. Her body felt nothing at all. She couldn't be standing here like this, out of doors. It was as if she were a hologram.

Ruby Greene and Melton were the characters that Jorx Crittendon had encountered holding sway in the n-scape. They had broken through the walls of the cave to erect Venusia in the System. Venusia, for Jorx Crittendon, for she was he, as she stood empty of all but knowledge on the far away moon, would have to destroy all of time, all and every entangled universe to kill them to make of the wide system his necessary deathscape. He had used Dr. Yang and Rogers and the dwarf, and she herself too, to raise up these myths. But the n-scape extended far to where others, in other times could enter as well. A war had risen up against him already; it extended everywhere, everywhen. Ruby Greene was its author and she still survived. Even Ruby ached with the Green Man's rage to be real.

The thick ice-floor cracked. Was there even gravity? Martha felt tremors echo through her feet, but heard no sound.

Very slowly, and far, far in the distance, something was approaching her underneath the ice. Its living, snakelike motion was revealed by the fractal wrinkles cracking, contracting, expanding the frozen wasteland between.

She felt suddenly aroused. There was very little time left in the world.

"Martha? Are you with me?"

"Johanna?"

Johanna's curls were bunched up against the blanket she'd wrapped around her head. She sat across the room, on a cot, charmingly un-fixed. "You know everything, don't you," she said.

"I know you're a—"

"Shhhhh. Never say it. Never ever. There's no time. We have work to do. While they're together."

"Who?"

"Jorx Crittendon, my love, and the boy he's making himself. His quest holds him in the past; opens up a husk for the Green Man to adopt, to enter our spacetime. Jorx will no longer be ... a projection. The Green Man will inhere, take us all away."

Martha didn't understand. "You're not telling me Jorx Crittendon is a hologram."

"There was once a real Crittendon. A writer and thinker, a second-wave immigrant to Venus. He is the boy you have seen by way of the neuroscape. But he died long ago, before the Princeps' ascension. The Princeps itself is an extraordinary machine, created by Melton and Morituri to handle the transition, and directed by Larry Held. It roamed the human n-scape, inhabiting the minds of the colonists. Before long it was able to control them to direct them in its single-minded quest.

"What was its quest?"

"To make itself real. But for the Princeps to be real, history itself would have to be proven un-written. Venusia, a dream. Terran life would have to unwind its potential and flip-flop into holographic fantasy. All Venusia would have to be irrevocably observed as unreal. So it was he who allowed, encouraged your friends to stretch out the neuroscape to accept the unresolved past into its scope. To defeat Melton and Ruby and their sway over your unconscious identities. If enough of us, if our whole society lost memory, lost death—well, then it would be true, Martha, or all that true means."

"But you said Larry Held was directing him."

"Larry, my dear, is not what he once was. He is so old, his body so re-structured, his mind so tired that he is spellbound by the power of his own puppet. He does the monster's bidding. "

"But Jorx touched me—"

"We use your senses, Martha, to make ourselves real for you. You, all of you, give us your power as you abdicate your own. We do your unconscious bidding. Even Jorx, especially Jorx, is at your command."

Martha's eyes had filled with tears. "Then you—you're not...?"

"Shh, my love. No more questions. All the world's a stage. You must be ready for the insurrection. What you've planned all along and trained yourselves to forget."

"The insurrection?"

Martha's Iye flew in from around the corner. It had taken some time, but it had found her.

"It is now," Johanna said. "Fix yourself up, my Martha. It is now, this moment, that the Green Man comes to stand on our ground. It is now he can be killed."

Chapter 28

It had been a long time since Nifty had seen so many people out after Feed. Something had changed; they knew it, but didn't know they knew it. They bumped around aimlessly, huddled confused, and he couldn't see much around their stupid hulking forms. He felt smaller than ever.

Yes, something was going on at the House of Sighs. V-lights lit the interior. Silhouettes of g-ops and V-technicians moved enshadowed before the stately entrance, operating flying Iyes and keeping civilians at bay. Nifty milled in with the growing crowd of stragglers.

Small and helmeted, he climbed the steps of the museum, and managed to get inside the spacious lobby. He didn't notice the little girl with a coconut bag slung over her shoulder who ran to follow him inside.

The new, larger Niftus Norrington was standing in a facing laundromat, watching "Windows on the Weird." He hadn't seen the original Nifty stroll by. He was glued to the stage.

"Access, if you will, this oddball, my Hoppies," Larry Held was saying. "A dad-sized cockroach crawling around the House of Sighs. You've never seen anything like it. Boys, Is Martha here? Are we feeding Martha Dobbs yet?"

The bug was unbelievable. Surely Larry could have come up with something more realistic. Still, it was fascinating to watch the precision of its movements, consider the fact of its possible existence. Shit, Norrington wanted to see what the model looked like in the real.

He lept up and made his way across to the House of Sighs. He could still hear "Windows on the Weird" all around as he pushed into the gathering crowd. A sudden female voice:

"This broadcast is being interrupted."

"By whom, doll-face?"

"By myself, Martha Dobbs, interrespondent. And by Johanna Zeep as well."

A hush came down. Norrington looked up with the others to find a flying V. Such a thing had never happened before.

"And by Johnny Ho too."

Pressed up for the first time among adults his own height, Norrington was one of the few who managed to see the bug on the far ceiling of the lobby. He saw it right away, and knew instantly that he'd been mistaken. It was real all right. It turned his stomach. The enormous, hairy bug hung there upside-down, quivering in fear. A sour stench wafted out over the crowd, as the creature sprayed the g-ops below it with its vomit.

The crowd around him craned their necks to see the lobby's huge, flying V. There was a moment of dead air, a blast of static and then suddenly the deep-eyed countenance of the girl reporter, Martha Dobbs, hovered there above them. Her eyes were red and swollen, her face bruised. She spoke forcefully, with clarity.

"We're interrupting the broadcast to declare the end of the Crittendon regime."

The crowd around him swelled. Norrington found himself, despite his size, roughly bumped and propelled forward, directly up to the force-binds with which the g-ops had sectioned off the remaining interior of the lobby.

"How could a gigantic bug like this... get out of the zoo.... hoppies…" Larry Held stumbled over the words. Norrington saw him standing there, talking to an Iye behind the force-binds.

"That's a dumb, misleading question," Johnny Ho interrupted. "Especially when the animals in our 'zoo' as you call it, are hologram projections and not flesh and blood at all. This rare creature is real."

"Dumb questions from a dumb guy, Johnny," Larry whispered. "What can I say? Is a bug—"

"It's not a 'bug', Larry. It's a Zoreckian.... Larry?"

Larry Held, not three meters distant from Norrington, was holding his hands tight on his ears—as if he were being assaulted by a sound that no one else could hear. Deep lines suddenly gripped his face like bands of fire.

"It's a plant," Larry mumbled. "What's it doing to my mind? How has it concentrated its waves so...?"

He stretched out his arms and rose several feet into the air. Free-floating, his wide mouth fell open. His tongue flapped mutely against his lips. A line of blood popped trickling out of his left eye. He covered his ears again, issued a blood-curdling scream, then collapsed on the floor.

The crowd, still riveted to the flying Iye, stepped back in wonder. The motion forced Norrington directly against the force-binds.

He saw then that Rogers Collectibles was inside the ring, far across the lobby.

Rogers stood back against the wall.

"They've killed it!" someone shouted. "The bug is dead!"

It was true, the bug was dead. Its hairy trunk was stuck to the ceiling with a bloody, silver sword. A great volume of yellow slime ran thickly down the wall as its twitching legs pedaled mechanically, obviously lifeless.

Jorx Crittendon stood flickering before the corpse, arm outstretched, green palm open. When he plucked his sword out, Zoreckian's husk stayed stuck to the ceiling. Jorx wiped the blood off of the blade; it glistened yellow on his black t-suit. The wide triangular grin stretched across his lean face. "This feels beautiful," he said.

He faced Rogers.

"To be legitimate. Real. Wow. I love it."

"That bug was real too," Rogers said. "I had an appointment to meet it here. It bought my book. I was going to deliver it." He held the book in his hands.

Crittendon's white eyes flashed. "You and your foarking book are annoying me Rogers. Don't you know it's a fake, fool? I killed Ruby Greene when I allowed her to entangle with the neuro-scop—so I alone could own...."

The flickering grew stronger, Jorx was becoming fully embodied. But he stopped speaking, looking past Rogers towards the crowd that had gathered anxiously behind them.

"G-op's," he murmured. "Gather Round. Increase force binds."

A ring of inviso-suited guards flickered into place around him—installing a band of electric force between the bug's body, Crittendon, Rogers and the crowd.

"You didn't kill Ruby Greene," Rogers said. "You killed Ae, the poet. Another writer but not the one you wanted. Her daughter in fact."

The angles in JC's face hardened. "You're too late. It doesn't matter. He is coming." Another being seemed to flicker out of him. He grinned terribly, as his cheeks swelled elastically outwards. "I am real," it said.

Rogers stood again in his ad-apt den, Jorx before him, hands outstretched. The white light of his eyes glistening as they pictured the hilt of a Japanese sword emerging from Rogers' chest.

"Oh Good," Jorx hissed. "Yesss."

Jorx yanked the blade out and Rogers realized that this time it had really passed through his chest.

Space suddenly yawning, he fell to his knees. His blood spilled black onto his chest. He had the sudden and fearful intuition that his business, in the grand scheme, amounted to nothing at all.

"There it is, Collectibles, you're real after all. Really dead."

"Show's over, folks," the Green Man smiled, flickering through Crittendon's face. "Why haven't you gone away? Why am I still here?" Jorx said, reappearing.

Jorx didn't yet own the n-scape, but time had changed. Events popped, temporarily resisting the flow to his infolding forehead.

This, then, was the final struggle. "Ah yes," Jorx said, still inhering. "The m-op."

"Kill him," said the Green Man.

The new Norrington's big body felt peculiarly light as he swung the needle-pistol out from under his robe.

The Princeps met his gaze with the Green Man's joyous eyes, sucking him in.

Norrington was struck with the fact that there were only the two of them. He and Jorx alone at the edge of a swirling event-horizon.

"Did you think I hadn't seen you coming? Your death is the last boundary." There were popping sounds all around, as the faces of the folks in the crowd emerged from out of their skin, fish-eyed, dribbling, kneeling before the thing that was coming.

Norrington perceived again the extraordinary burden of his solitude, a frozen picture forever stuck to his mind. "You will answer for the murder of Sylvia Yang," he said. But he was still lifting the needle-gun up and out from his robe; the events were slipping backwards. He was too big, too slow.

The ring of g-op's had fired. Seven of their own projectiles were pitter-pattering up his own chest.

He was on his knees, beside poor Collectibles. Yes, the real room was returning. Norrington wasn't sad. He knew from the mushroom that the subjectivity of experience is preserved not as a plurality of distinct and isolated meanings, but as a configuration of symbols ultimately leading to a total, single, and universal stream, enforced or agreed upon by other subjects, whose unconscious primacy was as necessary as his own. His life would, could, still be taken up by the stream. Perhaps only because he was prepared to die.

Indeed, as he died, Norrington saw a strange and uplifting sight.

What appeared to be flowers, the reddest, ruby flowers he'd ever seen, bloomed across the Princeps' inviolable chest.

"Now is the time, sir, if I may be so bold."

As his big double died, the other Nifty Norrington sprung into action. Jorx had't figured on two of him. The tiny man flipped firing over the bind-fields, emptying a clip of sixteen spikers sputtering up and across the Princeps' front. Crittendon, who'd never before been real, was caught without armor. Nifty pulled the weapon up to his head and with the last spiker, blew a hole in the Green Man's white eye.

The Green Man, in his final occurrence, folded into himself, moaning in outraged surprise. His triangular grin broke open into a stupid hole—he stood outstretched, caught in a million wars. Spears, bullets, daggers, knives, stones, lasers, the weapons of countless revolutions smashed his stream-crossing skulls in the bordering continua and his body spun in a whirlwind of gore.

As for Jorx Crittendon, the bulb of a plant had emerged from his mouth. His eyes went brown; weeds unwound his head from his torso. His flesh crumbled, as if carved of Venusian clay.

But no one was looking. A greater miracle had taken their attention. A small creature had landed on the great steps of the House of Sighs. The people parted as the little bird, the first they had ever seen, walked into the great hall, its little head mechanically jerking to the awkwardness of its steps.

It was a dove.

Chapter 29

The birds had returned. The crowd had broken into wild violence, dismantling the architectures, looting art, smashing v-lights, mobbing, suffocating g-ops. It was only when the V's gave way to a love scene between Johanna Zeep and Martha Dobbs that the violence began to subside. Eventually, at Martha Dobbs' request, all Venusia gathered by the sea-side. Not quite all, actually. M-op Niftus Norrington returned to the scene of the crime.

He didn't look at his own dead body, the larger him. And he couldn't bear to stop over Collectibles either.

Nifty placed his helmet on the floor. He was done with it. He approached the bug, cautiously, making sure no one was watching. The walls and floors of the lobby were splattered with yellow blood. The stink had settled, oddly enough, into something sad and beautiful. Nifty bent down and smelled it deep. It filled him with deep emotion. Gingerly, he took the creature's triangular, antennaed head and belted it around his waist like a coconut.

He turned, catching a sudden odor on the air. There, off to the side of the lobby, something was looking at him intensely. It was another large insect and it was alive. He burned with excitement. To meet its gaze sent a thrill through his heart. To catch her odor on the air was more delectable than anything he'd ever known. He knelt as she reared on hind legs; her head swiveled to fix him in its gaze. Her dainty mandibles were rubbing themselves in excitement. He was inexplicably certain she was a female. He understood her as if he were an insect himself. From all that distance away, he knew. She waved.

Nifty whispered. "Sylvia?"

Nifty had to scramble to keep up with the insect's gambling pace. There were wings on her back, he saw. She could have flown had she not wanted to be accompanied. As it was, her six long legs propelled her with a near magical ease.

"A new historian was needed," she said through a mechanical box strapped around her shoulder. "13th Zoreckian of the Great Leaf, whose head hangs from your belt, was something of an eccentric. He was so unconcerned with the future that the council decreed he should be given the past and that a 14th Zoreckian be selected."

"Let me guess," Nifty huffed. "You're the fourteenth Zorxian."

"Wrong. And it's Zoreckian."

"Slow down, can't you?"

She stopped walking.

"When you first looked at me," Nifty said. "I thought ... for a moment, I recognized something about you."

"I know you did, Nifty. Dr. Sylvia Yang is contained within me. I accepted her fact as it passed."

Nifty looked up at the slimy exoskeletal jaw, the hairy, slick beard glistening under its beak. Not even Sylvia possessed such beauty.

"Does that mean that when I'm talking to you," he asked, "I'm talking to her? To Sylvia?"

"Yes, only because you yourself have died. You were shot and spacetime rejected you when you died, because of the existence of your doubled dead self. That makes you the sort of anomaly morally suited for an implantation of an egg. I'm Sylvia. I'm a couple other girls too, Nifty Norrington." The metal box emitted a curious squeaking noise.

Norrington grumbled. "Egg?" Somehow a trick was being played on him. His arm loosened, and when he lifted it, he found it had dropped away to the ground.

He felt curiously light.

"13th Zoreckian of the Great Leaf was sacrificed to the good of the other selves."

A leg fell off. Nifty removed an arm.

"The egg of 14th Zoreckian of the Great Leaf was planted long ago."

"Amazing," exclaimed the 14th Zoreckian of the Great Leaf, as the flesh of Nifty's stunted body dropped away. He stepped out of the egg, beautiful and insectizoid. "I actually was that little man. I felt it so deeply—"

He broke off. Suddenly understanding who it was he was talking to, he knelt and rubbed his new head in the dirt. "My Queen," he said. "I do not deserve such honor."

"Nonsense. Arise. Let us cross the red water."

Rogers was standing on the cement floor beside her. Martha couldn't deny it, he saw. He was there among them.

"Johnny Ho himself," he said. "His castle."

He walked over to the bar, with its silver, eagle-headed beer handles. A mustachioed tap greeted him.

"Drink, Sir?"

"Beer," he said. "With ice."

Martha touched his shoulder. "How did you get here like that? I'm still ponging you."

He looked her in the eyes.

"I've decided to give up the book," he said.

Martha felt herself reddening. "You understand," she said. "We don't have time for personal matters right now. There's a colony to control."

"Well put." He turned away from her. "I won't be able to drink that sibble. I'm on the way out. The gates are still open. This is a visitation."

She saw that his front was wet with blood.

"Are you...?" Martha Dobbs reached out to touch him, but he

stepped back and away. "Quentin," she said. "I'm sorry. I'm so sorry."

Rogers Collectibles retained his composure. He fixed his hat tight to his head.

"Flower-taking should still be encouraged," he said. "But the option to desist must be there. Speaking of which, the plants—"

Martha grasped for his hands; her eyes flashed out before him.

"I am your Martha," she said. "I always was. And you're my Quentin. We had to forget."

He frowned. His eyes drew suddenly inward. "Yes Martha. I can remember that. I can remember everything...."

But he was gone, falling.

Epilogue

The drama was finished and the crisis passed. Martha Dobbs, as is well known, became by general election the de facto Minister of the Venusian ape government, helping to lead the colony through many painful transitions to come: the days of the comet, for instance, and the remembering. She would oversee, in her tenure, the de-industrialization of the flowers and the opening of planetary Venus to human exploration and settlement. "For the planet to accept us," she famously said, "we must first accept ourselves."

Consul Dobbs disliked the neuroscape. She outlawed Morituri helmets. With education and effort, the gates to the n-scape eventually closed. Once more, the general universal stream allowed the free, active expression of every individual life on the colony. Anomalies still occurred, as they must always do—strange balls streaked across the sky now and then, large talking insects appeared only to vanish. But the plants congratulated themselves on the reinstitution of an ordinarily navigable System. Oa had lived to continue its time. Signs of surviving life were detected throughout the system. The lunar colonies were already up and running and the Borstal on Mercury Station had survived. There seemed to have been some life detected even in the mother ocean of Terra.

One evening, many v-days and v-nights after the events related above, Martha Dobbs was seated by the fire in the old bookstore out beyond the Western edges of the colony. The place had been found long ago and she'd since made it her retreat. It was haunted, and from time to time, in the corner of her eye, she'd seen people passing—objects briefly inhering. Over the years, she had learned to read and write. Now, by careful chanting and delineation of arcane symbols, she finally managed to achieve time-space transition—without recourse to the neuroscape or the boiling of space—and raise a shade up before her.

Her fire grew in sudden intensity and she spotted Frank P. Hogart seated there, slumped over a chair by the green flames.

"You're Melton," Martha Dobbs said.

The old man opened a single, bright eye.

"A myth can't come into the real," he said. "I'm Frank Hogart."

There on his lap was the blue-jacketed book *Brane World*, the object whose provenance still haunted her dreams. Like Ruby Greene and the m-op Niftus Norrington, the little girl who could be seen picking up the book in the famous assassination footage had vanished from history.

"That was my friend's *Brane World*. Rogers Collectibles. He died trying to sell it to you."

The old man snorted. "Rogers Collectibles? A funny name for a man. I'll tell you this. Ruby Greene did not write the preface. There's a good sense of Ruby in it, of what she meant to the whole project, what she still means. The writer certainly knew her, talked to her, most likely, for there are details only she would have known. But it's not her. I know."

"The Preface was written by Ae," said Martha Dobbs, "a twenty-second century poet and—"

"Enough!" Hogart roared, suddenly.

The effort was apparently too much for the old man. He fell silent and slumped again in his chair. The book fell to the floor, open to its frontispiece.

Martha Dobbs picked it up.

"It has to be a grand lie," She said, reading the note below its title. "It's a book."

An inspiration came to her suddenly, from deep in her heart. Rogers Collectibles had been present to her so long in her dreams and memories. To send him a message, one that wouldn't disturb the delicacy of the streams that had brought them once together, something that would prod him gently forward to the moment, however brief... She took a pencil in her hand.

She wrote the words clearly and carefully. *"But it's a good one."*

She placed the book again in the old man's lap. It would be like a message in a bottle sent floating on time.

The fire cracked, and spat a shower of sparks into the room. The ghost was gone.

As for PHRED, the sentient plant, it was remembered by one of our friends and taken to a lovely casement window high up in the House of Sighs. It was placed in a little room with other artifacts arranged in honor of the insurrection: a Morituri helmet, a needle-rifle, a faulty watch, a ruby necklace and a Japanese silver sword.

From these objects it was able to secure memory of what had happened. There was good time to think dream. And there was much to think dream about, for the fact was that despite the effective end of its immersion (with the exception of Consul Dobbs its humans had all since died), the Senate had not yet made contact.

People used to appear to the plant as flickering germ-sacks of randomized emotional conflict, endowed with the arbitrary power either to destroy or to preserve its life. It was only after the occurrence of certain of the happenings outlined above, indeed after their very recording, that PHRED first began to appreciate the existence of a general tide of human history of great importance to the survival of vegetative life altogether.

A plant yearns mystically to garden. A sentient gardens humans. Personalized service and attention to each specimen's existence is part of the fun, and can lead, surprisingly, to exciting, unforeseen growth experience all one's own. Yet how could its garden be appreciated by the Senate—by the vegetative community as a whole—if the plant was to be forever immersed in human time. PHRED's duty was apparently not done. Its continued immersion therefore must have had something to do with its growing understanding of a legitimate human center to the Riemann surface of Oan history.

"If I might venture a suggestion, sir or madam," said the Morituri Helmet to PHRED one day. "A garden, if it is not properly weeded, will choke itself on its own wealth. The same is true of knowledge. To be alive one must know what not to know or the original plantings will cease to be relevant to the future fate of the ground. The past design will always disappear into its surviving elements, unless the plot is clearly delineated. In the abstract, Sir. If I may be so bold."

"*It might be—possible, even—that the past—since no one knew it quite as PHRED does—might again come unfixed?*"

"Precisely."

"*Are you suggesting—I write a true history of the insurrection—and the cruel murder—of Dr. Sylvia Yang?*"

"Sir, Madam, I would be willing to help."

"*—A book, helmet? Printed on the—dead flesh of—my comrades?*"

"If it's in the interest of the plants, and the wood used has already died, isn't it the most honorable of objects?"

But PHRED was immediately troubled. "Simply to observe the complications of the events that made the past of the current possibility," it complained to itself, "is far outside the scope of human language. Indeed human language is a stupid, bumbling thing and could never—

"Enough!" Interrupted the Senate at last, with sudden, spontaneous light. "PHRED shall write it. PHRED shall write it in the mysterious richness of the actual unfolding of Oa's veil, and not stoop to the limitations of the human mono-temporal narrative. The helmet will see that the work is printed; the humans that it is published, and the author, as is fit and proper, that its ambiguities shall be wide enough for plants to travel. For shall its text not be planted on the dried flesh of our own most hallowed and all-knowing dead? All presence to the light. All husks for the black rain."

The Senate had spoken.

Now, to work.

Maurice G. Dantec

SEMIOTEXTE SCI-FI

"Time to look beyond this rundown radioactive cop-ridden planet."
— William S. Burroughs

Reinhabiting the tradition of philosophical and political fable, Semiotexte is introducing a new science-fiction series under the Native Agents imprint. Debuting with Maurice Dantec's futurist-noir epic *Babylon Babies* and Mark von Schlegell's dystopian fantasy novel *Venusia*, these books speak to the present demise by assembling radical models for unlikely futures. Speculatively accelerated, Semiotexte Sci-Fi presents exciting new models for living the deterritorialized life.